YESTERDAY'S CHILDREN

YESTERDAY'S CHILDREN

BRETT HALSEY

KNIGHTSBRIDGE PUBLISHING COMPANY

NEW YORK

This edition of Yesterday's Children originally published by Janesway Publishing Inc. in 1984

Published in the United States by
Knightsbridge Publishing Company
255 East 49th Street
New York, New York 10017

Library of Congress Cataloging-in-Publication Data

Halsey, Brett.
  Yesterday's children / Brett Halsey.
    p.   cm.
  Reprint. Originally published: Janesway Pub. Co., 1984.
  ISBN 1-877961-55-8 : $19.95
  I. Title.
PS3558.A4115Y47   1990
913'.54—dc20   90-32254
                                                   CIP
ISBN: 0-877961-55-8

Designed by Stanley S. Drate/ Folio Graphics Company, Inc.

10 9 8 7 6 5 4 3 2 1
FIRST EDITION

*To Tracy, Terry, Dorris
and
my friends and colleagues,
the talented, hard-working performers
of daytime soap opera!*

When lovely woman stops to folly,
And finds too late that men betray
What Charms can sooth her melancholy
What art can wash her guilt away?

OLIVER   GOLDSMITH
(1766)

CHAPTER

1

"They aren't going away,"
Jamie Starbuck grumbled, listening to the persistent sound of
the downstairs doorbell while disentangling himself from the
disheveled young woman in bed beside him.

"I'm sorry," she pouted as she sat up, displaying her small,
firm breasts, and looping her long, brown hair into a knot
behind her head.

"Maybe you should take a look," he gestured through the
semidarkness toward the window.

She shrugged helplessly, then eased out of bed and padded
softly across the bedroom. Jamie's gaze followed her youthful,
well-defined curves as she moved to the heavily draped, sec-
ond-story window. He smiled and slid his fingers through the
mat of salt-and-pepper hair on his chest, feeling the flat, hard
muscles he struggled to maintain in defiance of a half cen-
tury's wear and tear.

A streak of sunlight illuminated her body for an instant as
she parted the drapes, then quickly closed them. "I . . . think
it's your wife," she gasped.

"Oh, shit!" Jamie exclaimed. The doorbell continued to
sound. "How could Erika know I'm here?"

"Your Jeep is in the driveway. What should I do?"

1

"Stall her!" He rolled out of bed and slipped into his polo shirt, jeans, and worn cowboy boots.

"She *does* know you're here!" The girl began to panic as she retrieved shorts and a tank top from the pile of clothing at the foot of the bed.

"No, she doesn't." Jamie tried to remain calm while his mind raced for an avenue of escape. "The only thing she knows for sure is that my Jeep is here. You'd better open the window and talk to her or she's never going to stop ringing that damned bell!"

"What shall I say?"

"Tell her . . . tell her I *was* here, but I left."

"Hello?" she called tentatively down from the window.

"Hello," Erika replied, an edge of hostility in her German-accented voice. Hands on hips, she arched her long, lean model's body to look up with wide, blue eyes flashing under the geometrically cut bangs of her white-blonde hair. "I'm Erika Starbuck. I have to speak with my husband. It's important."

"He isn't here," the girl spoke with more conviction than she felt.

"Tell her my friend, Bill Morgan, was with me . . . and we went off in *his* car," Jamie prompted as he finished dressing.

"He *was* here," she went on. "To drop off my little boy's ball that he left in Jamie's Jeep yesterday."

"That much he *told* me he was going to do." Erika's hostility came closer to the surface. "Then when I remembered seeing you at the children's soccer practice . . . I thought he might have stayed a while . . . *after* giving you the ball."

"Golf balls," Jamie hissed as he crouched by the telephone jabbing at the dial buttons. "Tell her Bill and I went to hit some golf balls!"

"Bill," Jamie whispered with relief into the phone as his friend responded at the other end of the line. "Remember the mother of that new kid on my boy's soccer team? The one with the great body? Yeah, that's the one," he nodded, his ruggedly handsome face breaking into a reassuring smile for the girl. "Well, I'm at her house now and Erika's about to break the door down. You've got to help me get out of here."

"If he's already gone," Erika baited, "do you mind if I use your phone? Jamie's agent has been trying desperately to find him for a very important interview."

"Keep her out for another few minutes," Jamie urged, hanging up the phone. "My friend's going to pick me up down the hill."

"Will it be all right to let her in?" she frowned nervously.

"It'll be fine," Jamie grinned before dashing out the door. "As long as she doesn't find me here, you have nothing to worry about."

After watching Jamie disappear, the pretty girl stuck her head out the window again. "I was in the bathroom," she explained to Erika. "That's why I didn't hear the door. Give me a moment, I'll be right down."

Jamie was down the stairs, out the sliding glass door to the brick patio, and halfway across the wide deck jutting out over the hillside when he remembered his jacket. "To hell with it," he muttered as he looked through the smoggy haze at the panoramic San Fernando Valley below him, then vaulted the railing at the side of the deck into a tangled cover of ivy, which extended to a thick growth of acacia along the downhill property line.

Erika said something about an interview, he remembered, struggling to keep his balance as he half slid and half ran down the incline. Jamie knew it must *really* be important, or she wouldn't be out looking for him. His agent had mentioned there might be something in the pilot for that new Western series they were planning at Warner Bros.

Jamie paused, turning his tall, athletic frame to peer up the hill as he pushed a graying lock of curly hair off his glistening forehead. It couldn't be another of those celebrity golf or tennis matches. Erika wouldn't bother me with one of those; they don't pay enough.

"Oh shit," Jamie cursed, as he caught a glimpse of movement on the deck and dove into the acacia thicket. He protected his face with his bare arms, tumbling blindly until he was stopped by a six-foot tall chain-link fence.

"Oh shit," he repeated as a pair of loudly aggressive Doberman pinschers charged from the opposite side of the fence. "Why do I do this?" he muttered to himself. "I'm getting too old to be losing my head over every new piece of tail that comes along!"

◆ Erika was nowhere in sight when Bill drove Jamie to pick up his Jeep. Nor was she at home when he arrived after stopping to phone his agent, Fred Wald.

"A soap opera?" he mumbled in the shower and again as he dressed in his neatly tailored, three-piece suit. "So this is what it's come to? Twenty-five years of starring in movies and TV to prepare me for this!"

He looked again at the memo pad next to his bedside phone. *Yesterday's Chldren—Producer, George Conley—Associate, Cathy Allison—Federated TV Network, 15th Floor—role of Spencer Franklyn, a dignified, middle-aged college administrator.*

"A dignified, *middle-aged* college administrator," he grimaced wryly, reflecting back over his career. First a teenage surfer in beach-blanket pictures, then a cowboy in the long-running TV series "Slim Chisholm," followed by his prosperous years in European Westerns. He grinned. It was a long time since he had played dignified. But in a *soap opera*?

Jamie checked his "dignified" image in the mirror, then hurried out to his Jeep and set out from the Valley side of the Hollywood Hills to the Beverly Hills headquarters of the Federated TV Network.

It's a job, he shrugged, driving along Santa Monica Boulevard. And as Fred pointed out with irritating regularity, jobs for Jamie Starbuck were not so plentiful these days. Apart from the money he owed Fred, there was Erika's teeth, Lori's back alimony, the house payments, and a host of other bills. He couldn't afford to turn down the part!

Jamie's gloom was covered by a quick smile for the security guard who saluted respectfully as he waved Jamie through the gates of the busy television studio. The guard's attention raised Jamie's spirits. He may be between jobs, but he was still a name.

After parking his Jeep, he tilted the rearview mirror to comb his hair and reacted somberly as he began to realize what was really troubling him.

It's all those stories I've heard about how tough it is to act in soaps, he thought. *The twenty or thirty pages of dialogue the actors have to learn, day after day, sometimes for weeks on end. It was never like that in the movies or nighttime TV.*

"I don't know if I *can* do it," he quietly admitted to his image in the mirror. "Or am I afraid that I can't?"

Jamie shook off his mood and glared into the mirror. "What kind of bullshit talk is that? Of course you can do it!"

As he strode toward the administration building, Jamie's bold, confident manner completely masked his growing awareness that show business might be passing him by and he was Goddamn scared!

◈ Cathy Allison heaved a sigh of relief when Jamie's interview was over and he walked out of the office.

She knew she was attractive. She could depend on her pretty face and voluptuous body to catch a man's attention long enough to make him aware there was a brain behind her intriguing green eyes. But the satisfaction she had gained from Jamie's interest in her femininity quickly disappeared as he shifted his attention to the men in the room when the discussion got down to business.

What a nerve! she thought, annoyed at the easy way he

returned his attention to her before he left; inviting her out for a drink. *Who does he think he is? Who does he think I am? I've never dated broken-down actors!*

Cathy's boss, George Conley, the network's favorite daytime producer, had checked him out. Jamie Starbuck had only worked occasionally since his return from Europe. A few guest spots on nighttime television, one or two commercials. His reputation was still blemished from ten years ago when he gave a beating to Russell Fisk on the set of his "Slim Chisholm" TV series.

Still, Cathy considered, looking over the photograph he left behind, *he could have saved some of the money he made from all those spaghetti Westerns. He doesn't look like he's having any problems. But with actors, who can tell anything by the way they look? They're all so darned phony!*

Tall and thin, George Conley displayed the effete, theatrical air of a New York showman as he rose to speak. "He's perfect, Cathy. I have to compliment you for suggesting him."

"Just doing my job," she replied, hiding her mixed feelings.

"What do you think?" George turned to the casting director. "The part begins in four days. Can we make a deal and have him ready to go to work in New York in four days?"

"His agent says he's sure he can talk Jamie into it if the money's right."

"Are you sure he can handle it?" Cahty injected doubtfully. "You know how some of these older movie stars fall apart when they have to play a whole show without stopping."

"Are you having second thoughts?" There was a twinkle in George's eyes. "Or are you just trying to protect yourself in case he doesn't work out?"

"No. Of course not." Her cheeks turned red.

"And consider how many choices we have," George went on. "Most leading men his age are either big stars, dead, or have given up show business to sell real estate or something."

"That's right," Cathy eagerly agreed. "And your demographic studies prove the show *needs* someone like Starbuck. Someone strong enough to play opposite Liz Barrett and famous enough to win back some of our audience."

"There will be a lot of publicity when the press finds out he's in the same show as Russell Fisk's daughter," the casting director added. "Remember how they got into it when Fisk was still head of TV at Burt Prinz Studios? 'Top executive and top star: Both knocked out the business with one punch!' Yeah, the press will have fun digging that one up."

"But he'll be working with Liz Barrett," George corrected.

"He could have something going with Leigh Fisk, too," Cathy prompted. "Don't you remember, I mentioned it to you before we left New York?"

"He does give the impression he can handle more than one woman at a time," George nodded, reflecting on how unsettled Cathy had been in Jamie's presence. "What do *you* think, Cathy?"

"I think he portrays a very sexy image . . . on the screen," she answered carefully. "*That's* the only impression I'm concerned with."

◈ Jamie spotted Erika leaning into her compact station wagon as he pulled up in front of their modest hillside home. She turned at the sound of the Jeep, her classically beautiful face exhibiting an indifference that, after fifteen years of marriage, Jamie recognized as trouble.

"They want to make a deal," he called, bounding up the driveway full of false cheer.

"Who?" she asked, arching her body into the car to hang her garment bag.

" 'Yesterday's Children.' The soap Fred told you about. In New York." Jamie's enthusiasm turned to curiosity as he noticed Erika's case of musical arrangements. "Are you going somewhere?"

"Rehearsal," she answered, taking the jacket he had left at the girl's house from her car and flinging it in his direction. "For Tony Mitchell's charity benefit tomorrow night."

"Tomorrow?" he squawked, bending over to pick up the jacket. "I may have to leave tomorrow. We have things to talk about. Anyway, you don't have to make a career of singing in Tony Mitchell benefits. It'd be different if you were getting paid!"

"I'm not going to argue with you about this," she reacted firmly. "Tony might be reviving his TV show. If he does, he's going to need a female singer."

"And Tony takes care of his friends," Jamie grimaced. "The whole world knows about Tony Mitchell's loyalty, especially to his female singers."

"Don't *you* start talking about loyalty to females," Erika warned as she got into her car and slammed the door. "And it's not as though you're earning so much money that I can ignore a chance of having a career of my own!"

"Wait a minute, Erika!" Jamie insisted. "Fred's waiting. I have to give them an answer."

"Does it pay?"

"Yes. Very well."

Erika raised her eyebrows into the same expression she used to express her disapproval upon their young son, Bucky. "Have you seen our bank balance, Jamie? How can there be any question about your decision?"

"The contract is for two years. In New York. I'll have to live there, and I don't want to go alone!"

"If I know you, you won't be alone for two minutes."

"Dammit, Erika . . ."

"And I'm not taking Bucky out of school."

"Not now, of course not," Jamie placated. "But later. Maybe next summer. Please, Erika, can't you miss one rehearsal and talk to me about this?"

"I thought you were busy tonight . . . with your football friends. Isn't this your 'game' night?" she asked sarcastically.

"Some things are more important than games!"

"Certainly more important than the games you want to play at home," she badgered. "You may think I'm dumb, but I know football doesn't last until four in the morning."

"Listen, Erika . . ."

"I've listened enough," she replied, starting the car's engine. "I'll try not to be very late tonight. And don't worry about dinner for Bucky. He's spending the night at the Kleinmans'."

"Like hell he is," Jamie protested. "If I'm leaving town, at least I'm having dinner with my son!"

"That would be nice," she smiled condescendingly, then drove away.

CHAPTER

Cathy was still numb with jet lag as the hot shower rinsed the soapy lather from her body. Why did George really send me back alone from Los Angeles, she wondered. He's been so secretive lately. Could he really be developing another show?

"Sam, honey," she called, turning off the water. "Would you hand me a towel?"

Through the steamy shower door she could see the indistinct motion of her husband's square, compact body moving from the bathroom mirror in response to her request. She stepped out of the shower to take the towel and began drying herself.

Sam turned back to the mirror to resume trimming his full black moustache but stopped still at the sight of his wife's round, firm breasts as she leaned over to dry her legs. "I'm glad you're back," he smiled longingly. "It seems like you've been gone a month!"

"It's only been three days," she said, pursing her full sensual lips as she looked in the mirror, her bright green eyes expressing the disapproval over the condition of her short, layered, glossy black hair.

"Well, it *seems* like a month," Sam reached to embrace her.

Cathy gave him a brushing kiss on the cheek and twisted out of his muscular arms to move into the adjacent bedroom. "Tell me again what they said," she asked.

"Who?" he responded, his dark eyes following her through the door.

"You know very well who. Hennigan and the rest of them at lunch Friday."

"How many times do I have to tell you?" he answered peevishly, trailing behind her. "They didn't say anything. Only that George Conley *might* be moving to the Coast."

"Only? If George moves to the Coast, that *only* means they'll be looking for a new producer. Since I am *only* the associate producer, I should *only* have a pretty good chance at the job! Didn't they say anything about me?"

"I already told you," he persisted.

"Are you sure? You know how hard I've worked to be ready for that job!"

"What do you want, Cathy? You've already gone from staff assistant to associate producer in little more than a year. Have some patience, will you? You want George to get the idea you're after his job?"

Cathy caught his unwilling glance as he watched her wiggle into her tight Donna Karan knit dress. "*Everybody* is after somebody else's job," she answered, turning her back to pull the dress over her shapely buttocks. "What does that have to do with anything?"

"Nothing," he yielded with accustomed resignation. "Look, when the time is right I'll do what I can. Don't I always?"

"Sure you do, honey," she smiled sweetly. "And I also know Federated didn't make you Director of Daytime Development because you're stupid."

"Then trust me a little," he answered, putting his arms around her trim waist.

"I do," she said, dutifully returning his embrace, then moving to her bedside table where she began sorting through a clutter of television scripts and story outlines. "I may be late tonight. George is due back this afternoon, and you know how late he makes me work when he's been away."

"But you just got home! Dammit Cathy, I *never* have you to myself."

"Never?" she pouted seductively. "If I get home early enough tonight, I'll make you eat those words."

"Really?" Sam's face brightened. "In that case, I'll be waiting for you!"

◈ Cathy struggled with her overloaded satchel as she pushed through the door into the outer office of "Yesterday's Children." The smell of coffee and the sound of Neil Decker's voice greeted her as she eased her load onto the receptionist's empty desk.

"Wait a minute, Mr. Conley," she heard Neil chirp. "I think she *just* walked in."

Damn that little fag, she thought, checking her watch. Even when I'm twenty minutes early, he has to make it sound like I'm late.

"Yes, it's me," Cathy called toward her boss's open office door. "Is that television's favorite producer you're talking to?"

Neil slid his large, rimless glasses over his forehead into his sandy curls and sprang from behind George Conley's desk. "Yes, and he doesn't sound too cheerful," he whispered.

Cathy snatched the phone from his hand and authoritatively settled into the producer's chair, ignoring Neil's impish smile as he presented her with a cup of coffee from his Thermos carafe.

"Good morning, George. You'll be happy to know I made it back to New York safe and sound. Is the sun shining brightly out there in California?"

"It's four in the morning," George's voice grumbled. "The sun doesn't shine at this hour, not even in Beverly Hills. I can't come home today and I haven't had any sleep; so don't call and bother me unless it's a matter of life and death!"

Recognizing his mood, Cathy refrained from answering.

"The network wants me to stay here and talk about changing writers. Our ratings have slipped again."

"Oh, no," she sighed. "Do they have anyone in mind?"

"Sure they do! They want the same three or four writers that everyone in daytime TV wants. Of course, we can't get them because all the good writers are working." He yawned. "Did Starbuck arrive all right?"

Cathy looked at Neil standing in the doorway and gestured for him to leave and close the door. "Neil met Jamie's plane and took him to an apartment he'd found. Jamie's coming in today to watch the rehearsal and taping."

Cathy took a deep breath and crossed her fingers. "I think you were right, Geroge. Jamie'll do fine. Are you planning to mention my idea of getting his character involved in a love triangle with Leigh Fisk and Liz Barrett?"

"Wait a minute," George interrupted. "Let's see how Starbuck works out before we start building the whole show around him. And what about Liz? How do you think she's going to react, losing her leading man to a pretty, young ingenue? You'd better learn a little more patience, Cathy."

Cathy cleared her throat, then forced a smile into the phone. "I'm sorry, George, but I can't help feeling we don't have *time* for patience. I know it's practically heresy to ask this about the biggest star in daytime TV, but if the world is so darned interested in what Liz Barrett has to say, why are our ratings going down?"

George's amusement was brief. "I'm not going to argue the point; just do as I told you."

"And what was that, my all-knowing leader?"

"I don't remember . . . but whatever it was, do it! I'm going to sleep." The line clicked dead.

Cathy slowly replaced the receiver, then leaned her head back in the chair. Patience, they say. The morning hadn't even started and already she'd had two lectures about patience.

She looked around the producer's office, unconsciously comparing it to her own tiny cubicle and to the larger, more opulent network executive suites. She wasn't going to sit around waiting for lightning to strike. If she had learned anything from George Conley, it was that she had to make her own opportunities. Cathy buzzed the intercom and Neil immediately appeared at the door. "Neil, go down to the rehearsal hall and see if Jamie Starbuck's come in yet. Make sure he's relaxed. Take him to breakfast or something."

"As much as I hate to admit it," Neil insolently leered, "I'm sure you could do a better job of it. You're more his type."

Cathy's face flushed angrily. "You're disgusting!"

"I was only kidding," Neil quickly retreated.

"Well, *stop* with your kidding. You aren't funny!"

"All right. I didn't know everyone was so touchy this morning. Did you talk to George? I mean, did you tell him about the story line we developed for Jamie and Leigh Fisk?"

"Yes. He said I should move a little slower. Evidently my neck is already on the line for suggesting we bring Jamie into the show in the first place."

"You won't get hurt," Neil assured, prudently not mentioning that he had planted the idea of hiring Jamie in her mind. "He's going to be good for the show. Believe me."

"If you're talking about Jamie Starbuck," a familiar voice addressed them, "we all certainly *want* to believe you." Cathy and Neil were startled by Liz Barrett's frosted blonde image of feminine authority standing in the doorway.

"Good morning, Liz," Cathy said politely. "Is there something I can do for you?"

Liz pointed a long, tapered fingernail at the telephone. "Thank you, but there's something I want to discuss with George."

"I talked to him a little while ago," Cathy offered as she rose from the chair. "He was out all night and was just getting to bed. I wouldn't bother him now. You know how he is when he hasn't slept."

"Yes, I know," Liz answered, a slight frown marring her always perfectly maintained, translucent beauty. "I was hoping to talk to him about the new writers, but I forgot about the time difference in Los Angeles. I'm always getting that mixed up."

"The new writers," Cathy repeated dumbly.

"Yes, didn't you know?"

"Yes, of course," Cathy faltered briefly. "I just didn't think anyone else did."

Liz arched her thinly penciled eyebrows into her petal curls. "After you've been here over twenty years, there's very little you don't hear about. One way or another."

"Then you've heard about the new story line I suggested for you and Jamie."

"No, *that* I haven't heard about."

Neil's eyes lit up with interest as he observed Cathy's calm expression while her mind raced to adjust their story idea to favor Liz.

"I haven't had time to develop it fully yet, but basically it involves a love story between your character and Jamie's . . . with the suggestion of a side affair with Leigh. Naturally, you'll win out in the end."

"How about a wedding?" Liz nodded thoughtfully. "Isn't it time for a big, beautiful wedding on 'Yesterday's Children'?"

"That's *exactly* what I had in mind." Cathy's eyes opened wide at the coincidence; then, with a quick smile of triumph to Neil, she continued. "Weddings are always good for the ratings. It's demographically sound and can run six months to a year. Assuming George likes the idea enough to push for it."

Liz's steely eyes darkened. "*I* like it. And if George doesn't, maybe his replacement will. Demographics and all."

Cathy's throat tightened. "I hope you understand, the way I laid it out for George was pretty sketchy."

"Don't worry, dear. I'm seated with the Vice President of Daytime Programming at the affiliates dinner in Washington, D.C., next week. I'll make sure that *he* understands it very clearly!"

"Got a minute?" Zev Brahms, the Unit Manager, intruded with a clipboard full of invoices under his arm.

"What is it, Zev?" Cathy asked.

"Good news," he responded. "Liz, you'll like this, too. I finally got the new furniture for your living room into the budget. It won't be as lavish as the set designer wants for you, but it'll be nice."

"Will I be able to look at the fabrics?" Liz asked.

"Sure. Come to the department anytime today."

"Thank you, Zev," she smiled warmly. "How is your wife?"

"This weather doesn't do much for her asthma, but what can you do?"

"I'm sure you're doing all you can," Liz responded supportively. "Give her a big hug from us, will you, Zev."

"She'll appreciate that," he grinned shyly. "Thanks, Liz."

Cathy felt a tug of resentment as Zev, favoring his lame leg, turned to leave. "It's about time they okayed that new set," she coughed, then returned the conversation to the subject uppermost in her mind. "You mentioned something about George's replacement. Have you heard anything definite? I mean . . . about his leaving?"

"Nothing is ever definite in this business," Liz replied, glancing at Neil. "But if he does leave, I hope those ridiculous demographic studies go with him!"

Neil began moving toward the door as Cathy opened her mouth to speak. "Bye, girls," he gushed, hurrying out of the office. "I've got work to do."

◈ *What a nerve,* Neil thought as he stepped into the elevator. *What colossal nerve, trying to sell two versions of the same story. Only she can get away with something like that. Even with George Conley! Cathy got that closet queen into bed and look where it got her. When I went to bed with him, all I got was a headache worrying about AIDS.*

The elevator door opened on the second floor and Neil scurried through the familiar maze of corridors that connect Federated Television's business and production offices to the studio area. He poked his head into the stark, neon-lit rehearsal hall across from Studio 41, and briefly surveyed the still-drowsy group of actors assembled around a long table.

Vico Fellouris, the large, overweight staff director, turned and fixed Neil with an accusative glare. "Where's the goddamn coffee? We've been here half an hour and there's still no goddamn coffee!"

Neil looked at the empty table where the morning coffee and sweet rolls were usually found. "I don't know. I'll go down to the commissary and check on it right away."

"Well, make it snappy. I don't know how they expect us to get started in the morning when they don't have the coffee here on time." Vico's dark, bleary eyes and unsteady hands signaled the reason for his hostility.

"You're right," Neil agreed. "Oh, by the way, Jamie Starbuck hasn't been in here has he?"

"He doesn't start until tomorrow," Vico growled. "Now go bother someone else. I've got a show to get to the floor."

Bitch, bitch, bitch, Neil thought as he left the rehearsal hall, cutting through the cavernous videotaping studio on his way to the commissary. *It isn't my fault Vico's become fat and unhappy because of what he might have been. He's a great director. He could've been as important as any of them, but he chose to stay with "Yesterday's Children." That's nobody's fault but his own.*

Neil stepped through the soundproof door at the opposite end of the studio into a wide, main corridor where he spotted a man nonchalantly pushing a cart with a large, stainless steel coffee urn. "Hey," he called. "Is that for rehearsal hall 41?"

"That's right."

Neil looked at his watch. "Do you realize that coffee should have been delivered there over forty-five minutes ago?"

"Hey, man. Don't talk to me about late. When the coffee's ready I wheel it over. That's all, man. That's all I get paid for!"

"Okay," Neil retreated. "Then, let's not waste any more time talking about it."

My God, Neil coughed, continuing toward the commissary, *everybody is so touchy. They can't all be having their period at the same time!*

The smell of frying bacon tantalized his small, lightly freckled nose, as he walked past the cafeteria-style serving area into the large dining room. His gaze swept over the tables, pausing briefly on an attractive young man from the network news department, then continuing until he spied Leigh Fisk.

Now, there's a girl who doesn't have anything to be touchy about, he mused, watching her dawdle over a plate of scrambled eggs while intently reading a paperback book. *She's everything I'm not! She's tall, pretty, and doesn't have to diet to stay thin. She can wear funky clothes and still look like a lady. Her family money goes back to Rupert Fisk, so she can afford to work for the pleasure of it. She has the reputation of being a professional virgin, but no one resents her for it.*

Leigh glanced up as she turned a page and drew Neil to her table with a warm smile. "Hi, Neil. Want to have breakfast with me?"

"Thanks, cutie, but I'm looking for someone. Jamie Starbuck hasn't been here has he?"

"Is he coming in again today? I heard he was here yesterday, but I wasn't in the show yesterday."

"Yes. He wants to observe for a couple days before he actually begins."

"That's really great. I'm dying to meet him!"

Neil settled into the chair opposite her. "I thought you knew him. I mean . . . your father and everything."

"That happened when I was a little girl. I never knew him like a real person or anything."

Neil pulled his chair closer and lowered his voice. "Come on, cutie, just between us girls, did it happen the way I read it?"

Leigh's long, honey blond hair fanned across her shoulders as she shook her head. "I honestly don't know. After he broke

Daddy's jaw, his name became a dirty word that wasn't to be mentioned. I never thought much about it, actually . . . until this morning when I heard he was coming on the show."

"And now?"

Leigh's clear blue eyes twinkled merrily. "Now? Now I'm as curious as you are, but who do I ask? You know I'm not living at home anymore. Besides, Daddy's in Europe and Mommy's in Palm Springs for a tennis tournament."

"You could ask Jamie," Neil teased.

Leigh saucily wrinkled her patrician nose. "All right, I will. And I'll tell him *you* told me to."

"You would, wouldn't you?" he laughed. "But if you ever find out, you'll tell me, won't you? In exchange, if you promise to keep your mouth shut, I'll tell you a little secret."

"A secret? You know you can trust me, Neil. Come on, tell me!"

"Well, I have it on very good authority that you and Liz and Jamie are going to be in the same story line. And that prissy little Penny Archer character you play may end up having an affair with him."

"An affair . . . with Jamie Starbuck?" Leigh's expression was blank for a moment, then a mischievous grin spread across her face. "Oh, my God. Daddy will have a stroke! But Mom will love it. I've got to call her!"

"Why should your mother love it?"

"I don't know," she answered, still grinning. "But she will. I have a feeling."

"I thought you said I could trust you."

"Oh please," Leigh sweetly cajoled. "Just let me tell Mom. She won't say a thing. I swear!"

"Sure. On your grandfather's Bible."

"I'll ask her about Daddy and Jamie," she bargained. "And I promise, I'll let you know everything she tells me. Even if it's something disgusting." She glanced at the clock. "Oh my! Vico will kill me if I'm late! I've got to run!"

CHAPTER

It's like a goddamn loony bin in here, Jamie silently exclaimed from his vantage point in Studio 41's control room. He was leaning forward to follow the action on the wall of television screens in front of him.

In the center were two large color monitors—one showing the shot Vico Fellouris was taping at the moment from camera 2 and on the other, the preview monitor, the next shot he was planning to use. Below was a row of smaller black and white monitors labeled "1," "2," "3," "SLIDE," "FILM," "ON AIR," "ABC," "CBS," and "NBC."

Through the jumble of talk Jamie tried to fix his attention on the voices closest to Vico.

"Ready camera 3 and keep it tight," the associate director called into his headset.

"Thirty seconds too long," the production assistant intoned.

"Three!" Vico commanded with a sharp snap of his fingers.

The technical director's hands moved swiftly over his complex console of levers and buttons, and Liz Barrett's image popped to the center monitor.

"Ready Two," the associate director called and the somberly aesthetic, young face of one of the show's stars, Annie Holland, appeared on the preview monitor.

"Tighten it up!" Vico ordered the cameraman operating camera 3.

"Watch that mike shadow on Two," the associate director warned.

Jamie quickly glanced through the double glass window into the audio room where the technician adjusted his dials and levers while giving instructions to the man operating the microphone boom in the adjacent studio.

"Two!" Vico snapped his fingers.

"Ready Three! Ready commercial film!"

"Still thirty long."

Jamie leaned back on his stool and slowly shook his head. It looked and sounded like they were all crazy, but when you pieced it together somehow it all made sense.

"Three!" Vico snapped his fingers again.

Annie Holland's gaunt, boyish figure spun into view on the center monitor; her yellowish, catlike eyes glowed with intensity as the scene became more strident. Sweet and tough, Jamie observed. That's a hell of a combination. Not very sexy, but damned effective.

A blur of movement from camera 1's black and white monitor caught Jamie's attention as the camera was moved into position for the scene following the commercial break. A table in a corner of Webster University's library sharpened into view and Jamie recognized Leigh Fisk arranging her schoolbooks while whispering across the table to the square-jawed young actor, Stanley Gordon, who played her boyfriend.

So that was Russell Fisk's scrawny little daughter. She turned out pretty well. It was a good thing she took after her mother. He wondered if she knew Erika was almost her stepmother.

"Annie's up!" the production assistant tersely announced, scanning the written dialogue in her script. "She's ad-libbing."

"Oh shit!" Vico groaned.

Jamie felt a knot tightening in the pit of his own stomach as he saw the panic begin to show in the young actress's eyes.

"Three!" Vico called. "Loosen it up, Three. We'll hold on

Liz long enough for Annie to look at the prompter and get back in the scene."

"Forty long!"

"Two," Vico spoke into his headset, watching Annie on camera 2 and the preview monitors. "Can you move a little more to your left so the prompter is more in her eye-line?"

"Can't do it, Vico. I'm right up against the set."

Liz gamely began ad-libbing, trying to jog loose the block in Annie's memory.

"Fifty-five second long."

"Look at the prompter, goddamn you!" Vico yelled at the girl's image in the monitors.

Ralph Marks, the stage manager, spoke over the intercom. "The prompter's broken, Vico. They're working on it."

Annie reluctantly shifted her gaze to the camera lens, her pathetic expression of defeat filling the preview screen in full color. "I'm sorry," she said. Then, with her eyes brimming with tears, she turned away from the camera.

"Stop the tape," the assistant ordered as the telephone began to ring.

"It's Cathy," the production assistant said to Vico. "She wants to know what happened."

"She has a monitor in her office," Vico barked. "She knows what happened as well as any of us!"

Liz came flying into the control room. "I'm sorry, Vico. I did what I could, but Annie's in such a terrible emotional state. I think she needs a rest."

"I know what she needs," he growled, searching through the remainder of his script for a possible cut to eliminate the extra seconds they were running over.

Liz turned to Jamie and smiled. "I hope this hasn't been disturbing for you. It really doesn't happen very often."

"No," he grinned sheepishly, stepping from the stool and straightening his body to its full height. "It doesn't disturb me. It scares me to death!"

Liz's smile brightened as she placed a comforting hand on his arm. "You don't have anything to worry about."

The unexpected firmness of his bicep under the rough corduroy of his tailored jacket caused her to almost involuntarily pull her hand away. "Not a man of your experience."

"Well, my experience hasn't been in *this* kind of work. I really admire you people, learning all these lines every day."

"You'll get used to it. There're a lot of movie actors who've come to daytime. Macdonald Cary, Rory Calhoun, Dame Judith Anderson, even Janice Paige. I'm sure they went through the same doubts you're having right now."

"How about you?" he asked, mentally noting the tell-tale signs of recent plastic surgery on her finely planed face. "Did this frighten *you* when you started?"

"Oh my," she responded, her fingers fluttering over the delicate scar in her hairline. "It was so long ago I can hardly remember. I still get a bit of stage fright before my concerts though."

"Concerts?"

"Yes," she answered, not understanding his ignorance. "I sing. Colleges, dinner theaters. You haven't heard my albums?"

"Well, I was out of the country for a long time," he lied. "And before that, I ah . . . You don't get much time to watch soaps when you're working during the day."

"Yes, that is a shame, isn't it."

"How much longer?" Vico demanded of his associate director.

"At least another five minutes. There's a glitch in the computer."

"What does that mean?" Jamie quietly asked Liz.

"I'm not sure, but I think it has something to do with the fact that we shoot 'live'."

"What do you mean?" Jamie gestured toward the video console.

"Of course, it's on tape," she clarified. "But we *pretend* it's live. That's how we maintain our special quality. We're the only show left that tries to shoot from start to finish without stopping."

"Maybe that's why they get so excited when an actor forgets his lines."

Vico spoke to the stage manager through his headset. "How's it going in there, Ralph?"

"It looks like Annie's all right now. Cathy's been talking to her."

"I have a couple of cuts. I'm coming in." Vico turned away from his console. "Liz, I made some cuts in your scene with Annie. Let's go run through them with her." His mouth twisted into a crooked grin as he shifted his look to Jamie. "It sure as hell ain't like the movies, is it?"

Before Jamie could respond, Leigh Fisk came bounding through the door.

"Hi, everybody," she called brightly. "I thought I'd come in and help out."

"Thanks," Vico grunted affectionately. "You can take over. I have to go out to the stage."

Liz started to say something to Jamie but instead dropped her gaze and followed Vico out of the control room.

Leigh extended her hand and boldly approached Jamie.

"Hello, Mr. Starbuck. I'm Leigh Fisk."

Jamie couldn't help but smile as he returned her firm handshake. "Hello, Leigh. We've met before. But I guess you've forgotten."

"Oh no! It's just that I didn't think you'd remember *me!* You were my favorite actor until . . ."

"Until the disagreement with your father," he assisted.

Leigh's clear eyes danced with suppressed amusement. "Yes, the disagreement. I spoke with my mother during our break. She said to give you her regards."

"Thank you. How *is* your mother?"

"She's terrific! She's out in California." Leigh looked up into his dark eyes. "Mommy said she saw your wife the other night at Nicky Blair's restaurant. What a coincidence. They haven't seen each other since Erika was working for Daddy. And that was *before* the disagreement. She asked if you're still together?"

Jamie was a bit taken aback by her directness. "Sure. We're still together . . . more or less."

"I asked her if Erika mentioned your being here in New York, but Mommy said they didn't get a chance to speak. When is she coming? It'll really be great to see her again!"

"Yes, great," a reluctant smile tugged at the corners of his mouth. "But she hasn't decided . . ." Jamie breathed a small sigh of relief when he saw Vico briskly reenter the control room, followed by Cathy and Neil.

"Okay, honey," Vico said to Leigh. "I'll take over again. You'd better get out there. We're ready to start."

"Is Annie all right?"

"She'll get through it," Cathy assured.

"One minute to tape," the assistant announced over the PA system.

"I'd better run," Leigh said as the control room suddenly became alive with activity.

Jamie's attention was drawn to a grandfatherly figure coming through the door.

"You haven't met Karl yet," Neil said, moving to Jamie's side. "He plays Dr. Bayard. You're sharing a dressing room with him."

Jamie smiled with faint recognition at the sight of the elderly actor whose fringe of white hair seemed almost like a halo.

"I'm Karl Herbert," his eyes sparkled kindly. "Welcome to the show. We're all very pleased that you decided to join us."

"Thanks," Jamie nodded graciously, catching a scent of gin through Karl's walruslike moustache.

"Karl," an assistant interrupted. "You're wanted on the set."

"Excuse me," he said to Jamie. "I'm in the following act. We'll get acquaintd later."

"Sure," Jamie replied as Karl waved and hastened out of the control room.

"Jamie," Cathy spoke. "Would you mind stepping outside?"

"Of course not." He put his arm around her shoulder in a friendly manner.

Cathy moved ahead, deftly slipping from under the weight of his arm. When they reached the corridor she turned, her face a mask of cheerful efficiency. "I'm sorry about the confusion."

"I don't see how I'm ever going to remember all these names." He looked deep into her pretty green eyes. "And there are a few other things I'm unclear about. What do you say we have a drink later?"

Cathy's face colored slightly as she glanced at Neil, who was trailing close behind.

"I'm afraid that's impossible. Neil can answer any questions you have. The costumer is busy with something else so Neil's going to take you shopping for wardrobe. That is, if you don't mind?"

"Mind?" Jamie shrugged off her rebuff as he put his large hand on Neil's shoulder. "Of course not. You know, the last college picture I did, the wardrobe was easy: Levis, button-down shirt, and a letterman sweater."

"The All-American," Neil spoke up. "With Lori Doone."

"I'll be damned," Jamie grinned at Cathy. "The kid's a historian!"

"I've been a fan of yours since I was only . . ."

"Don't remind me how long it's been!" Jamie protested good-naturedly. "Instead, why don't you tell me how this 'middle-aged' college administrator fits in with the rest of 'Yesterday's Children'?"

Neil shook his head as they moved away, assuring Jamie that he looked as youthful as ever.

Cathy watched Jamie disappear down the corridor. "Actors," she hissed under her breath. "They all think they're so damned irresistible!!"

CHAPTER

"Demographics," Liz muttered to herself, as she pulled her mink on over her faintly patterned suit and stepped out of her dressing room.

It doesn't matter that "Yesterday's Children" has been on top for almost twenty years. It doesn't matter that we're still in the top ten, both with the ratings and the magazine polls. Now they've dreamed up demographics to worry about. If they really want to know how many are watching, why don't they count everybody? What about the thousands of people in hospitals, even prisons? Nobody thinks to count them!

She looked down at the script protruding from her bag as she proceeded toward the artists' entrance. *I'll be glad if George Conley really does leave. I hope he chokes on his demographics!*

Liz pushed through the double doors into the chill of the gray afternoon and noticed Annie Holland trudging up the street to the corner bus stop. Her knitted cap was down tightly over her mousy brown hair and her head was hunched into the turned-up collar of her long, cossack-style coat. Liz's eyes shifted undecidedly from the row of heated taxis waiting at the curb to the forlorn figure slowly walking away from her. *I wish I could understand that girl,* Liz thought. *She's the best heavy we've ever had. Maybe the best in television. It isn't easy to hate a person with her waiflike quality, but our viewers don't have any trouble hating her!*

Liz drew her fur coat more tightly around her body and hastened after her young colleague. "I'm going right by your neighborhood. Would you like to share a taxi?"

Annie gave a frightened start at Liz's sudden appearance. She had removed her makeup and the hollow darkness of her eyes seemed more pronounced than Liz had ever remembered.

"No, thank you. I think I'm going to walk."

Liz shivered, sinking deeper into her warm coat. "Do you mind if I walk with you? Walking is such wonderful exercise."

Annie didn't answer. She continued her methodical pace, keeping her eyes cast down at the sidewalk in front of her.

"I love to walk on these cold days," Liz said. "It makes your whole body feel kind of tingly, doesn't it?"

No reaction came from the preoccupied young actress.

I wonder if it's drugs, Liz thought. No. She had seen people on drugs. It was all that hate mail Annie was getting. It was wearing her down.

"You can't let those letters ruin your life. The postal authorities and network security are looking for the moron who wrote them. Chances are it's just another harmless lunatic who's satisfying his neurosis with his poison pen."

Annie reacted with an almost imperceptible shrug.

"And have you considered that, in a way, these letters are a tribute to your acting ability?" Liz continued kindly. "They prove that people believe—*really* believe—in the work you're doing."

Annie nodded wordlessly.

"You're not the *only* one. I've received some pretty disturbing mail through the years, too. And you know how *everyone* loves Jennifer Wells."

Liz noticed an almost imperceivable waver in Annie's expression. *Maybe it is drugs,* she speculated. "Annie," Liz said, assuming the motherly role of her television character. "Are you in some kind of trouble? Is there something you'd like to talk about? Something I may be able to help you with?"

Annie raised her head, taking a deep breath. She blinked back what might have been a tear, then pensively shook her head. "No, Liz. I'm fine. Really I am. I'm just . . . tired. I haven't been sleeping well." She shakily turned her head at the lumbering sound of the uptown bus approaching the nearby stop.

"Have you seen a doctor?" Liz continued.

"That's my bus," Annie cried, dashing for the opening door. "I'm okay, Liz! Honest I am!"

Annie caught a glimpse of Liz's troubled face as the bus lurched away from the curb. She made an instinctive move toward an empty seat, but changed her mind and reached for the overhead handrail instead, allowing her body to sway listlessly with the movement of the vehicle.

Annie knew Liz meant well. But how could Liz understand when Annie couldn't understand herself? This wasn't like what happened to Michael J. Fox or Jodie Foster. Not even that poor Rebecca Shaeffer.

Annie mechanically inserted her keys into the three safety locks in the door of her second floor walk-up apartment. She glanced up and down the narrow staircase of the renovated brownstone building on West 68th Street and then quickly slipped inside.

She paused a moment, studying the moderate disarray of her sparsely furnished studio apartment. Apart from her large brass bed, the few remaining pieces of furniture would have been more appropriate in a child's room. There was a small, hand-painted table surrounded by three matching chairs, a miniature sofa, a Tiffany-style glass lamp, and a tiny color television set.

She shed her cap and coat and moved into the cramped alcove-kitchen where she put a copper tea kettle on the fire, ignoring the dishes in the sink. She selected a flavor from an assortment of exotic herb teas in the cupboard, measured a portion into a dainty porcelain teapot, then filled it with boiling water. She stared at the pot until the tea began to steep, then slowly crossed to the brass bed.

After removing the rumpled handmade quilt, she looked

first at one, then the other set of silver-plated handcuffs attached to the brass posts at either side of the head of the bed.

An unfamiliar noise from the hallway caused her to glance warily at the door. Hearing nothing more, she hurriedly stripped the gaily patterned sheets from the bed, trying not to notice the spattered stains of blood mixed with traces of black ink.

She deposited the soiled sheets on top of a bloodied towel in the bathroom hamper, closed the hamper, then lifted her eyes to her unhappy reflection in the mirror. I must be out of my mind, she thought. But what can I do?

After putting fresh sheets on the bed she poured a cup of tea and lowered herself into one of the small chairs around the table.

A cry of pain escaped her lips as she involuntarily jumped to her feet.

Dropping her skirt and panties as she moved, she returned to the bathroom. Her eyes began to well up with tears when she looked over her shoulder at the large inflamed welt on the side of her buttocks spelling out the crude, freshly tattooed words 'BAD ASS.'

She blotted her eyes with a paper tissue, then took a can of spray disinfectant from the medicine cabinet and awkwardly applied it to her wounded backside.

"This *has* to stop," she uttered aloud with finality. "I can't let him destroy me!"

The sound of the telephone jarred the first cracks in her newfound resolution, and the man's voice at the other end of the line cause it to crumble completely.

She nodded submissively, replaced the receiver, and numbly changed into a short, flimsy nightgown.

She climbed onto the bed and locked her left wrist into one of the handcuffs. Lying on her stomach, she struggled to secure the other handcuff on her right wrist, but her clumsy position made it impossible.

"Oh, my Lord," she gasped, her efforts becoming more frantic. "I'll be punished! He's going to hurt me, I know it!"

CHAPTER

 Sam Allison's hard, deliberate strokes churned the water in the West Side YMCA's swimming pool into boiling froth. He executed a proficient racing turn and began yet another lap.

Sam's concentration on his swimming form began to wane as his thoughts strayed to Cathy. *I can't win,* he reflected. *Cathy doesn't really want to be a producer. It's all some kind of a power trip with her. As soon as she has that job she'll be looking to the next one. Before I know it she'll be my boss and I'll still be doing her work as well as my own.*

Sam executed another turn when he reached the other end of the pool, but his steady rhythm had drifted away. He rolled onto his back and propelled himself with an easy kicking motion. *She'll never be able to produce that show. She can't write! Everyone knows a good soap producer must be able to write along with everything else, and she can't write dialogue worth a damn.*

Sam decided he never should have helped her the first time. Once she found out he could doctor her scripts, she'd get a headache every time he wouldn't.

Still floating on his back, Sam gazed at the ceiling high overhead, and a wry smile spread across his face. Maybe he could develop a new show around that idea: *The Joy of Making Your Husband Pay for Sex. Since he was the expert, he'd be the moderator . . .*

"Hey!"

Sam turned to see the large, pasty figure of his longtime friend and college roommate, Devon Rudin, impatiently striding along the pool deck. "What are you smiling about? You're supposed to be thinking!"

"I *am* thinking," Sam shot back. "About this new show I may put into development; a new twist on the wives against the husbands game shows."

"That should be easy for you," Devon smirked. "Cathy's had you in training for weeks now."

"You're a born smart ass," Sam responded as he chopped the pool's surface with his hand, spraying Devon with a fan of water.

◆ After leaving the pool and showering, Sam and Devon squeezed into the crowded, white-tiled steam room. Devon carefully adjusted the towel covering his genitals while suspiciously eyeing the other occupants. "One more thing," he said in a low voice. "Our deal is going to include a membership at the New York Athletic Club. This place always did make me nervous."

"The 'Y' was good enough back in Chicago."

"A lot of things have changed since Chicago. You and me, for example."

"Yeah, you've put on about twenty pounds."

"Don't try to joke your way out of this. I can't stall much longer, Sam. You're going to *have* to make a decision." Devon shook his head. "What the hell is wrong with you? You hate your job at Federated. You've told me so a dozen times. I'm offering you a partnership with no investment in a company that can't lose. We'll have six million to spend on the Saddle Cologne account alone! If the agency never lands another client, you should *still* make twice what you're earning now. And we've already talked about the tax advantages."

Sam sighed as he wiped the perspiration from his face and chest. "I know, Dev. It's just that I have other problems to consider."

"How many times do I have to tell you, Sam? Our office isn't going to be in Timbuktu! We'll be right here in New York City. You'll be spending every night in your conjugal bed."

Sam's face reddened. "It isn't that . . ."

"That's *exactly* what it is," Devon persisted. "We've been planning something like this since the mail room at Leo Burnett. What's happened to you? I admit Cathy has a great set of knockers, but you never had any problems getting laid. It's not as though you're some little putz who has to run around jerking off in his raincoat."

Sam rose from the tile bench and rubbed the perspiration from his body. "You've got it all wrong, Dev."

"Prove it then!"

"Just a couple more days."

"All right, Sam," Devon said, also rising from the bench. "Day after tomorrow. I don't want to push you, but I'm committed to make a move."

"I know," Sam nodded.

"And I hope you also know you're not the only one with wife problems. Ruth's father thinks you're already in."

"You told me."

"Papa Roth knows you're a goy, but he thinks you look Jewish."

"It's all right with me. When a man like your Papa Roth owns half the world, he can think anything he wants."

"*Except* that his only son-in-law is a fool and a liar!"

Sam smiled ruefully. "You've made your point, Devon. And, speaking of beards, there's one over there that's watching you like you're a kosher delicatessen."

Devon didn't look, but quickly wrapped his towel around his waist and stepped through the door into the shower room. After a quick shower he hurried on to the locker room and was nearly dressed when Sam joined him.

"I believe that since you're standing me up for dinner you owe me the pleasure of a large healthy martini," Devon called as he knotted his tie and slipped into his impeccably cut, three-piece gray flannel suit.

"How about the Ginger Man?" Sam called back from his locker. "It's just around the corner."

"Fine. They have a pretty active bar. Maybe I won't have to go home for dinner after all." Devon stepped back from the mirror. Satisfied with what he saw, his attention wandered to the reflection of the man behind him changing into a worn, sleeveless sweatsuit. His idle curiosity flashed into intense interest when he suddenly recognized the man's face. "Hey," he said, sidling over to Sam's locker. "Isn't that the actor who used to be Slim Chisholm on TV? What's he doing here?"

"Probably the same thing we are."

"But, he a *star*. Stars don't go to the 'Y'!"

"Sure they do. I see stars in here every once in a while."

Devon's head bobbed with excitement. "I see stars all the time, but this guy was my idol. God, it's been years!"

"Would you like to meet him?" Sam asked with false nonchalance.

"Hell yes, I'd like to meet him. Do you know him?" Devon hesitated as a new idea illuminated his countenance. "Wouldn't he be great for the Saddle Cologne campaign? He could sell a train load!"

"Don't go jumping the gun, Dev. We don't *have* a Saddle Cologne campaign yet," Sam cautioned, then turned away to approach Jamie.

"Excuse me, Mr. Starbuck, but I'm Sam Allison. Cathy Allison's husband . . . from 'Yesterday's Children'?"

Jamie's blank expression changed into a cordial smile as he offered his hand to Sam. "Nice to meet you, Sam. I didn't know she had a husband. But I reckon there's a lot going on over there that I don't know about yet. Do you work on the show too?"

"Not directly. I'm in daytime development. My office is in the tower over on Sixth Avenue."

"Slippery Rock," Jamie nodded. "I was there when they opened that building. I was in nighttime then."

"I remember. My friend over there says Slim Chisholm was his idol. Would you mind if I introduce him to you?"

"Course not," Jamie answered as he bent over to secure the laces of his sneakers.

Devon effusively responded to Sam's introduction, and as the men conversed, Sam became fascinated by Devon's obvious hero worship. He was also intrigued by his own attraction to the actor's easygoing charm. Devon's right, he mused. Starbuck's a natural. He could sell a ton of Saddle.

Sensing Jamie's desire to end the conversation, Sam hinted that he and Devon be on their way. Devon grudgingly assented, but not before giving way to his enthusiasm. "Listen," he said. "Let's have dinner some night. Sam and I are working on a project you'd be perfect for. That is, if you're interested in doing commercials?"

Jamie shrugged noncommittally. "I don't have anything against commercials. What's the product?"

"Saddle Cologne," Devon blurted.

Sam spoke the same instant. "It's really premature to talk about it." He shot Devon a warning look. "We've been discussing the *possibility* of getting involved with the Saddle advertising campaign. *Nothing* definite yet."

"That's correct," Devon conceded. "But *if* we do the campaign, how would you feel about becoming a part of it? Maybe as the spokesman."

"Saddle's all right," Jamie replied, betraying no eagerness. "I used it when I was a kid. In fact, I think the first time I ever shaved I used Saddle. Sure, let's have dinner and talk about it. Cathy has my number at home."

Sam hurried Devon through the good-byes and Jamie made his way to the exercise room where he began a routine of light calisthenics.

Would I be interested in doing the Saddle Cologne spots? Jamie thought ironically. *Those sonsabitches. From the time I came back to this country, my agent has been doing everything he could think of to get them to use me in that commercial!*

◈ The cold night air didn't penetrate the sheepskin coat Jamie had purchased in Munich a few years earlier.

After leaving the YMCA he turned up Broadway past Lincoln Center, then on to Columbus Avenue in the direction of the West 69th Street furnished apartment that Neil had efficiently located for him.

The new facade of Jamie's remodeled apartment building stood out amongst the older, more sedate brownstones of the West Sixties and Seventies. He entered, checked the mailbox, then took the elevator to the third floor.

The small, one bedroom apartment had a homey atmosphere. Its furnishings were inexpensive but obviously chosen with taste and care, and the cramped but handy kitchen was an amateur chef's delight.

He poured a glass of chilled Chablis, seated himself on the sofa in front of the television, and deliberately placed the wine glass on his script. He gazed at it for a moment before picking up a TV Guide which was also lying on the table.

They're getting later and later, he mused when he discovered one of his early films listed in the all-night schedule. *RUMBLING REBELS,* starring Jamie Starbuck and Lori Doone.

"Here's to you Lori," he said, raising his glass in mock salute. "You're as responsible as anyone that I'm about to launch a glorious career in soap opera! You and your back alimony!"

His attention turned to a photograph of his son on the mantle. He glanced at his watch, mentally calculating the three-hour time difference in Los Angeles. Was Bucky home from school yet? No. He had soccer practice today.

Damn this business! It wasn't right for the coach to have to leave so close to the championships. Jamie frowned as he disinterestedly watched the world news flickering across the TV screen. He'd fix something to eat and phone later. Bucky should be home in an hour or so.

After finishing his meal of a simple salad, some hard cheese, and another cold glass of Chablis, Jamie nervously began prowling around the small apartment.

The more he tried to ignore it, the more his attention was drawn to the script lying on the coffee table. *I don't know what I'm worried about,* he thought. *I know the damn thing. So what if they do it like it's live? It's only a half-hour show. Live television isn't any tougher than doing a play.* Jamie had done a few plays at Pasadena Playhouse. He didn't have any problems then. *But Christ, that was over twenty-five years ago. I didn't know what real problems were in those days!*

Jamie snatched up the script and once again began reviewing his dialogue. His confidence grew as the lines came easily. Suddenly the image of Annie Holland's panic-stricken face intruded itself into his consciousness.

What's the next line? He tried to force his memory, but it only recalled the scent of gin on Karl's breath.

A brushing glance at the page restored the forgotten line, along with his confidence, and he continued easily to the end of the script.

"I knew I could do it," he uttered, going for another glass of wine. "I've made more movies than all these TV stiffs put together. If they can do it, there's no reason *I* can't!"

Jamie tossed the script back on the table. He looked at his watch and the telephone again. An instant later it rang.

His face broadened into a warm smile as he recognized his son's voice at the other end of the line.

"Hi Daddy!"

"Howdy, Bucky boy."

"You wanted me to tell you about the new coach. He's not very good, Daddy. Couldn't you find a soap opera show here? The other kids think you're a better coach too."

A wave of emotion warmed Jamie. "You have to give him a chance, Bucky. He'll improve. And if the show works out, next season we'll play on a new team, here."

"Okay, Daddy," Bucky conceded. "But I think it would be better if you came home."

"So do I . . . So do I, son . . . but I can't."

"I wanted to stay home tomorrow and watch your first show, but Mommy says I can't miss school."

"She's right. The show we tape tomorrow won't be on until next week, anyway."

"Are you coming home for my birthday?"

Jamie sighed. "It doesn't look like it. According to the advance schedule I won't even have a long weekend."

"Aw!"

"But we'll be together for Christmas!" Jamie quickly added. "Mommy promised that if I can't get off, she'll bring you here. It'll be fun. There'll be snow in the park, and everything!"

"Okay, Daddy," the boy responded unenthusiastically. "If you don't come home, Mommy says we'll probably go to Palm Springs for my birthday."

"Palm Springs?"

"To Tony Mitchell's house. We went there Saturday, after you left."

"Oh. . . ." Jamie tried to keep his rising jealousy out of his voice. "Is Mommy there now? Can I talk to her?"

"She's in her room. Just a minute."

"Hello," Erika's soft German accent purred into the phone.

"Hi, Erika. Just checking to see that everything's all right."

"Everything's all right here. And with you? Have you started the show?"

"No, it's tomorrow."

"Yes, naturally . . . tomorrow."

"I hear you and Bucky were in Palm Springs?"

"I sang at the benefit I told you about. With Tony Mitchell."

"You didn't tell me you were taking Bucky to stay at his house."

"Don't be silly, Jamie. Tony has a big house. There were many people. Bucky had his own room."

"And you?"

Erika laughed nervously. "Jamie, sometimes you ask the

most insane questions. Oh, you'll never guess who I saw there."

"Nancy Fisk?"

Erika paused. "How do you know?"

"Palm Springs isn't as far from New York as you might like to think," Jamie answered dryly. "Her daughter Leigh is a regular in 'Yesterday's Children.' Leigh talked to her mother today."

"What about her father? Russell must be thrilled to know you're with his daughter."

"I'm not *with* her. We'll be in the same show, that's all."

"But Russell knows your reputation . . . and he knows your type. I wonder if he was told the same thing about you and I when *we* first worked together?"

"I don't care *what* anyone tells him," Jamie snapped, then contained his rising anger. "It's not going to work, Erika. What Russell Fisk thinks or says about *anything* has nothing to do with your having Bucky sleep at Tony Mitchell's place while you're . . . sleeping there too!"

"You have a mind like a pig," she spat. "My relationship with Tony is purely professional!"

"Don't bullshit me, Erika. Everybody knows about Tony and his professional relationships!" Jamie realized he had gone too far, but before he could retreat, the phone clicked dead in his ear.

"Goddammit!" he swore after dialing his number at home and reaching a busy signal. "I don't want to fight with her, but I'll be damned if I'm going to let her take Bucky along while she's doing house calls!"

Jamie picked up his script, then threw it back on the coffee table. *How do I solve this mess,* he thought with helpless frustration. *Erika just doesn't give a shit anymore. As far as she's concerned, her husband is just another horny, over-the-hill relic of late-night reruns.*

But that could change. I could make a comeback. With a little luck, "Yesterday's Children" can open the door to a lot of things!

CHAPTER

6

The dark phantoms began scurrying to the recesses of Annie Holland's mind as she slowly awakened from her troubled sleep.

At first she felt a chill on her naked back; then as she drowsily reached for the bed quilt the dull pain of her lacerated buttocks crept into her consciousness. She curled more tightly into her fetal position but found the pain less intrusive when she turned to lie on her stomach.

As her mind began to clear, pangs of hunger, then revulsion, gripped her belly, and she squeezed her eyes shut trying to block out the memory of the night before.

She moistened her lips as she remembered the dry, stifling taste of the tampons Zev had stuffed into her mouth as he repeatedly punctured her skin with his thread-wrapped, ink-soaked needles. She recalled how he made her watch in a hand mirror while he added embellishments to the tattoo across her rear.

He wasn't always like this, Annie thought. When she first came on the show he was so sweet and helpful. They had said he was one of the best unit managers they'd had at Federated. Everything went so smoothly when he ran things. She hadn't even noticed his crippled leg until he started coming here. And when he wore those special shoes he hardly limped.

Annie suddenly froze as she felt the touch of a finger lightly tracing over the letters etched in her buttocks. She turned her head and through the early morning darkness she saw Zev lying on his side, his chin cupped in his hand, carefully studying his handiwork.

"You really *are* bad, you know," he quietly spoke. "That's why you're so good on the show. Because you're really bad."

"Is that why you punish me?" she asked plaintively. "Because I'm bad?"

"That's part of it," he answered. "That . . . and because you like it so much."

"No, Zev, I *don't* like it. But I like *you*. That's my problem."

"You think you deserve to be punished and you like me because I *know* you do."

"Oh Zev," she sighed, dropping her head on the pillow. "I'm so confused."

Zev silently continued running his finger over her swollen wounds. He put his fingernail under a freshly formed scab and sharply lifted it off, causing Annie to cry out in pain.

"Do we need some more tampons?" he asked.

"No! No," she said, gritting her teeth.

He gave her a light pat, then slid off the bed and limped into the kitchen. Annie watched him return with a bottle of whisky and a wad of cotton.

"We don't want this to get infected," he said, dousing the cotton with the liquid.

"Please, Zev," she cried.

"Maybe we *do* need the tampons!" he said as he extracted some from a container near the bed and forced them into her mouth.

Zev's penis began to come to life as he stood beside the bed watching Annie's frail body shake with morbid anticipation.

He hooked his hand under her hips and drew her to a kneeling position at the edge of the bed, then dropped to his knees, placing his face a few inches from her naked backside.

The sound of Annie's muffled sobs filtered through the tampons as Zev daubed at her ink- and blood-speckled skin with the whisky-soaked cotton. Convulsive waves of pain racked her body while he applied the whisky more liberally and roughly licked it off with the flat of his tongue.

Annie couldn't help gagging on the tampons as the pain grew more intense. She prayed that her body would reach its maximum tolerance and go numb, but it didn't.

Suddenly he stopped. She waited in fearful anticipation until she felt Zev jab his rock-hard penis into her body and forcefully begin pounding his pelvis against her torn buttocks, driving himself deep into her vagina.

Again and again she came, her mind floating off into another dimension of excruciating torment and passion. Time had no meaning until through the haze she heard Zev gasp, throw his body across her back, and frantically clutch her breasts as he joined her in an explosive orgasm.

Annie collapsed in a state of semiconsciousness after Zev withdrew and went into the bathroom. She became vaguely aware of his reappearance now fully clothed. He stood by the bed and explained that he had to stop by his apartment before going to work. His wife worried about him if he didn't come home at all.

Somewhere deep in Annie's subconscious she wanted to laugh, but the most she could manage was a small fluttering motion with her fingertips and an inaudible groan of farewell.

CHAPTER

Sam walked into the bedroom and placed a vitamin capsule and a small glass of orange juice on Cathy's vanity table; it was cluttered with pills and makeup.

Cathy applied a light, final touch to her eye makeup, popped the capsule in her mouth, and drained the glass. "There," she said, looking with satisfaction into her mirror.

"As I was saying," Sam turned and spoke with a forced nonchalance while redoing the knot in his tie. "Devon's hard work is beginning to pay off. The old man has okayed the agency idea and given Devon the Saddle Cologne account to get it started."

"That's nice for Devon," Cathy reacted. "But what does that have to do with the script?"

"What script?"

"*Today's* script!" she acidly replied. "The one that's over five minutes short . . . that you promised last night you'd look at."

"I *did* look at it. But dammit, Cathy, I'm trying to talk to you!"

"I don't understand you, Sam!" Cathy jumped to her feet. "You know how important this is to me. You know they're watching to see how capable I am without George. Don't you care? Don't you want me to get ahead?"

"Sure I do," Sam retreated.

"Then is it so much to ask for a little help from my own husband? Or is it that you're so busy with your fat friend that I should find someone else to help me?"

"Of course not," Sam placated, tentatively putting his hands around her waist.

"I hope not," she purred, responding to his touch by delicately pressing herself into his groin. "I wouldn't know what to do with anyone else. You've spoiled me."

"I don't like to hear you talk like that," Sam said, embracing her more tightly. "I forgot about the script because I don't see any special problems. So it's short? Add a flashback or two. Let Liz sing a song. You've had short scripts like this dozens of times before. Why panic over *this* one?"

"Because *I'm* in charge," she answered, slipping away from his embrace. "I'll get the script. You show me where we should put in the flashbacks."

"Okay," he shrugged. "But I still want to talk to you."

Cathy took the manuscript from her bedside table and fanned through its pages trying to anticipate Sam's suggestions.

Sam breathed sharply through his nose, then plunged ahead. "Devon's offered me a full partnership in his new advertising agency."

Cathy's eyes didn't waver from the pages in front of her as she smiled. "That's the funniest thing I've ever heard. Devon offering a job to *you*. Please, Sam, I don't have time for joking. What do you want to talk about?"

"That's it," he mumbled defensively. "I told him I'd think about it."

"Think about what?" she demanded, unwilling to believe he was serious. "Devon Rudin is a nincompoop. And if it wasn't for his rich wife he wouldn't amount to even that much. *You're* almost a vice president of one of the most important television networks in the world."

"I'm not a vice president yet."

"But you *will* be. They love you at Federated. You know that."

"Yeah, but, I don't . . ."

"Please, Sam," she murmured, closing the subject by tucking her body into his embrace. "I'll be in a better mood for kidding later . . . maybe tonight. But now, I'm worried about the script." Cathy accepted a brief kiss, then pushed the script into Sam's hands and returned to her vanity table where she once again inspected her makeup.

Sam rolled the manuscript into a tight cylinder and withdrew to the small dining area in the living room. He was seated at the table skimming the pages when the sound of the doorbell jarred his concentration. He gazed curiously toward the door, at his watch, then toward the bedroom.

"That must be Neil," Cathy called. "Will you let him in?"

"All right." Sam looked through the peephole, unbolted the night latches, and opened the door. "Morning, Neil."

"Morning, Sam." Neil stepped spritely into the living room. "Is Cathy ready?"

"Almost," Sam replied as he returned to the open script.

Neil ducked into the kitchen and soon reappeared with a steaming cup of coffee. "How's things over at Slippery Rock? Any new developments?"

"New developments?" Sam guffawed, then leaned back in his chair. "Do you know what I do, Neil?"

"Sure," he answered good-naturedly. "You're a director of daytime development. I would suppose that means you help create and develop new ideas for daytime television."

"That's right," Sam answered, staring nostalgically at his two gold-plated Emmys prominently displayed in the living room bookcase. "I sit at my desk all day creating and developing new ideas."

"And darn *good* ideas," Cathy emphasized as she breezed out of the bedroom. "Like letting Liz do a song. Can you find a place in the script to put one?"

"Why not?" Sam shrugged.

"What about George?" Neil interjected. "Liz did a song *last* week. George isn't so crazy about letting her sing that often."

Cathy's voice took a tone of gentle admonition. "Think a minute, Neil. George is in L.A. and Liz is here. George is undoubtedly going to move to L.A. while Liz is staying right here. Who is it we want to keep happy?"

"How about here?" Sam interrupted, indicating with his finger into the script. "In this last scene, right after Spencer Franklyn leaves to walk to the university with Penny. Thinking about Spencer can start Lizzie reminiscing about her poor, dead husband. Cut in a few flashbacks. Get the famous Jennifer Wells tears rolling while she sings to her dear departed love. *That* ought to get them!"

"Not only *them*," Cathy's expression brightened. "Today's show will air on the same day as the network affiliates dinner in Washington, D.C. I think they'd really like it if we give them the same song live that they've just seen on television."

"What a great idea!" Neil grinned appreciatively. "George *has* to like it. And you know Liz is going to *love* it!"

"Good creative public relations," Sam agreed. "Maybe you're in the wrong end of this business."

"No I'm not," Cathy pointedly corrected. "And neither are *you*!"

CHAPTER

"Don't you want to say something to Jamie?" Neil urged, trying to slow Cathy's rapid pace as he followed her along the dressing room corridor.

"First things first," she clipped, before putting on a radiant smile and stepping through Liz's open door. "We should have taped dress rehearsal!" she cried enthusiastically.

"The song is super," Neil grinned over her shoulder.

"Thank you," Liz rose graciously from her makeup table. "I knew you'd like it, but I still want to thank you for getting it approved. I know how hard the network resists using new material."

"I had to go all the way to Jim Hennigan, but you know how I am. I believe anything that's good for the show is worth fighting for."

"So do I, Cathy." She cast a glance to Neil. "Which is one of the reasons I'm taking the trouble tonight of meeting that new, young arranger you recommended, Neil."

"Eddie Irving is new in town, but I know you'll be happy Liz," Neil replied confidently. "He's a real find!"

"We'll see. In view of all the changes in music today, I'm always reluctant to get my hopes up. . . . Speaking of disappointments," Liz returned her attention to Cathy, "have you heard any news about when George is returning?"

"He said he's being delayed another day or two. He didn't say why."

Liz looked thoughtfully at Cathy, then smiled. "If he knew how little we need him he would never have left."

Cathy's eyes gleamed enthusiastically as she returned Liz's look. "I'm happy you feel that way, Liz. Your opinion has always been terribly important to me. You have a better grasp of what the audience wants than any actress I've ever known."

"It's a question of honesty, Cathy." Liz's voice took on a note of seriousness. "If you don't lie or try to cheat them the audience will trust you and stay with you forever. It's so simple I'm surprised more people don't understand it."

"I couldn't agree with you more," Cathy chimed. "I remember you saying when I first began working here: 'Honesty is the key to the audience's heart.' It's been a sort of watchword for me ever since."

"Good," Liz warmly responded. "Now, if we could convince everyone else connected with the show to feel the same way, we'd be number one again before you know it."

"We will be," Cathy answered with bold confidence.

"Hey, Neil," a voice sounded from down the corridor.

Neil saw Zev Brahms moving toward him with the slight, rolling gait he affected to hide his limp. His pleasantly handsome face wore its customary friendly expression as he asked Cathy's whereabouts.

Neil pointed through the open doorway and Zev looked in. "Excuse me, Cathy," he said. "But Vico is trying to find you. He thinks he's found some better flashbacks to use with Liz's song."

"Thanks, Zev," she said. "Neil, call Vico. Tell him I'm on my way."

"Oh, Zev?" Liz spoke as Neil picked up her dressing room telephone. "How is your wife's asthma? Is she feeling any better?"

"I'm afraid not. I'm seriously thinking of taking that station manager job with the affiliate station out in Albuquerque. They seem to feel that my experience in Special Projects

and now with this show qualifies me to run the whole operation."

"But Albuquerque?" Neil echoed while dialing the phone.
"There's nothing but Indians out there. What will you do for
fun?"

"I've been a little concerned about that myself," Zev replied. "New York is much more exciting. But what can I do?
Alice has to breathe."

"I'm sorry," Liz said.

"If there's anything *we* can do," Cathy added.

"Thanks, I appreciate it," he responded with a tinge of
embarrassment, then turned to leave. "I'd better get back to
work. Oh, by the way, I don't know who's responsible, but I
sure am glad Liz has a *real* leading man for a change. You and
Jamie work great together."

"I don't know for certain," Liz smiled. "But rumor has it
that it was all Cathy's idea."

"Well," Cathy reacted with guarded satisfaction, "I'll reserve comment on that rumor until we have the show on
tape."

◈ Eddie Irving dreamily
closed his eyes while his fingers caressed the keyboard of Liz's
baby grand piano. As the tempo of the tender ballad quickened, Liz's shoulders began to sway and she moved sensuously
around her living room, crooning the tune softly.

After a complete tour of the room she returned to the
piano where she stood behind Eddie, resting her hands on his
thin shoulders until the last note. "Oh, Eddie, it's wonderful,"
she exclaimed, bending over and pressing her cheek against
his.

Eddie's eyes sparkled through his oversized, tinted glasses.
"I have to admit," he said, "it sure feels good. But that's as
much the way you sing it as the way I wrote it."

"Thank you. And thank you for bringing it to me. It's

definitely going into the new album!" Liz peered intently at him, then turned and paced across the living room. "I suppose Neil told you that I'm also looking for a new accompanist. I'm going to do one or two numbers at the network affiliates dinner in Washington, D.C., next week. Would you like to play for me?"

Eddie fidgeted with one end of the narrow, woolen scarf draped over his neck. "Sure I would. What kind of material do you want?"

"Well, first we'll do something uptempo to catch their attention, and then we can do *this* song. I just love it! I wish I could sing it on 'Yesterday's Children.' "

"Why can't you?"

"You know Jennifer. From time to time she gets a chance to sing for herself at home, sometimes at weddings . . . ar d on rare, special occasions at the local nightclub. But our writers are always arguing that it isn't easy to work in songs for the Dean of Women."

He looked at Liz with amusement in his eyes. "Isn't there an old 'Singing Nun' series on late-night cable?"

Liz laughed. "I believe you're thinking of the 'Flying Nun.' I'd love to see George Conley's face if I suggested *that* one to him."

Liz was swept by a feeling of warm familiarity as Eddie's face broke into a good-natured grin. She noticed the crooked, upturned corners of his mouth and his small, pearly teeth. Raising her gaze to his, their eyes held briefly, then the familiar feeling passed as Eddie looked away, retreating back into his reticence.

The awkwardness of the moment was alleviated by her mother, Fern, coming into the room with a tray of tea and cookies. "I didn't hear any music so I thought you might be ready for a cup of tea."

Liz's annoyance at the interruption disappeared when she noted her mother's fresh makeup and the pretty scarf around her stringy, white hair. "Thank you, Fern. Would you care for a cup of tea, Eddie?"

"No thanks," he replied, looking at his watch. "If we're finished I'd better go. If I show up in time, I can play a late gig at this little club down in the Village."

Liz nodded unhappily as she watched him neatly place his music in a worn valise. "I have a show tomorrow or I would come along. I'd love to hear you play some more."

"*You'll* have a cup of tea with me, won't you, Liz?" Fern interposed as she arranged two cups. "I'd like to hear you too. I've been listening from the other room and I like what I heard. But I don't go to *late* shows anymore."

"I think you'll be hearing a lot of Eddie's music," Liz said over her shoulder, leading Eddie to the foyer.

"Wait," Fern called as she hurried to wrap some cookies in a paper napkin and offered them to Eddie. "Take these to eat on the subway. Ask anybody at Federated. Fern Barrett makes the best cookies in all New York!"

"Thank you. Good night, Mrs. Barrett."

Liz opened the door to let Eddie out as he pulled on his coat. "Come by the studio tomorrow, if you like. I'm free between ten and eleven. You can look through the rest of my music."

"Ten in the morning," he smiled. "Yes, I'll be there."

Liz closed the door behind him and returned to Fern, dreamily carrying the image of Eddie's liquid gaze in her memory. "He's a nice boy . . . and talented."

"Yes, talented," Fern answered, thinking of the other talented boys Liz had brought home. "New York must have more talented people than any city in the world."

CHAPTER

Leigh felt good about having passed through another "phase" in her life as she packed the last of her possessions in the apartment she had, until today, shared with her friends, Beth, and the diminutive, shapely redhead, Mindy Shrafft. She didn't want to appear a prude, but it offended her private nature when Beth's boyfriend, Dave, became a fourth roommate in their one bedroom, one bath apartment.

Sharing the bedroom with Mindy and having to listen, night after night, to the lustful couple on the squeaky rollaway in the living room was bad enough, but the confusion over who got the bath—and when—was impossible. She had never shared a bath with anyone, let alone a leering, oversexed, young man. And she was heartily relieved when a confrontation with Dave led to a "one of us has to go" situation.

Why not go back home? she reasoned. Her bedroom suite in her parents' spacious Fifth Avenue apartment was just as she had left it. Her independence would be maintained by a rental agreement she negotiated with her mother, Nancy. Her privacy was assured by the fact that her parents were seldom in New York anymore, and almost *never* at the same time.

Nancy would soon be returning from Palm Springs and Russell, if he passed through New York at all, would stay only a few days before going to Florida for the rest of the winter season. It was the logical, sensible thing to do.

"But what's going to happen to me?" Mindy wailed as she helped carry a bundle of books down to a waiting cab. "I'll have to move too. It's all right for you; you're an actress. But what do you think they'd say at the bank about one of their rising executives living in a ménage à trois?"

"I was against his moving in from the beginning," Leigh reacted defensively. "You were the one who said 'live and let live.'"

"I know," Mindy conceded. "And I can't even blame Beth. She's so hooked on Dave she can't think of anything else. You'll never catch me so involved in a sexual relationship. That's all it is, don't you think?"

"Of course that's all it is," Leigh responded. "You and I have had dozens of boyfriends, but we've always managed to avoid falling into that trap!"

"Not yet, anyway," Mindy grinned.

"Meter's running, girls," the cab driver urged them along. "Let's go . . ."

"Okay, okay," they grumbled.

"Don't forget we're meeting for dinner," Mindy reminded Leigh.

"I won't. And don't forget to watch the show today. You'll see Jamie Starbuck."

"What's so hot about Jamie Starbuck? He's too old to get excited about."

"Who said you have to get excited?" Leigh countered. "Just watch. He's terrific."

"Something special?" Mindy teased.

"Make up your own mind," Leigh replied, smiling. "You know where I'm going to be while I'm watching?"

"Where?"

"In my nice, hot, leisurely bathtub—alone!"

"You rat!" Mindy called out as Leigh's cab pulled away from the curb.

◈ Leigh waited until the doorman brought her belongings up to the apartment in which she had lived more than half of her life, then dragged the bundles into her room where she paused to sit for a moment, savoring the contentment of being back in her own nest.

After stripping out of her clothing, she added a double measure of bath oil to the water flowing into her tub, switched on the television, then eased into her steaming bath.

"Perfect timing," she sighed contentedly as she turned her head to look through the open doorway as the strains of "Yesterday's Children" theme music drew her attention to the television screen.

After carefully watching the opening scene where Penny and Jennifer discussed Spencer Franklyn's impending arrival, Leigh's attentiveness waned as she realized she would not reappear until later in the show when Penny and Spencer meet.

She sopped a sponge full of sudsy water, daubed it lightly to her face, then lazily stroked the length of her thin, pretty legs. *I wish I could understand what's happening to me,* she thought, pressing her mouth into a tight line. *It's been only eight days since Jamie started the show and I feel . . . I feel excited. That's what I feel. I've never spent so much time thinking about a man before.*

She wondered if he knew. Sometimes he looked at her as if he did. What a ridiculous situation! She couldn't even talk to Mindy about it. She pretended to be so liberal, but she thought more like a banker every day.

Leigh's thoughts continued to focus on Jamie. He's an older man. He's married. With children . . . almost as old as I am. He's an actor. Daddy *hates* actors.

Leigh ran the sponge over her shoulder and began to stroke her breast, watching with fascination as her nipple grew and hardened.

Could it really have been Jamie's fault that Daddy had to leave Hollywood? I've heard lots of stories where actors and producers have gotten into fights. It must have been more than that . . . I'll have to ask Mommy again . . .

The sound of the telephone jangled Leigh out of her reverie. She twisted to her knees and strained her glistening body to reach the receiver hanging on the bathroom wall.

"I'm glad your old number still works," Neil's voice cracked with exhilaration. "It's official! George has quit. He isn't even coming back to clean out his desk!"

"Oh," Leigh responded uncertainly. "What does it mean? Does it affect you?"

"It affects me a lot," he puffed. "They're not making any permanent assignments yet, but for now I'm your new, temporary associate producer and Cathy's got George's job. Even though she's on trial, you know Cathy. Once she's in, it'll take an atom bomb to get her out!"

"That's wonderful. I'm really excited for you! And Cathy must be in heaven. What did Liz say?"

"She's in Washington at the affiliates dinner. But when Cathy called her, she said she already knew, and she'd help Cathy in any way she could."

"That *is* exciting. They do seem to like each other."

"So far they do," Neil answered with a trace of irony. "It'll be interesting to see what happens."

"What do you mean?"

"Nothing," he hedged. "It's just that with the new writers and everything, it'll be interesting to see which direction Cathy's going to try to take the show."

"Wait a minute," Leigh interrupted, as the sound of Jamie's voice snapped her attention to the TV screen. "Jamie's first scene is coming on."

"You want me to call you back?"

"No. Just be quiet a minute."

The balance between Jamie and Liz seemed just right. And

observing her own image coming down the stairs to join the scene filled Leigh with a pleasant glow.

After her exit with Jamie, the camera angle tightened to a close-up of Liz's bemused expression.

"They're very good together," she said.

"Yeah. Too bad the chemistry isn't as good between *you* and him."

"What do you mean? The scenes we taped yesterday were terrific!"

"I know cutie," he laughed. "Auntie Neil is just teasing. You *are* terrific together. Just be careful."

"Careful about what?"

"Let's put it this way. You're watching the TV in your bedroom, right?"

"Yes."

"But you're in the bathroom—in the tub, right?"

"How do you know?"

"I know you're holding the phone in one hand—where's the other?"

Leigh suddenly became aware of the warm, sodden sponge she had firmly pressed between her legs.

"Neil, you're sick. You're *really* sick!"

"Well, now you know what I'm talking about," he laughed.

"Just keep your degenerate advice to yourself. I don't need it!"

"Okay, sweetie, but watch yourself just the same . . . I gotta go. I'll see you tomorrow."

"Tomorrow," she repeated vaguely. "My God, I almost forgot! Tomorrow we're doing the publicity stills with Jamie and Liz!"

"I don't know why I put up with you," Neil groaned amusedly. "You get *everything* backward! You're not supposed to become temperamental, forgetful, and bitchy until *after* you're a star!"

"I didn't forget," she insisted weakly. "It just . . . sort of slipped my mind. . . ."

"The mind that's famous for being slipperier than a mud-

wrestler's bottom," he mocked, then changed to a more serious tone. "But I'm used to it . . . And you know I'm always
here if you want to talk."

"You can always talk to me too," she responded warmly.
"You have a lot more problems than I do, you sick thing!"

"I love you too, cutie. By the way . . . where was it?"

"What?"

"Your hand."

"Good-bye, Neil," she hissed. And hung up.

CHAPTER

"Outrageous," the pretty stewardess in Jamie's bed purred with total contentment. He had met her on his flight from L.A. and now they were lying together, watching the final credits of "Yesterday's Children" roll across the screen of his bedroom TV. "Really outrageous! I've never slept with anyone while I was watching him on TV!"

"Didn't it kind of divide your concentration?" Jamie grinned and got up to turn off the set.

"No," she wiggled her receptive body close to his as he returned to bed. "If anything, it *doubled* my concentration. Seeing you here . . . and there. And feeling you *everywhere!*"

"In three-dimensional stereo," he joked.

"*Four* dimensional!" She peppered his neck with kisses and hopped out of bed. She took her stewardess uniform from the back of a chair and with the measured step of a Las Vegas showgirl glided toward the bathroom. "Wait until I tell the other girls," she enthused.

"An actor's first duty is to his fans," he smiled, watching her close the door.

Jamie's mood grew somber as his thoughts drifted to the show. He remembered a feeling of discomfort at the sight of Leigh's image gazing out from the TV screen.

He recalled her perky smile, her trusting eyes, and the urge he had to touch her hair during the scene they had taped the previous day.

She was young, pretty, full of hell. Just his type. But she reminded him of someone.

Of course! No wonder she was his type. She was just like Erika was at her age. Naturally he was attracted to her. She was the type that had gotten him into trouble all of his life!

◈ Leigh had put on a pair of worn jeans, a loose sweater, and woolly socks and, while keeping an eye on the TV, finished restoring her room to its familiar state.

"Yesterday's Children" was followed by "Eternal Spring," Federated Television's only soap opera taped in their West Coast studio, a constant rival in the seesaw ratings competition.

Leigh harbored a secret resentment against "Eternal Spring's" producers for taking advantage of their location in the movie capital and their ability to lure important film stars into guest roles on the show.

Now *we* have a movie star too, she thought, as she curled up on her bed to watch the closing scenes draw to an end. He may not be as important as Elizabeth Taylor, but he once was. And there would undoubtedly be thousands of his loyal fans who would start watching the show because of him. Leigh was grateful they, and not "Eternal Spring," had snagged him.

When she awakened from a fitful nap, Leigh's room was in darkness.

Realizing there was plenty of time before meeting Mindy, she went to the kitchen for a Coke. As she passed the open door to her parents' bedroom, she stopped to notice some partially unpacked Louis Vuiton suitcases on the floor at the foot of the rumpled bed.

"Mom's home! Daddy too," she cried with delight, then flew down the hallway, past the kitchen, through the stately dining room, to the entry of the dramatically decorated living room.

The joy in her heart turned to stone at the sight of her father and a strange woman, standing arm-in-arm, sharing a glass of champagne while gazing out of the window at the wintery, early evening activity in Central Park, far below.

"Dad," she gasped, barely able to speak. A tray of cheese and crackers and a champagne bottle stood in front of the glowing fireplace. The couple paled with surprise at Leigh's unexpected appearance.

"Princess," Russell exclaimed, sharply releasing the woman's arm. "I . . . didn't know you were here. . . . I . . . we arrived from Paris this afternoon and I. . . . What are you *doing* here?"

Leigh struggled to control rising hysteria. "I live here." She glared at the woman in tastefully seductive, silk lounging pajamas and casually arranged hair. Before Russell could answer, Leigh questioned, "Is Mom here too?"

"No. She . . ."

"If you'll excuse me," the woman coughed and began to edge out of the room. "I think it best if I . . ."

"Wait, Millicent." Russell's normally erect posture seemed to sag as he tried to take control of the situation. "This is my daughter, Leigh. And Leigh, this is . . . ah . . . Millicent Lipton."

"How do you do," Millicent nodded embarrassedly, then fled to the bedroom.

"I thought you were sharing an apartment with Beth and Mindy," Russell plodded on. "I was going to call you . . . You've complained so often that I don't treat you like an adult . . . I was hoping we all might have dinner at El Morocco."

"All?" Leigh repeated, her shock turning to disgust. "Does that include Mom?"

"I've already phoned your mother. She won't return until

next week," he said softly. "I'm sorry you had to meet Milli-cent this way, but . . . Well, we've become . . . very friendly."

"That's what someone told me they read in a magazine. I said it wasn't true."

"Leigh," he smiled appeasingly. "I thought we were best friends?"

Not since I was eleven years old, she thought to herself.

"Not only as father and daughter, but as equals. Adults. Millicent is a wonderfully decent person and in all honesty, she has nothing whatever to do with the differences between your mother and me. Please, have dinner with us."

"I have a date."

"Fine," he breathed with relief. "Bring him along. Do I know him?"

The taste of revenge blossomed in Leigh before she opened her mouth. "Yes, I think so. Jamie Starbuck?"

"Jamie Starbuck," he echoed incredulously. "You don't mean?"

"Yes I do. The actor. I believe you knew each other when I was a little girl."

"That's preposterous! How could you know Jamie Star-buck?"

"He's in 'Yesterday's Children.' He's really great . . . we've become very 'friendly.'"

"That's enough young lady," Russell cut her off. "I'd hoped you could be serious. Obviously I've given you credit for more maturity than you deserve."

"Oh, I'm serious, Dad," she said standing her ground in cool defiance. "And if maturity means abandoning your sense of values and your loyalties, then maybe you're right, you *have* given me too much credit."

"Loyalty?" he blurted. "How can you even joke about Jamie Starbuck? He's a married man who . . ."

"He's separated," she lied.

"I'm not surprised," he grunted. "But he's not divorced!"

"Neither are you! You're not even separated. At least as far as Mom knows."

"Dammit, Leigh, will you stop this! Our situations aren't at all comparable. You know what Jamie Starbuck's done to me. He . . ."

"No, I *don't*," Leigh interrupted. "The only thing I ever heard was that you two had a fistfight and he broke your jaw. What else happened to make you hate him so much?"

Already on the defensive, Russell felt his distress heighten by this unexpected turn of the conversation. "What *else*?" he sputtered. "What more do you need?"

"What were you fighting about?" she persisted. "Was it another woman? Was it Mom? Was it Erika?"

Leigh was surprised by Russell's visible surge of anger. He retreated a couple of steps, passed his hand over his mouth, then brought himself under control and answered with quiet intensity, "My distaste for Jamie Starbuck has nothing to do with your mother. He is a man without honor, scruples, or a modicum of talent. He repaid me for trying to save his career by attempting to destroy mine."

Leigh shook her head and eased down on the edge of the sofa.

"Why do you think he's interested in you?" Russell persisted as he sat beside her. "Couldn't it be that he's using your innocence to humiliate me again? He knows there's nothing he could do to hurt me more than to break your heart."

"But, Dad, if we're just 'friendly,' how can he hurt you *or* me?"

"There are many ways," Russell emphasized as he rose to his feet. "Your reputation, for example. How do you think it looks to the young people of your peer group for you to be so closely involved with a married man? Even if he *is* separated, how can they respect you?"

"Well, Dad," she replied with glacial calm. "If my friends will lose respect for me because of a mere friendship with Jamie, what must *your* friends think of Millicent? You're making it pretty obvious that you're more than just traveling companions."

"That's different!"

"Why is it different?" she pursued. "Is morality only for the young? Tell me, at what age does one outgrow their need for moral values?"

"Won't you *try* to understand?" he changed to an almost pleading tone. "I'm your father. I . . ." Russell's head snapped around at the sound of the telephone. "Who's that?"

"It's probably Mom. She said she would call."

"You wouldn't say anything?"

"Why not, Dad? Mom's from your generation. She wouldn't make any moral judgments about another woman using her bedroom."

"Don't answer it," Russell ordered in rising desperation. "There's no need to say anything about this to your mother! You'll only hurt her! Just give me half an hour. I'll take Millicent to a hotel."

"All right," Leigh acceded as the phone stopped ringing. "But what's wrong, Dad? Don't you know that Mom still loves you?"

"No, I don't know," he hesitated. "Things aren't always the way they look. I . . . I don't have time, but . . . try to be understanding. I didn't want it this way."

Leigh listened to the sounds of Russell and Millicent getting ready to leave as she slowly walked down the hallway to her bedroom.

She closed the door, locked it, and sank onto her bed. *You talk about the mess he's made of his life,* she silently lamented. *What about what you've done to yours and Mom's? Is that Jamie's fault too? Or was it Mom's? Was it Mom's fault that she made a success with her fabric business after you screwed up in Hollywood, then lost all your money producing those bad plays?*

Leigh glanced to a photo of herself as a little girl, sitting astride a pony that was being held by her smiling father. *And I suppose it's my fault that you pretend to be my best friend when it's been years since you've shown the slightest interest in knowing who or what I really am.*

After refusing to respond when Russell knocked on her

door to say good-bye, she moved across the room to the dresser where she turned the photo face down, then returned to her bed and quietly succumbed to the loathing in her heart. "You want me to be understanding, Daddy?" she whispered. "Maybe it's time to see how understanding *you* can be."

CHAPTER

11

The photographer tried to create an air of excitement as he posed Jamie and Liz on the false marble steps of the set representing the entrance to Webster University's administration building. He was methodically shooting the last of the photos illustrating their impending romantic entanglement before bringing in Leigh for the group poses and, subsequently, her solo poses with Jamie.

"Dignity and controlled passion" were the instructions continually repeated by the photographer while he changed their positions and adjusted his camera.

"Controlled passion should be easy for you," Jamie said quietly to Liz, holding her in his arms. "After performing last night, then flying in this morning from D.C., you must be exhausted."

"Not yet," she smiled. "But I will be tonight. It usually takes me a day to come down after a successful concert."

"Then it *was* successful. Congratulations!"

"Thank you. Yes. And I think it was especially important to be successful in front of the people from our affiliate stations. They're the spine of our network."

"Yeah," Jamie smiled. "And as far as daytime is concerned, you're the heart."

"I try," she nodded modestly. "I do feel the responsibility of my position. 'Yesterday's Children' is the most important thing in my . . ."

"That's it!" the photographer interrupted. "Let's take ten, then I'll call makeup and have them send Leigh down."

"I can't tell you how happy I've become, now that you're a part of the show." There was no questioning her sincerity, as she poured each of them a cup of coffee.

"I'm happy too, I guess. I'd never thought before about doing a soap, but the more I'm in it, the better I like it."

"Is it becoming more comfortable? I mean, compared to your work in films?"

"Well," Jamie grinned. "It's more comfortable than falling off horses, I can assure you of that! But, seriously," he went on, as Liz blinked uncomprehendingly, "I am getting a kick out of it. I've had a lot of challenges in my acting career. It's been a long time since I've had a genuinely new one like this."

"What about your wife?" she casually probed. "How is she finding all this?"

"Well, it happened so fast, I don't think she's made up her mind yet."

"Not even about relocating here?"

"She . . . has a couple of things going on in Hollywood. She may not be able to move here."

"Two careers in one family is difficult. Mother says she's seen your wife—Erika, isn't it?"

"Yes. Erika."

"My mother has seen her on a Tony Mitchell Telethon. She says she has a nice singing style, rather like a German version of Linda Ronstadt."

"Yeah," Jamie conceded. "That's what they used to say in Europe."

"Kind of 'sixties,'" Liz added. "I hope that style comes back. It was a wonderful era for female vocalists."

"It's been tough for her. The only place German accents are very popular is in World War II movies . . . We'll have to wait and see. She said she'll bring our son, Bucky, here for Christmas if I can't get home. Beyond that . . ." he gestured emptily with his hands.

"I understand how you feel," she put a comforting hand on his arm. "We're in the same position except my son, Teddy, is out there in California. He goes to school at USC. I won't see him until Christmas either." Liz paused to take a nervous breath. "You must be awfully lonely. Perhaps you and I could . . ."

"Hi, everybody!" Leigh announced, gingerly coming onto the set. "I hope you're not waiting for me!"

"No, we're on a break," Liz answered and impersonally returned Leigh's kiss on the cheek.

"It's terrific that your show went so well in Washington," she said over her shoulder to Liz. "Neil told me how great it was!"

"Neil?" Liz questioned.

"Eddie must have told him," Leigh clarified, brightly returning her attention to Jamie. "Neil and I are going out for spaghetti tonight. If you're alone, we'd like you to come along."

"If it's spaghetti you want," Jamie smiled, "you should come to *my* place. I make better spaghetti than you can get in any restaurant."

"Really?" she asked enthusiastically. "And it wouldn't be too much trouble?"

"No trouble at all," he smiled. "Just tell me what time."

"Anytime!"

"About seven-thirty okay? How about you, Liz? Do you want to come too?"

"I can't," she replied, covering her resentment. "I'm in the show tomorrow, and after last night . . . I'll need my rest."

"We'll be the guinea pigs, Liz," Leigh said, masking her relief. "You can see how good he is next time."

"Next time," Liz forced a smile. "Yes. I'll be looking forward to it."

◈ Cathy planted her elbows amidst the mound of paperwork that had accumulated on her desk, and wearily kneaded her fingertips into her temples.

"Neil, do you realize this is all mine?" she moaned. "All of George's stuff has been cleaned out of here."

"Do I realize it?" Neil huffed. "I'm the one who cleaned it out and it's all in *my* office!"

"We'll have some help tomorrow. They're sending us a new production assistant to take your old job."

"Good. We'll let him worry about George's things. Who is it?"

Cathy shrugged her shoulders. "Someone with experience, I hope. I don't want to have to be teacher along with everything else."

"It's been a long, exciting day," Neil soothed. "Relax. We're doing fine."

"I know," she sighed. "It's just so darned hard when you have to do everything *alone.*"

"I've heard how lonely it is at the top. Still, I wouldn't say you're totally alone—unless you haven't been able to find Sam."

"Oh, I found him," she snipped. "Finally. He was in hiding all day—his secretary too. If she wasn't old enough to be his mother . . ."

"Where was he?"

"He *finally* left a message on the service at home to meet him for dinner at Twenty-One. He could have called here, but he knows I wouldn't go. He's with that idiotic friend of his, Devon Rudin."

"Well, I wouldn't be too hard on him. If he's been away from the office all day, he probably doesn't know about your promotion."

"It's his *job* to know," Cathy protested. "He's a major daytime executive. He's supposed to know *everything*. How does he expect us to get ahead if he doesn't pay attention to business?"

Sensitive to her mood, Neil abandoned any attempt to

defend Sam. "I don't know about getting ahead," he quipped. "But I know I passed up a free spaghetti dinner to be here and I'm starved! Let's take a break and go to Kerry's."

"All right," she yielded. "But we're coming back and finishing this mess."

"You haven't forgotten the new writers are coming in tomorrow?"

"No, I haven't forgotten." Cathy returned to sorting and arranging the confusion on her desk.

"They're going to want to start on their 'bible.' What are you going to do?" Neil queried. "According to what you've been saying, your projected format is of a *youth*-oriented show revolving around Jennifer Wells's story line. Have you figured out how to *do* that?"

Cathy's body sank into her executive chair. "It would be so easy if Liz Barrett wasn't such a *monument* around here. Sam was supposed to think about it, but his head's been off in the clouds lately. And you've seen how busy *I've* been."

Neil nodded perceptively. "Have you thought of . . . moving slowly? Sort of picking at her base? Eliminating the cronies her stories are usually involved with, until there's no one *but* the kids for her to relate to?"

Cathy's interest locked in on Neil's well-reasoned suggestion. "It's an idea I've been considering," she bluffed. "You mean like Dr. Bayard, Madge, and the Fosters?"

"Yeah. Like, one could die. Another get married. Maybe the Fosters could retire and move to Florida . . ."

"I'm not sure," she hedged. "They've been in the show a long time too."

"But they aren't indispensable. They aren't momuments like Liz." Neil could see Cathy's imagination begin to spark.

"Sure," she said. "A longtime regular's death is *guaranteed* high ratings. So is a marriage. Little by little we get rid of all the old-timers and replace them with young people. Before long we'll have a fresher-looking cast than 'The Young and the Restless.' " Cathy looked dubiously at Neil. "I wonder if Jamie was a mistake?"

"Hell no," he exclaimed. "Jamie's doing great. The mail's

already starting to come in. And he's a perfect device to symbolize the changeover. He can be the pivot on which we swing the show's accent from mature characters and stories to our new interest in the tribulatons of the young. Don't you see it? The symbolic swing from Liz to Leigh?"

"Of course I see it," Cathy purred contentedly. "It's beautiful. And what makes it *really* perfect is, Liz will never know what hit her."

"I'm glad I'm on *your* side," Neil grinned sardonically.

"You're also on Jim Hennigan's side. Our vice president of daytime *started* this business of paying attention to George's demographic studies. If I get the show back on top of the ratings, Liz's opinion won't amount to a pile of beans."

"But you'd better be careful along the way," he cautioned. "Liz is still the major name in 'Yesterday's Children,' and you're still a *temporary* producer. If she gets wind of what you're trying to do before this assignment becomes permanent, the only side we'll both be on is *out!*"

◈ Jamie stood in front of the stove in the small efficient kitchen of his sublet apartment, pretending not to notice Leigh's skittish discomfort as he concentrated on the large kettle of water about to come to a boil.

"I'm sorry I was late, but I was on the phone with my mother. Once she gets started, she just goes on and on. I thought she was never going to stop talking."

"It's all right. I'm happy you came. I thought you'd cancel too when Neil couldn't come."

"Poor Neil," she shrugged sympathetically. "Since Cathy got that advancement he hasn't had a moment to himself. But there was never any doubt about *me* showing up, especially since it was my idea. I feel badly enough just being late!"

"No problem," Jamie smiled, giving no indication of the

suave seducer Leigh had pictured him to be. "There's hardly any preparation for spaghetti carbonara. Once the water's boiling, it goes very quickly and it doesn't hurt the salad to sit a while in the fridge."

"I love Italian food," Leigh commented, looking over the neatly arranged ingredients on the chopping block. "Where did you learn to cook, in Italy?"

"Some, but mostly from an Italian cook in Germany," he rambled, discretely marking the soft curves under her clinging woolen dress. "When you've spent as much time as I have making movies in places where the food is barely edible, you learn to cook just to survive."

"I can imagine," she said, slowly beginning to doubt her ability to play the femme fatale. "May I help? My mother is coming home next week. She loves Italian food too . . . And it would sure impress her if I could fix an authentic Italian spaghetti."

"Do you think she'd mind where you got the recipe?"

"Not a bit," she shook her head. "She didn't mind at all when I told her I was coming here tonight. In fact, she said to say hello."

"She did?" Jamie raised his eyebrows. "In that case, next time you talk to her, return the greeting—and if you really want to help, you can begin with chopping the parsley while I pour us a glass of vino. As they say in Italy, 'A meal without wine is like a day without sunshine.' Although I've never seen them drink wine with breakfast."

"Not even on their cornflakes?" her mouth curled into a grin.

"Not that I've seen," he laughed, then handed her a glass of wine and raised his own. "Cheers."

"Cheers!" she responded provocatively.

"Well," Jamie said, resisting the invitation in her eyes, "if you're going to chop the parsley, I'd better get you a knife."

"Yes," she answered, feeling a rush of color in her face. "Yes, I'm going to need a knife."

Putting aside for a moment his own growing conflict of

emotions over Leigh, Jamie stirred the chopped onions lightly sauteing in bacon grease, then opened a fresh box of imported spaghetti. "Annie didn't look so well at work today. Do you have any idea what's bothering her?"

Leigh kept her eyes on the knife blade, which she methodically stroked through the sprigs of parsley as she spoke. "For one thing, I know she's upset about some particularly creepy fan letters."

"I thought they stopped that."

"Security is screening her mail and they say they're trying to trace down the nut who's writing them, but Annie insists that they continue forwarding the letters on to her."

"She reads them?"

Leigh's brow knitted into a frown. "Yes. Remember how David Hinkley wrote those letters to Jodie Foster before he tried to kill President Reagan? And that pretty girl from 'My Sister Sam,' Rebecca Shaeffer? That guy didn't try to talk to her or rape her or anything. He just waited until she opened the door and shot her."

Jamie paused as he removed a bundle of spaghetti from its box. "We never worried about those things back in my day . . ."

"The world was saner then," she replied reflectively.

Jamie turned away to silently chastize himself for his unintended reference to the difference in their ages.

"Yeah," he replied. "But I still don't understand why she wants to read them."

"Me neither," she agreed, unaware of his discomfort.

Jamie was about to drop the spaghetti into the boiling water when the telephone rang.

It was his agent, Fred Wald, calling from Hollywood. Jamie lowered the fire under the onions and water and asked Leigh to hang up the phone once he picked up the extension in the bedroom.

Leigh replaced the receiver when Jamie's voice came on the line and diligently began chopping the parsley.

Warmed by the wine, she was surprised at how comfortably at home she felt in Jamie's apartment.

Is this the way he's going to ruin my life? she thought, remembering her father's warning. A glass of wine and a cooking lesson didn't seem very sinister to her.

This can't be the man that Dad hates so much. All my life I've heard what a bastard he is, but no one ever told me why. Her chopping became slower and more methodical. *I wonder if I could ask Jamie. Or would it be better to wait, and try again with Mom? Could it have something to do with Erika?* She paused to shake her head. *I'd leave it alone if I wasn't so darn nosy . . .*

Leigh finished the parsley and stepped to the kitchen door where she could hear Jamie's low baritone coming from the bedroom.

More than ever she was convinced her father's fears for her regarding Jamie were unfounded. A man who looked at her the way Jamie did certainly wasn't going to hurt her.

She turned back to the kitchen as Jamie appeared, phone in hand, at the bedroom door.

He made a gesture indicating he wouldn't be long, then disappeared from her view.

"That's what I said," he emphasized into the phone as he sat on the edge of the bed. "Two hundred thousand dollars."

"They won't go two hundred thousand," Fred's voice came back to him. "They say it's too much. The most they'll go is a hundred."

"Tell them to stick it," Jamie replied firmly.

"They say they can get Robert Conrad for one fifty."

"That's bullshit, Fred. You know it as well as I do."

"All right," Fred breathed heavily. "I won't give up on the two hundred thou if you're sure you want to take the chance."

"I'm positive I'm reading these guys right." Jamie was adamant. "Just be sure they don't screw up with the time! If they forget about the four weeks notice I have to give according to my contract, it may blow the whole deal."

"I'll take care of the details," Fred replied. "Everything else all right?"

"Yeah, if we don't talk about the weather. How's things out there?"

"Everything's fine, except for one thing, maybe. I forgot to tell you, Erika was in yesterday. She needed a thousand dollars. Said an emergency came up."

"What kind of an emergency?"

"She didn't say."

"Did you give it to her?"

"I know I should have checked with you first—you don't have a thousand. But you were busy at the studio so I gave it to her out of my personal account."

"Oh, shit," Jamie groaned. "But thanks anyway, Freddie. I don't know how I'm ever going to catch up, with the goddamn taxes, the ex-wives, keeping up this place here and the house out there . . ."

"You really *need* this Saddle deal, Jamie. It's the one way you'll get even. I hope you realize we're taking a chance—holding out for another hundred thousand."

"I know it, Freddie. But it's a chance I've got to take. I'm goddamn tired of being broke!"

"Okay, kid. I'll call you as soon as I have some definite word."

Jamie shook his head, then took a deep breath and stepped out of the bedroom. Leigh was standing in front of the mantle with a framed photo in her hands.

"Is this your little boy, the one you have with Erika?" she asked, worried by his new and more somber mood.

"Yeah, that's Bucky. He's the real star of the Starbuck family."

"Do you miss them?" she probed.

"Yeah," he sighed. "If I can't get home before, I won't see Bucky until Christmas."

"Why is that?" she almost held her breath.

"Erika. She's too busy to spend any time in New York."

"Not ever?"

"Who knows," he shrugged. "Maybe someday."

"Bucky's cute," she said with a surge of optimism as she reached for the second photo on the mantle. "And these others? They must be the twins you mentioned at Kerry's Tavern the other day."

"Cheryl and Sean," Jamie answered with a suddenly renewed awareness of his age and how much nearer Leigh's was to his children's.

"You don't feel as close to them, do you?"

"No. They were almost babies when we divorced. Their mother and I haven't been very friendly . . . and I was out of the country most of their growing up years."

"Out of the country?" she repeated with her most convincing display of innocence. "Why was that?"

"Why?" he responded with a slow, ironic grin. "No particular reason . . . . except I like to work, and there was more work at the time in Europe."

"What about the problem with my father?" she succumbed to her curiosity. "Did that have something to do with it?"

"Don't you know?"

"I've heard some of it," she bluffed. "But not everything."

"Well," Jamie began, unsure of how much he was willing to reveal. "Your father became the producer of my TV series, 'Slim Chisholm,' during the last two years of its run. We never did agree what the show was about. And . . . there were some other things we didn't agree on . . ."

"Like what?" she interjected.

"Like . . . personal things."

"Too personal to talk about?"

Jamie laughed. " 'Inquiring minds want to know,' eh?"

Leigh blushed. "No. It's just that I've heard little bits and pieces all my life, and . . . and I'm curious."

"Our personal disagreements weren't nearly as important as the professional ones," he answered evasively. "Your father wanted to make our gutsy, down-to-earth Western into a highbrow, intellectual drama. We had a few 'intellectual' yell-outs, which I finally settled one day with a 'down-to-earth' punch in the mouth."

Leigh felt a warm sensation of perfidious pleasure. "That was it?"

"The scandal magazines had a couple different versions, but, yes, that was about it."

Before Leigh could ask what the scandal magazines had

written, Jamie glanced toward the kitchen and asked, "Did you finish the parsley?"

"Yes, it's all ready for you," she answered. Then, making the decision to forge ahead with her ambiguous plan of seduction, she looked up to him with a tempting smile. "Is there anything else I can do?"

Jamie avoided her glance and turned away toward the kitchen. "No, I can handle the rest. We'll eat in a few minutes."

Leigh's determined good cheer and her apparent zest for the excellent meal he had prepared bolstered Jamie's spirits and detracted him from his cares of the outside world.

She listened with genuine enchantment as Jamie recounted some of his favorite stories about the problems and pleasures of filmmaking in Europe.

Leigh's fascination with this large, gentle man couldn't silence the voice in her subconscious, which whispered its doubts about the morality of being with a married man. Another, more accommodating voice argued, *If Erika cared about her husband,* she'd *be here instead of me!*

Leigh didn't allow the moral voice to interfere with her growing attraction to Jamie. After dinner, as she helped tidy up the tiny kitchen, she could sense that their physical closeness was affecting Jamie as well. Although they kept their conversation light, each time they touched, the sensation brought them closer and closer. By the time they finished washing the dishes, the air was charged with electricity.

Jamie knew he was increasingly attracted to this lovely young girl, and as the urge to take her into his arms began to cloud his reason, he moved deliberately to the living-room bar.

His mind was a confused jumble of images: his children, her father, Erika, the phone conversation with his agent, the romance that was building between their soap opera characters. He poured a shot of cognac and downed it in one gulp.

How do I get myself into situations like this? he thought. *There were ten thousand reasons why he shouldn't get in-*

volved with this sensuously sweet young woman, and they all spelled trouble.

He felt a flash of spite. Seducing her would be a surefire way to get back at her father. He crushed the thought instantly.

Jamie set down his glass and started for the coatrack. "Come on," he ordered, putting on his coat.

"Where are we going?" she asked with surprise.

"I'm taking you home."

"Home?"

"Listen, Leigh," he gripped her shoulders and held her at arms' length. "I like you. I like you perhaps a little too much. You may think I'm nuts, but that's why we're leaving."

The feel of his strong hands on her shoulders enflamed her whole being, but at the same time she was tremendously impressed by this surprising show of gallantry. He was not, after all, the compulsive womanizer the gossip columns intimated he was.

"I may seem young . . . in a lot of ways," she answered solemnly, "But I don't think you're nuts." She clasped her hands on his forearms and gazed into his eyes, her own eyes glowing with promise. "What I do think is, I know what you're doing . . . and I should appreciate it."

"It's better, that's all. Better for both of us."

"I trust you, Jamie," she smiled warmly. "So I guess I'd better believe you."

Jamie grinned. "Maybe that's why I like you so much. You're smarter than most."

He gave her a light kiss on the forehead, then hurried her into her coat before he could change his mind.

CHAPTER

12

Neil whistled quietly to himself as he sat in his office leafing through the script that had just been delivered from the writers.

"Liz is going to crap," he said under his breath. "They should be a little more subtle about this thing that's developing between Penny and Spencer. Jennifer would have to be blind not to notice."

"Okay, Miss Cathy," he leaned back in his chair. "I'm dying to see how you're going to bullshit your way out of this one." He sprang forward at the sound of Liz's voice entering the outer office.

After a moment he saw Liz sweep past his doorway into Cathy's office. As the door closed behind her, Neil picked up his briefcase from the floor and withdrew the new writers' 'long story' outline he and Cathy had been reviewing the night before. He placed the pages in a neat pile and sat back, awaiting the summons that came almost immediately.

"Believe me," Cathy was saying as Neil slipped into her office and laid the pages on her desk. "I'm as frustrated over the material we have to work with as you are, but the new writers' scripts won't begin coming in until next week. What can I do?"

"The first thing you can do," Liz responded firmly, "is stop referring to them as 'new writers.' There is nothing at all new about them. The Kirklands have been writing soaps as long as I can remember—and badly at that. The next thing you have to do is see that someone puts a stop to this nonsense developing between Leigh and Jamie before it goes too far!"

"George Conley said they were the only daytime writers who were available," she said, struggling to deflect the issue.

"Of course they were available. Mark my words, it won't be long until we have the same problems with them that we're having right now."

"I hope not," Cathy sighed, staying away from the object of Liz's anger. "The old writers are just turning in the minimum number of pages to fulfill their contract. I'm doing what I can on the dialogue, but I can't tamper with the story line, you know that."

"Cathy," Liz emphasized, "there is no story line! They're making a fool out of me. It's ridiculous!"

Cathy's expression was helpless as she slowly shook her head. "If they would make me the *real* producer—I mean, make the assignment permanent—I'd be able to assert myself, make demands. The way things are, I simply don't have the power."

"I know . . . I know," Liz shook her head enigmatically. "That's why we have to work together. We can't let them ruin our show." She began a light tapping on the desk with her lacquered nails as she looked thoughtfully into Cathy's eyes. "The Kirklands appear to have power. Their contract says they don't have to answer to anyone except Hennigan, no matter *who's* producing the show."

Cathy's quick glance to Neil revealed her discomfort over Liz's seemingly endless supply of inside information. She picked up the pages and went through the motion of checking to see that they were in proper order. "It's more difficult than you think," she said, relieved to be off the subject of Leigh and Jamie. "They've decided to begin with a real bang."

"A real bang?" Liz was instantly apprehensive. "That usually means somebody is going to die. Who is it?"

Cathy cleared her throat. "Well, they say it's good for the ratings."

"Yes, it's good for the ratings—temporarily. So is good, intelligent writing and plot development good for the ratings, and not so harmful to the basic structure of the show!" Liz took a calming breath. "Forgive me. You were about to tell me who's being sacrificed on the altar of the rating services."

"I didn't want it either, but they wouldn't listen to me. Dr. Bayard."

"Dr. Bayard!" Liz shouted in disbelief. "That's Karl Herbert. He's been with the show for over fifteen years!"

"Which, according to the Kirklands, means his death will make that much greater an impact."

"It'll make quite an impact on Karl, I can promise you *that*. This show is his whole life!"

Cathy looked miserably at Neil, then back to Liz. "That's the trouble with this job. Even though it isn't my decision I have to take all the responsibility. I think Karl is a wonderful actor. I don't care much for the gin bottles he sneaks into his dressing room—but it doesn't seem to be affecting his performances."

"Not a whit!" Liz insisted. "He's taken his little drink of gin before taping every day since he came on the show. It calms his nerves, that's all." She opened her handbag and began rummaging through it, nervously. "It's times like this I'm sorry I quit smoking. It just doesn't make sense. He's our *doctor*. Do you realize how many times he's saved my life? Why not someone else—one of the newer characters?"

"Like Stanley Gordon, for instance?" Cathy asked.

"Well," Liz was wringing her hands. "I don't know."

"Stanley's going too," Cathy sighed glumly.

"What??"

"Yes. Our fearless football hero is going to be an innocent victim."

"Oh, dear," Liz moaned. "Who else?"

"There's no one else," Cathy tried to reassure her. "Not for the time being."

"I don't know why I'm surprised," Liz said, regaining her composure. "Next thing you know, they'll be after me."

"After you?" Cathy cried with a self-conscious laugh. "What a ridiculous notion! You're the heart of the show. Everyone knows that."

"Yeah, everyone," Neil echoed.

"Poor Karl," Liz shook her head compassionately. "My mother will be so disappointed. He always writes such nice notes when she sends him cookies."

"Her cookies are sensational," Neil smiled.

Liz responded with a puzzled look.

"Eddie Irving had them," Neil clarified. "It was a couple of weeks ago. She must have given them to him about the time you decided to work together."

"Yes," Liz concurred. "She did give him some cookies then."

Cathy caught a glimpse of the speculation on Liz's face as she looked at Neil. "I've been meaning to ask your opinion. The reaction to your performance at the affiliate dinner last week was so positive that I was thinking it might be a good idea to put Eddie under contract. Create some role for him in Webster's music department. Nothing terribly important, but enough to make sure he's available when you need him."

"That might be a good idea." Liz tried to sound casual. "He's very talented . . . and young. Isn't that what the network wants—more talented, *young* people?"

"Yes, that's right," Cathy agreed ingenuously. "It's just something I've been thinking about. Naturally, I wouldn't *do* anything before consulting you. He'd be your . . . ah . . . he would probably work more closely with *you* than anyone else. I wonder if he can act?"

"I'm sure he can," Liz spoke out.

"He said he did some acting in school," Neil interjected. "Hey, we'll be testing some new actresses next week. Why don't we let Eddie assist on the tests? That way we'll have him on tape without making a special thing about it."

"That sounds reasonable," Liz said, looking to Cathy.

"Yes, it does sound reasonable. Then after the test we can talk about it again. I'm positive that if we put our heads together, we can do something."

"I'm sure we can," Liz smiled, rising to leave.

"Thank you. I appreciate your support."

Liz paused at the door. "Are you coming to Kerry's Tavern for Zev Brahm's farewell?"

"I almost forgot he took that job in Albuquerque," Cathy sighed, looking at her watch. "I'd really like to, but there just isn't enough time in the day. When I've finished here, I have to dash over to Slippery Rock for an executive meeting. Then I'll be working at home. I often wonder if people know what it's like to be a television producer."

"I often wonder that myself," Liz replied, bemused. Then she smiled warmly and walked out of the office.

Cathy's intercom buzzed. "Yes?" she answered. "Oh. Yes. I'll talk to Mr. Hennigan. Just a second." She poised her finger over the flashing button on the telephone and glared at Neil. "Don't you have to get things wrapped up so you can go over to Kerry's?"

"Sure." As he closed the door behind him he heard her voice soften sweetly as she agreed to meet Hennigan later for dinner. What a pro! he thought. At least Hennigan would know he was getting screwed. Poor Liz didn't have a chance.

Sam sat morosely staring at the telephone as Devon came bursting through his office door.

"You won't believe what that fucking agent is demanding," Devon exploded. "Two hundred thousand dollars! Who needs Jamie Starbuck? For two hundred thousand dollars I'll get Clint Eastwood!"

"Then get him," Sam responded listlessly.

"What's the matter with you?" Devon demanded. "You know we couldn't get Eastwood for a million! I wish you'd pay more attention to what's happening around here!"

Sam leaned back in his chair, putting on an outward show of concern.

"I've been concentrating on the storyboard, that's all."

"Storyboard my ass, I know what you're concentrating on. Hey, pal, I don't want to be a kvetch, but she doesn't have the only big tits and tight ass in this town! Look around you. Models, actresses . . . they're coming in here by the dozens every day, dropping off their pictures and résumés."

He glanced toward the door, then leaned over the desk, nearer to Sam. "You should listen to me. It doesn't take much to get them to drop everything else if you put your mind to it."

"I know," Sam replied.

"Then let me take care of it. I'll get us a couple of bimbos. We'll do the town. I know one with a body like Cathy's, only better."

"Naw."

"Don't be so fast with your no's," Devon insisted. "You're not getting any at home and it's affecting your work. Do it for the company—and the girls, they appreciate it when a big executive like you shows an interest in them."

Sam was amused by his friend's deft rationalizations. He rubbed the tense muscles in the back of his neck. "What I want is . . . Dammit, if I could only understand! What the hell difference does it make to her if I'm at Federated or here? I can make a lot of money here and I can become an important force in the television industry. Hell, advertising is just as important as programming. A lot of people think it's more important. A hell of a lot more!"

"The smart ones do," Devon concurred. "They know that the purpose of programming is to keep the audience watching between commercials. The networks don't care if the programmers put on soap operas, the Olympics, or pig-fucking contests so long as enough people stay tuned to the commercials."

"But Cathy doesn't understand that," Sam added resignedly. "She thinks I've blown my whole future by leaving the network. She hasn't talked to me since she found out I quit to come here and make commercials."

Devon stepped away from Sam's desk, measuring his thoughts before continuing. "Sam, normally I don't stick my nose in people's personal affairs, but you're my best friend so I guess I have the right to put my two cents in. What I want to say is, who gives a damn what Cathy understands about commercials? And why does she *have* to understand them? It isn't natural. Get her pregnant once or twice. That'll straighten out her thinking."

Sam put his elbow on his desk and rested his forehead in his hand. "I wish it were that easy. I don't think it would work with Cathy. She's too . . . I guess she's too ambitious to settle for just being a housewife."

"What are you saying, *just* a housewife?" Devon exclaimed. "That's the kind of thinking that has you screwed up! Look, I'm not a chauvinist about this. I believe in equality and all that stuff. I believe everybody is entitled to their rights. I also believe in what's natural, and women in business isn't natural." Sam's look of skepticism only goaded Devon on. "Sam, it's in the Bible! A woman's place is in the home! If it's in the Bible, that means even God agrees. I'll tell you someone else who agrees—Papa Roth."

Not wishing to be overheard, Devon moved to the office door and closed it.

"Papa Roth is nuts on the subject. He says you got to have balls to be in business. And God didn't give balls to women, so where do they get them? They reach out and try to steal them from some man. Usually the man closest to them. That's probably why Cathy's pissed that you left Federated. She probably figured that as long as you were there, she had your balls."

Sam rose from his seat and began pacing back and forth. "I don't like to think about that, Devon. Even if you're right, I don't want to think about it."

"Okay, okay," Devon conceded. "Don't think about that. But how about *you?* Can we think about you, so maybe you'll be some use around here? We've got to get moving. Get this campaign in the saddle." Devon grinned at his pun, then moved to give Sam a friendly pat on the shoulder. "I may think you're stupid getting all messed up over Cathy, but like I said, you're my best friend so I want you to be happy. Listen to me, why don't you do this: On your way home tonight, stop at one of those shops where you can get some champagne, some fancy hors d'oeuvres or whatever it is that turns her on. Then create a nice, sexy atmosphere in your apartment, so when she gets home at least the mood will be right. Wine her. Dine her. Give her some soft music and smooth dialogue—then jump on her . . . Wait a minute," Devon interrupted himself. "Don't move, I'll be right back."

He hurried out of the office, then returned with a small silver pillbox in his hand. He took out a white pill and set it in front of Sam.

"What is it?"

"It's a Quaalude," Devon answered simply. "You know . . . Quaalude."

"I don't use drugs."

"Aw, don't be such a child. Don't think of it as a drug. It's not like crack or anything. I even use this with Ruth once in a while. Just break it in half. You take half, give her half . . . and it's, ah . . . it's great!"

"Really?" He was weakening.

"Sam, would I do anything to hurt you? Try it. I promise, both you and Cathy will thank me in the morning."

Sam picked up the pill and gingerly rolled it between his thumb and forefinger.

"Just put it in your pocket," Devon persuaded. "If you use it, use it. If you don't, you're crazy. I mean it."

◈ Cathy was exhausted by the time she unlocked the door to her apartment and let herself in. By the light of the television, she noticed the curled-up figure of her husband asleep on the sofa. Her mind registered a vague curiosity at the sight of the partially eaten tray of hors d'oeuvres but not enough to deter her from her singleminded purpose of collapsing into bed.

She moved to turn off the television but, deciding she'd rather not deal with Sam, instead crept softly into the bedroom. After quietly closing the door, she shed her clothing, leaving it in a pile at her feet, and went into the bathroom where she mechanically removed her makeup, creamed her face, and brushed her teeth.

A glimpse in the mirror at her tired, bloodshot eyes reminded her of her pulsating headache. Was it all worth it? she wondered. Jim wasn't so bad, but how important an executive did she have to become before she could sleep with anyone she wanted to?

"Hi, Cath," Sam's voice jarred her senses. He set aside his annoyance as he moved into the doorway, holding two brimming glasses of champagne in his hands. "Now I know why I quit Federated. Look at the hours they make you keep."

She looked at Sam, catching a familiar glimmer in his eyes as he surveyed her nude figure.

"Did you have a party here tonight?" she yawned, easing past him and heading for the bed.

"Yeah, a party for two, but only one of us showed up."

Cathy sat on the edge of her bed and set the alarm clock.

"Don't go to bed yet. You have to drink this," he insisted, handing one of the glasses to her.

"Oh, no," she groaned. "I'm tired. It's late. I just brushed my teeth and I have a splitting headache."

"Oh, come on," Sam cajoled. "It'll make you feel better. It'll make both of us feel better. This . . . this thing between us has gone on much too long."

"Sam, I don't care to discuss it tonight," she protested. "I just want to get to sleep. I have to get up early and I've had a *long* day."

"Well, *I* care to discuss it," Sam said, fighting to keep the belligerance out of his voice. "If you're going to be coming home so late, the least you can do is leave word on the service."

"Word? Why should I leave word when we're not talking?" Cathy reacted. "But, please, let's not argue about it. I'm not exaggerating, I have a terrible, terrible headache."

"Come on," he pleaded. "Have just a sip. One little drink with me."

"All right," she reluctantly yielded. "I'll take a sip. But only on one condition—that you bring me an aspirin."

"An aspirin?" Sam repeated suddenly remembering the Quaalude. "Okay, I'll get it. Just a minute."

Sam dashed into the bathroom where he had hidden the Quaalude. He popped half into his mouth and brought out the other half with a glass of champagne and handed it to his wife.

When she hesitated, Sam casually explained that it was a new headache remedy the agency was testing and that the pills of the first batch were too strong, so half was more than adequate.

Accepting his explanation, Cathy washed the drug down with some champagne and took a second sip before crawling between the cool sheets.

Sam hurried into the living room, stripped out of his clothing, and switched off the TV before returning to bed. Cathy had turned her back to him, but he snuggled up close and began caressing her.

"Please," she begged. "Not tonight. I really can't, Sam, honest to God, I *can't*."

"Just relax," he soothed. "You don't have to do anything. *I'll* do it. I'll do everything."

Oh, dear God, she lamented. She was *never* going to get to sleep. Sam's efforts were becoming more and more irritating as her mind slipped back to the warm hotel room bed she had left only a half hour earlier. How cozy and peaceful she had felt after Jim had left to go home; how tempted she had been to remain where she was. If only she had taken a bag and another outfit . . . she would be sleeping tranquilly right now . . . getting her needed rest for the onslaught of tomorrow's problems.

A subdued feeling of giddiness crept over her as she reflected on her evening of lovemaking. Her mind began fantasizing that Sam's advances were merely a continuation of Jim's and it was all becoming an intermingled experience.

"Hey," she heard Sam's voice ring with delight as his fingers touched the dampness of her recent sexual encounter. "You're wet! You're *really* wet, Cath. You're not fooling me with this cold, sleepy act."

She sighed resignedly and retreated into the twilight world of semiconsciousness.

"Come on honey," he urged. "You don't have to pretend . . . you know how good it feels!"

Cathy turned her head to avoid his attempted kisses, forcing him to redirect his attention down her neck and smooth, pale shoulders to her swollen nipples. She was too tired and unknowingly spaced out on the Quaalude and champagne to resist anymore. Sam's probing fingers and impassioned tongue grew more aggressive, as he slowly licked his way down over her flat belly—and then buried his flushed face into the moistness between her legs. His determined tongue could evoke no more than a few involuntary tremors of her pelvis, so, ignoring his disappointment, he eased his weight on top of her and entered her in one smooth thrust. "Come on, honey," he lovingly repeated before pressing his lips against hers, plunging his tongue into her slack mouth.

Sam ejaculated, then rolled over and accepted the unhappy realization that Cathy had fallen asleep before he finished.

◈ Jamie enjoyed the invigorating chill in the air. He was still warm from his workout and steam bath. He strode briskly up Columbus Avenue and turned the corner onto 69th Street toward his apartment.

A pretty girl crossing the street reminded him of Leigh. And the thought of her freshness of spirit and unrepressed animation gave him a pleasant stir of emotion.

Dammit, Starbuck, he thought ruefully as he let himself in his building. Was he becoming a dirty old man? Still, twenty or twenty-five years didn't make that much difference anymore. Everyone was doing it! More important, he didn't *feel* too old for her. It could work into a mutually satisfying arrangement, he reasoned, unlatching his front door locks, if Leigh were the type to be content with a discreet affair. But intuitively he knew she wasn't. And at heart he wasn't either—not with a girl of her exceptional quality.

Finding a message on his answering machine from Fred Wald in Hollywood, Jamie quickly dialed his number.

"We got it!" Fred announced proudly. "We got it all! The whole two hundred thousand!"

"Thank God," Jamie plopped on the edge of the bed. "I'll be able to breathe again."

"It's a relief to me too, kid," Fred said kindly. "I have to admit, I was a little worried."

"We all were," Jamie heaved a sigh. "Have you told Erika? She's been nervous as hell."

"I saved that pleasure for you. Why don't you call her now, then go out and celebrate. I'll get back to you next week when the contracts are ready."

"Okay, Freddy," he said affectionately. "And thanks . . ."

"Don't thank me," Fred said before hanging up. "I'd have taken the job for *fifty* thousand!"

"Erika!" Jamie boomed as she answered the phone. "Fred just called. We got the Saddle commercial! They're paying two hundred thousand dollars, just like we asked!"

"Oh, Jamie," her voice quavered. "It's marvelous! It's more than marvelous. It's . . . I've been so frightened. Jamie, the soap opera money is starting to come, but we're so far behind."

"You should have more confidence," he crowed happily. "Have I ever failed to show up with the cavalry in time to head them off at the pass?"

"But you always let them get so *close*," she laughed through tears of relief.

"I'm sorry," he said, feeling the intimacy of their mutual struggle as his eye fell on the calendar where he recorded his taping schedule. "Hey," he looked at his watch. "I don't work again until Wednesday. If I hurry, I can catch a late plane tonight and have four days at home! What do you think?"

"Tonight?"

"Yeah. There's a flight that leaves here at nine and gets in there around midnight. Don't worry about picking me up. I can take a cab."

"Midnight tonight?" she suddenly sobered. "I wish I'd known before."

"I didn't know I could *afford* to come until a few minutes ago. What's the matter? Is there a problem?"

"No problem, except I'm going to Las Vegas tonight. Tomorrow starts Tony Mitchell's mental health telethon at the Sahara. They asked me to sing. It's *national,* Jamie. It will be seen all over the country."

"Oh," Jamie's exuberence plummeted. "What about Bucky?"

"He left a few moments ago. Don't you remember, he told you he was going to the mountains this weekend with the Kleinman family?"

"Damn," he swore in frustration. "If I'd only known sooner."

"Yes, Bucky will be so disappointed."

"And you?"

"Me? I am always happy to see you, Jamie."

He thought he detected a note of ambivalence in her voice but he wasn't up to calling her on it. "Okay, then. How about this. I'll meet you in Vegas. You do what you have to do. We'll see a couple shows, then go home Sunday in time to be there when Bucky gets back. I'll return here on the late flight Tuesday night."

His proposal was met with a long silence from the other end of the line.

"What is it, Erika?" he pushed. "Another problem?"

"Jamie," she replied, with some difficulty. "Jamie, I must

talk to you. All week I have been trying to find the words . . . and the courage, but I could find neither. Now, I must. I have always tried to be a good wife, not to embarrass you—even if I have sometimes foolishly let you think things that weren't true."

Jamie's throat tightened in anticipation.

"But now . . . there are some photographs. They are in *Alles.*"

"The Kraut scandal magazine?"

"Yes."

"What kind of photographs?"

"Not as bad as they appear, but not very nice. It must have been a paparazzo with a tele-lens shooting over the wall."

"What wall?" Where?"

Erika's voice become very low. "The wall behind Tony Mitchell's house in Palm Springs. A little party. A few people by the pool. Swimming. Dancing. You know how I despise swimsuits and you know how hot it can be there—also at night. I was a bit tipsy. Maybe I sniffed something, I don't remember. Soon we all were . . . naked. It wasn't a sex party. We merely didn't wear anything."

Jamie fought back the outburst rising in his throat. "Did Bucky see it?" he asked with affected calmness.

"I have the magazine hidden. He'll never find it."

"I mean the *party.*"

"No. Never, he was sleeping. I could never be so foolish as that!"

The line again was still as Erika awaited a response.

"The photos aren't very clear," she said, trying to ease the outrage she was expecting from her husband. "It was night. In truth, the photo with Tony . . . it could be anyone . . . even you."

"Me," he exploded. "Who would ever think he was me? He's at least a foot shorter than I am."

"Yes. You are right," she conceded meekly.

"Oh hell," he said, filled with distaste.

"I am sorry, Jamie . . . and ashamed."

"Sure," he responded, feeling oddly detached from the situation. Instead of anger he now felt empty. Ironically, hazy images of Leigh entered his mind. "So am I."

"I'm so confused," she managed to continue. "It's been so difficult. I don't have many chances left. You know I can sing, Jamie. But what's the good if I don't have a chance?"

"I didn't realize it was that important," he said quietly.

"Nor did I. Until I began to think of what would have happened if you didn't find your soap opera. That terrible ex-wife of yours, that Lori Doone, would have taken *everything!* I have to think of Bucky!"

"Oh, bullshit," he reacted, his anger now breaking. "I've always taken care of you two. Don't tell me you're chasing after Tony Mitchell for Bucky!"

"I didn't say that!"

"Like hell."

"I didn't!"

"Okay, you didn't. What does it matter?"

"You hate me, don't you Jamie?"

"No, Erika, I don't hate you. I guess right now I just don't feel anything." He heard Erika blow her nose and realized she had been crying.

"It's my fault, Jamie."

Leigh's image popped into his mind again. "No, Erika. It's probably my fault as much as yours."

"What do you mean?"

"Nothing," he answered, not wishing to reveal any more. "Look, I'd better go now. Tell Bucky I'll call Sunday night. And good luck in Vegas."

"I'm sorry." She laughed bitterly. "I keep saying that."

"Well, I'm sorry too, if that means anything. But like you always used to say, 'That's how the cookie crumbles.' "

Without any further ado or even a good-bye, Erika hung up, leaving Jamie holding the silent receiver to his ear. He was slow to put it down, feeling in his heart that a major part of his life was painfully ending.

He sat a moment, a sense of relief gradually replacing his sadness.

"Erika, it looks like you've finally pushed me over the edge," he uttered aloud, reaching for his telephone book and thumbing through the pages in search of Leigh's number.

CHAPTER

13

Neil felt comfortably at home sitting in the director's chair in Studio 41's control room. Even though it was only a test and he was assisted by minimal staff, one might get the impression from watching Neil's behavior that he was directing one of the network's most prestigious prime-time dramas. All eyes in the control room were focused on the large "ON AIR" monitor, where the striking black actress, Joyce Pagent, was electrifying the screen, playing a test scene opposite Eddie—all eyes with the exception of Liz, who was concentrating on the small 2 Monitor where Eddie's close-ups filled the screen.

"God, she's good," Neil said to no one in particular.

Liz nodded silently, suppressing her impulse to draw attention to Eddie. *He's doing quite well,* she thought. *Especially for someone without any experience. They have to take into consideration his lack of experience.*

Liz switched her attention to Joyce's image on the monitor.

How strange it is, she mused. The part of Ned's defense attorney in his trial for Dr. Bayard's murder would be just another role if it were played by a white male. But by casting the role with a black female it automatically became socially significant.

Liz's gaze drifted back to Neil as he concentrated on his work. And homosexuals, her musing continued. There's *never* been a homosexual in daytime. Her gaze rose to Eddie's image on the monitor, then quickly back to Neil. Her cheeks began to burn with embarrassment as she realized what she really wanted from Eddie.

Suddenly feeling as if everyone could read her mind, she stood up, brushed at the imaginary creases in her skirt, and started for the door.

She hesitated as she saw through the soundproof window that Cathy was coming from the opposite direction.

Cathy asked Liz to wait a moment, spoke a few words to Neil, then beckoned for Liz to follow her into the hallway.

"What do you think?" Cathy asked as they stepped away from the door.

"I think he's doing very well," Liz answered. "I mean, we knew he hasn't had much experience."

"Yes," Cathy smiled knowingly. "And the girls . . . what do you think of the girls?"

"Oh, they're very good. Especially the last one, Joyce Pagent. I don't know how the rest of them will do, but she's the best so far."

"She'll probably get the part, but we had to test them all. You know how it is with minorities."

Liz nodded her understanding. "We don't see many female lawyers in daytime. I think it's a marvelous idea."

"I've wanted a woman to play that part from the minute I read the outline. Then I thought, why not a black woman? That way we'll have a little bit of controversy—not enough to offend anyone—and a lot of good public relations."

"And another jump in the ratings," Liz smiled admiringly. "I've been meaning to thank you for helping to straighten out that little problem with the script. A romance with Jamie and me is more natural . . . and much more dramatic."

"It's for all of us," Cathy spread her arms in a selfless gesture, then grew serious. "I was hoping I would find you. I just left Karl. I told him what's going to happen to Dr. Bayard.

He seemed to be all right, but . . . well, you're so good at things like this. I thought you might want to . . ."

"Where is he?"

"I think he's in his dressing room."

Karl, in a sleeveless undershirt, was seated at his makeup table, smearing his makeup remover with a facial tissue, when Liz walked in on him. His usually sparkling eyes were veiled with a dull mistiness as he smiled a greeting. Liz was shocked to see that for the first time in fifteen years, Karl's gin bottle was standing in full display on the table. She swallowed a well of tears as she returned his smile.

"Oh, Karl," she exclaimed, unable to suppress her sadness any longer.

"There, there. It's not as bad as all that." He moved to embrace her. They stood for a few moments, clinging to each other in heartfelt anguish. Then Liz lifted her head, blinked away a tear, and kissed the tip of his nose. "Do you have anything for nervous hysteria, doctor?" giving a meaningful glance to the bottle of gin.

Karl reached for a clean glass. "They haven't taken away my prescription pad yet, so I think I'll fix us both up before it turns into mass hysteria."

Liz grimaced involuntarily as the raw, undiluted liquor burned her throat, causing Karl to smile through the tiny beads of gin hanging onto the tips of his moustache.

"I forgot that some of us don't take our medicine straight," he grinned. "Sit down. I know where there's some lemon soda and maybe a little ice."

Karl ducked out of the door and returned shortly with an ice-filled glass and a bottle of lemon soda. He mixed a new drink and handed it back to her.

"Dr. Bayard's cure-all for delicate ladies," he announced with a flourish.

"That's better," she responded, setting her mouth in what she hoped was a gay smile. "Much better than all the popular remedies we've had sponsoring the show."

"Much, much better," he agreed, settling wearily back into

his chair. "I should have been a sponsor instead of an actor. I'd be a millionaire today."

Liz had seated herself in front of Jamie's makeup table, which stood adjacent to Karl's. As Karl cleaned off the last of his makeup, she turned to study her own image in Jamie's mirror. The face she looked at seemed oddly unfamiliar. She was a *star*. Perhaps the most important star in daytime television, but the image she saw in the mirror only reflected her growing sense of unfulfillment. In spite of a lifetime of success in show biz, she still felt incomplete and lonely.

"You'd think it would get easier," she muttered. "We've said good-bye so many times to so many people."

The two actors avoided each other's eyes, gazing at their own mirrored reflections.

"Well," Karl spoke softly. "You know how it is with show people; we're just too damned emotional about things. Good-bye doesn't always have to mean good-bye. We could be doing another show together before you know it."

"Not me," she brooded. "I was born here and it's here I'm going to die."

"Just a moment," Karl chuckled. "You're getting our roles mixed up. *I'm* the one with whom we're supposed to be commiserating. *I'm* the failed old has-been in the winter of his discontented life. Look at yourself. You're a beautiful, talented woman, and a damned good actress. That's the trouble with soaps; sometimes we get such a long run that we forget all the other actors out there who do very well without a steady job."

A spark of light returned to Karl's eyes as he peered into the mirror, toying with his moustache.

"I think I'll shave this thing off," he said. "I'm tired of it getting into everything I put in my mouth."

He covered the walruslike growth on his lip with three fingers, trying to see how he would look without it.

"I'll tell you something else I'm tired of—Dr. Bayard. He's developed into an unbearable old codger in the last years. I've never said anything, but I was getting bored with him. I've been so busy running the little theater up in Deer Creek that I haven't thought about acting in another role for too many years."

Liz fought back another urge to cry as she watched her friend attempting to smooth down the frizzy wreath of white hair around his head.

"My agent's been after me to do something on the summer theater circuit. Maybe I'll do *The Man Who Came to Dinner*. I used to do a lot of comedy."

Karl's posture became more erect as he buttoned his shirt and knotted his tie. When he finished, he again studied his moustache.

"I'll tell you another thing I'm tired of. I'm an actor. My name is Karl Herbert. I've been an actor all my life, and I'm proud of it. I'm damn tired of everyone coming up to me on the street with their medical complaints. You know, I could walk into any hospital in the country, go into the operating room and start cutting, and no one would say a word."

The familiar sparkle was back in his eyes as he turned to Liz.

"Maybe I should do it." He paused a moment in amused contemplation. "A couple more doses of my cure-all tonic and I probably could."

He gently pulled Liz to her feet.

"Liz Barrett, you're a fine lady," he said with love in his eyes. "You're a great actress and an even greater friend. And if you like listening to this kind of dialogue, get your coat and come with me to Kerry's. All this cheering you up has made me very thirsty."

CHAPTER

14

Cathy stared at the blinking lights over the double bank of elevators in the Federated Broadcasting Tower as she tried to anticipate which would be the next car to make the ascent to the executive offices. Bearing the weight of her heavy Gucci satchel in both arms, she scurried toward the first of the gleaming, stainless-steel doors to slide open. As she dropped the satchel between her feet and leaned against the wall, her eye caught a glimpse of a tall, slightly stooped man striding toward the street entrance.

Foreboding passed over her at the thought of how much the retreating figure resembled George Conley, the former producer of "Yesterday's Children."

If it was George, what would *he* be doing here? He had his own production company on the Coast. He wouldn't come back. No. It couldn't be George.

Cathy breathed easier as she stepped through the elevator doors into the network's spacious brass and glass reception hall. No matter how low her spirits, every time she moved along the richly modern corridor she secretly appraised the senior executive suites, deciding which of them she would claim as the prize of her inevitable success.

As she stepped into Jim Hennigan's office, her little game was quickly forgotten at the sight of his gloomy expression.

"Sit down," he said in a tone empty of its usual intimacy.

George Conley's image flitted through her mind as she lowered her satchel and settled uneasily into the chair facing his desk.

"I just got this," he said, picking up a confidential inter-office memo. "It's bad enough that our strongest shows, 'Yesterday's Children' and 'Eternal Spring,' have slipped another point in the ratings, but ABC's dropping the one show in your time slot that we've never had any trouble with."

"'County Medical'?"

"The boneyard of doctor shows," Jim nodded. "It's been on the edge for the last couple of years, but it looks like they were holding on until they felt they had a shot at us."

Cathy moistened her lips with her tongue. "What are they scheduling in its place?"

"They're giving it to us with both barrels."

She raised her eyebrows in curious anticipation.

"Daily reruns of 'Dynasty.'"

"Oh, dear God!"

"I think it's the *dear Kirklands* who are going to have to help us this time," Jim responded ironically. "We're going to have to think of every device possible to keep our audience from switching channels—murder, rape, marriage, babies, suicide. Whatever it takes."

"Have you talked to the Kirklands? Are they willing to write a new format?"

"It won't be new. They'll just have to speed up the original long-range story line. Don't worry, they'll write it. I intend to phone them as soon as dawn breaks over their Beverly Hills swimming pool."

Cathy reached into her satchel and withdrew a manila folder containing a sheaf of projected story ideas. "Do you think you can get them to come to New York? It would be a lot better if we could work on this in person instead of by phone."

"Exactly," Jim answered. "That's why you're going to the Coast." He continued speaking before she could protest. "It's in their contract, remember? They came here once in the beginning, but they don't have to come back to New York for any reason."

"It's crazy." Cathy was resentful.

Jim's gaze drifted blankly to the wide-yoked neckline of her knitted dress. "I was hoping to go with you, but I don't know as yet if I can. 'Yesterday's Children' isn't the only problem I have to think about."

"When do I have to leave?"

"Tonight. We don't have any time to waste on this." He tore some handwritten sheets from a yellow, lined tablet and slid them across the desk. "Here's some ideas I jotted down."

She efficiently ran her finger down the page, checking the notations. "This won't work," she said, tapping her fingertip halfway through the list. "We can't speed up the romance between Jennifer and Spencer. Jamie's leaving for three weeks to make that stupid commercial."

"Oh," Jim grimaced. "Well, suppose we get them in bed just before he leaves. He's going to Boston to try and raise money for the college, right?"

"Right."

"We won't say when he's coming back. Jennifer can be waiting every day, anxious to know his reaction to their sexual encounter. Will he still respect her? Will he want to marry her?" Jim's face broke into an impish grin as he stood up and moved away from his desk. "Will the women of America diddle themselves into senility with anticipation?"

A small laugh escaped from Cathy's lips. "Seriously, though," she said. "It's a good idea. We can maintain a strong interest in the Jennifer character and not have to spend too much time with her."

"While heating up the other stories. I'd like to see Ned and the black girl get together before the doctor dies. I saw the tests. We'll sign the pretty one."

"Joyce Pagent."

"Yes, she's good."

"I think so too. So does Liz."

Jim paused as he was about to return to his seat. "When did *she* see the tests?"

"She watched the taping."

"Of course she did," he expelled, sinking into the chair behind his desk. "I don't know why I bothered to ask."

Cathy smiled inwardly at his annoyance. "I think she may have been there to watch the boy who was *assisting* in the tests."

"Her accompanist?" Jim questioned, then stopped as the germ of suspicion planted itself in his mind. "Is something going on between those two? Now that I think about it, they *were* pretty chummy in Washington."

"I don't know," Cathy answered innocently. "She's taken an unusual interest in his career. She's been after me to find a continuing role for him in the show. But as far as any personal involvement—well, he is awfully young."

"Young?" he scoffed. "Try gay! But I don't care what he is. If he can keep her mind off the show long enough for me to do what has to be done, he can be whatever he wants. Tell the Kirklands to write a part for him."

"Yes, sir."

"Don't think I'm not aware of what you're up against, because I am. When we get 'Yesterday's Children' back on top and I can make the producer's assignment permanent, I won't forget all that you've done."

Cathy crossed her legs and smoothed the hem of her skirt. "I've tried my best."

"I know. And to show my appreciation, I'm assigning one of my best former assistants to your staff. Her name is Marnie Reardon."

"Oh," she replied, displaying a gratitude she wasn't sure she felt. "When does she start?"

"Right away."

"That will be a help."

"Maybe I can make it out to the Coast for the weekend," he said with a significant look from across the desk. "If I can't come before . . ."

"It would be wonderful if you could."

"I'll try my best," he smiled intimately.

I'm sure you will, she thought, with private delight.

Flushed with a sense of accomplishment, Cathy returned her attention to Jim's list of story suggestions.

◈ Eddie Irving manipulated the multiple locks to the front door of his Greenwich Village apartment and stood to one side to permit Liz to enter.

In a glance Liz took note of the old kitchen table and chair, which also served as his desk; the sofa bed; the converted closet containing a small refrigerator and hot plate; and the gleamingly new, upright piano that dominated the small room. Other than the piano which she had leased for him, the only other object of value she could see was a quality stereo tape deck.

They lost no time getting to work. After perusing Eddie's new arrangements together, he seated himself at the piano and ran through them with Liz humming along.

More than two hours passed rehearsing together in an atmosphere of work and enjoyment until the telephone finally interrupted their session. After a short, guarded conversation Eddie returned to the piano, but in a different mood. He was obviously disturbed about something.

"That was Neil," he said quietly. "He wanted to talk, but I told him we were busy . . . working." Eddie removed his glasses and cleaned the lenses with the end of the long scarf still draped around the collar of his shirt. "I hope you don't mind," he said, doubtfully.

"Oh my, no," she smiled. "I love it when we work on the music. I must say, Neil has remarkable energy. The way he works, I should think he'd be ready to collapse at night."

"I would too, but he never does. Not even on the week-ends."

Liz deliberately rejected the sordid thoughts forming in her mind. "Well, I'm happy you don't have to sleep on his couch anymore. It must have been difficult for you when you were tired."

"It wasn't always easy," Eddie mumbled, then turned away to make a notation on one of the music sheets.

Liz, as anxious as Eddie to end the discussion of his previous sleeping arrangement, moved to the window where she was greeted with a view of a dirty, red brick air shaft. She moved back to the piano and struck a few simple chords.

"It's a terrific piano," Eddie said. "You'll never know how much I appreciate it."

"You deserve it," she smiled. "And a lot more. If your career continues as it has, very soon you'll have your own baby grand."

"I've been very lucky," he replied. "Not many people have come to New York and gotten ahead as fast as I have. Meeting you was the best thing that's happened to me."

"It's been good for me too," Liz answered. She glanced at the refrigerator. "Do you have anything to drink?"

"I'm sorry. I should have asked. There's some Pepsi here. I like Pepsi when I'm working."

"Oh," she replied halfheartedly.

"You mean alcohol. Gee, I don't have any. I hardly ever drink anything stronger than Pepsi."

"That's all right. Pepsi's fine."

Eddie took the ice tray to the bathroom basin, broke loose some cubes, and put them in a glass of cola which he offered to Liz.

"Do you smoke grass?" Liz heard herself ask.

Eddie looked up with surprise. "Sometimes," he answered warily. "Sometimes I use it when I'm working. Sometimes it helps me see music from a different angle. Do you?"

"Well," she grinned sheepishly. "I tried it once. After my son, Teddy, went away to school I found some in his bureau. One night while Fern was asleep, I locked myself in my bedroom and . . ." Liz laughed, self-consciously. "You should have seen me!" It took over half an hour to get one rolled—even then it looked like no cigarette you've ever seen—I couldn't finish it because I was afraid of waking Fern with my coughing."

"Did you feel anything?"

"I don't think so. A little guilty perhaps . . . and foolish. And I was a little concerned about the *smoking* aspect of it. I'd quit cigarettes only about a year before."

"It isn't the same as cigarettes."

"Yes, I've heard that."

Eddie took a measured sip from his glass; then, with studied casualness, he leaned back with one elbow on the piano. "If you ever think you might like to try again . . ."

"Do you have some?"

"A little."

"Why not? Maybe we'll come up with a Top Forty tune."

Liz moved to the couch as Eddie retrieved the necessary paraphernalia from his little kitchen cabinet and rolled a perfectly symmetrical cigarette.

He lit it and drew deeply. He then inserted the joint into a hole in a glass tube which had its center section formed into a series of coils.

"Watch," he said as he blocked the end of the tube with his finger, put the other end to his lips and breathed in until the coils were filled with smoke. Then, in one motion, he removed his finger and inhaled sharply, emptying the tube into his lungs. "It's called a carburetor," he rasped, trying not to lose any smoke as he spoke. "You get more smoke and don't lose any."

He extended the device to Liz, keeping his finger on the other end.

She tentatively put it to her mouth and watched with rapt attention as the smoke filled the tube, then disappeared down her throat. The hot smoke stayed down for a moment, then involuntarily burst forth from her nose and mouth in a spasm of coughing. "I can't," she gasped.

"Try it again," he said, handing her the glass of Pepsi. "And drink this. It'll cool your throat."

She made a second attempt after gulping the cooling liquid. This time she managed to hold it a while longer before she began to cough. By her fourth attempt she could retain the smoke in her lungs without coughing.

"That's enough for now," he said, before the cigarette was completely burned. "This is pretty good weed."

Liz leaned back preparing to assess her reaction as the narcotic flowed through her system.

"This is what I'd like to do," Eddie remarked as he inserted a Chopin concerto into his cassette player. "Previn does classical *and* pop, and he's successful at both."

"There's no reason you can't do the same. You have the talent."

"And movies," he continued as he refilled the cola glasses. "Henry Mancini plays the piano. And Bill Conti used to play in bars just like I do."

"You won't have to play in bars anymore."

"That's right," he said, sitting beside her. "It's all because of you. Someday I'll show you how much I appreciate it."

"You do show me, Eddie." She gently patted his leg. "With your music. You make such beautiful music for me."

"Someday I'll show you what I can really do. Maybe someday I'll write a new theme for 'Yesterday's Children.' Something people will listen to and know it represents *you*."

"What a lovely thought," Liz said feelingly.

" 'Yesterday's Children' *is* you," Eddie continued. "I don't understand why they fight it."

"Who fights what?"

"You know, like Cathy Allison and some of the others who want to change things. They don't realize that 'Yesterday's Children' is in a class by itself. It's the only half-hour show on television that maintains the classic live TV tradition."

Liz smiled serenely as she closed her eyes and rested her head on the back of the sofa. "The business is full of little people who don't recognize class. Don't worry about Cathy. She thinks she's clever, but I know exactly what she's trying to do."

"You do?"

"Do you know how many would-be producers we've had on the show?"

"No," Eddie shook his head blankly.

"Do you know how many Jennifer Wellses we've had?"

"Just *one*. You started the show."

"Exactly. If Neil Decker is really a friend of yours, you might remind him of that."

"I think he knows."

"Good."

"Neil wants to be a director. Cathy said she'll help him."

Liz chuckled. "Cathy helps Cathy. Neil should be wise enough to see through Cathy by now."

"I think she has him a little blinded."

"I know what she uses to blind most men, but I don't understand how it works on Neil."

"Well . . ."

"I don't want to talk about Neil," she said, rolling her head onto Eddie's shoulder and maneuvering her fingers between the buttons of his shirt. "Or Cathy either. I just want to talk about how I feel."

"How *do* you feel?" he asked, awkwardly placing his arm around her.

"Good," she said, squirming closer to him. "Good and warm . . . and wonderful." Liz slid her hand under his shirt and lightly stroked his chest.

Eddie responded by kissing the top of her head. Suddenly she lifted her face and he put his lips to hers.

They continued exploring each other's bodies and mouths until Eddie pulled away to turn off the lights in the apartment. He stumbled his way back to the sofa bed. In the darkness, Liz removed her clothing and helped Eddie out of his.

Whether or not she was influenced by the marijuana, Liz didn't care. She had abandoned the last shred of her inhibitions and she was not to be denied.

She dropped to her knees and grasped his limp penis in her hand, at the same time running her tongue and sensuous lips along the curve of his abdomen, nibbling and biting as she inched downward. When she reached his organ she teased its shaft and head with her lips, then greedily engulfed its entirety into her mouth. Minutes passed as Liz did her utmost to stir Eddie to arousal but the erection both were praying for failed to occur. She caressed his muscular buttocks and continued to suck until her mouth became dry and cottonlike. But his member refused to respond. Her passion turned to frustration. *I am better than you, Neil,* she angrily thought to herself. *I will turn Eddie on! I will!*

Please, Eddie! Please!

Please respond.

CHAPTER

15

"And say hello to Sam!"
Neil called after Jamie as he hurried out of the studio for a
meeting with Sam and Devon.

"I will," Jamie waved over his shoulder without slowing his
pace.

I wish Jamie were more interested in Liz, Neil frowned to
himself, trudging down the hallway toward his office. *She's
always happier and more manageable when she has a leading
man who gives her a little now and then . . .*

*And I'm not sure I like the way things are developing
between him and Leigh . . .*

*But who am I to judge? Maybe I just want to get Liz paired
off so she'll leave Eddie alone.*

Neil snapped out of his reverie when he saw the new
assistant, Marnie, waving her plump arms in his direction to
tell him Cathy was on the phone from Los Angeles.

He dashed into the office, took a deep breath to compose
himself, then leaned back in Cathy's executive chair with the
phone nestled between his shoulder and ear.

"Don't worry!" he assured. "Today's show couldn't have
gone better. You'll love it, I promise! The audience will be so
worried about Ned that they'll never dream it's Doc Bayard
who's really going to die."

"Have you contacted Joyce Pagent?" Cathy's voice filtered through the receiver.

"Yes. There's no problem with her starting the first of next week. Except she's pretty unhappy we can't give her a script."

"Well," Cathy bristled. "Before she complains to Oprah Winfrey, tell her she's not the only one being discriminated against. None of us has a script!"

"I know it, Cathy! Vico's been in here bellowing like a wounded bull. Threatening to quit again. The whole cast is bitching at me because they have to go home this weekend without next week's scripts to study."

"They have Monday's script, don't they?"

"Yeah, but just barely. The copy machines broke down again. The scripts just got here about half an hour ago. We didn't even have time to check them for mistakes."

"How's the new girl, Marnie, doing?"

"Fine. She'll never win any beauty contests," he added lightly. "But she knows her business."

"That's why I hired her," Cathy snapped. "Don't worry about Vico, I'll call him later."

"What about Liz? She says you haven't returned her calls."

"No." Cathy paused, on sensitive ground. "And I'm not going to. I suppose I should, but, listen, Neil, tell her we're really tied up but we're developing a sensational idea for her. It's exactly what she's been looking for. Tell her . . . tell her I'll let her read it Monday morning before anyone else sees it."

Neil shifted his position in the chair. "This sensational idea. You're talking about the sex thing with Jamie, aren't you?"

"Yes, of course, but don't *you* say anything. *I* want to tell her."

"It might not be a bad idea to discuss it with her. You know how she feels . . ."

"Don't be stupid, Neil! If I needed Liz's advice to produce this show, I'd ask her for it. I don't need her approval either. It was Jim Hennigan's idea and it was one of the first things he laid out for the Kirklands when he got here this morning. If she has any complaints, she can go to him."

Neil masked his reaction to Cathy's rebuff. "Whatever you say, cutie."

"Good," she answered coldly. "And be available when I get back Sunday night."

"Oh, I will," he assured.

"Is there anything else?"

"No," Neil responded. "Except there's a rumor going around about a scandal in the production manager's department."

"I've heard all about that," Cathy flared. "Don't waste my time with other peoples' problems."

"You're right," he retorted. "Why reach for the moon when you have the stars?"

"What?"

"That's advice from your late great favorite, Bette Davis."

"Are you trying to get fired?"

"No. I'm trying to lighten your mood."

"Well, don't. There's nothing wrong with my mood that a little cooperation won't cure, so stop trying to be funny and stick to business."

"Yes sir . . . I mean, ma'am. I'll stick like crazy glue," he continued as the line clicked dead in his ear.

"Stick it in *your* business," he mimicked at the phone before slamming it back into its cradle.

"Whatcha doing, Neil, practicing to be a producer?" Leigh's cheerful voiced teased from the doorway.

"And you're practicing to be funny, I suppose," he retorted.

Leigh blinked, pretending to be crushed by his reaction. "Sorry to have disturbed you," she muttered as she made a move to leave.

"No, wait," Neil jumped from his chair and took Leigh's arm, leading her back into the office and closing the door. "I'm the one who's sorry," he smiled contritely. "You know how it is at that time of the month. You get pretty crazy too."

"Oh, Neil," Leigh's face broke into a grin. "I wish you *would* get your period . . . even once. Then you wouldn't think it was such a joke!"

"Maybe not, but I do envy all those things having your

period excuses. And *missing* one. *That* excuses almost any-thing!"

"You're the most disgusting person I know!"

"And you're the sweetest." Neil pecked her on the cheek. "That's why I'm going to ask, how's it going with you and Jamie?"

"Why do you ask a question like that?" she was at once defensive.

"Because I care about you," he smiled. "Because I see how you are when you're together. And because yesterday you went to the teleprompter once and today you needed it twice. That isn't like you. You usually know your dialogue better than anyone in the show."

"What's wrong with everyone today?" she stormed. "Why is it a man and a woman can't be friends without the whole world thinking they're going to bed together? I really didn't expect it from you!"

"That isn't what I meant," Neil retreated.

"Oh yes, you did!" she insisted. "And if you *really* want to know what's bothering me, it's my mother. She came home yesterday and went right into the hospital."

"Why? What's wrong?"

"They don't know. They're checking to find out."

"I hope it isn't serious," he grunted, now feeling like a complete rat. "Ah . . . Monday's script is the only one that we'll have today."

"I don't work Monday, but I do Tuesday."

"We'll have Tuesday through Friday's scripts on Monday afternoon."

"Not 'til Monday?" she wailed.

"I feel the same way," Neil sighed. "But it's for the good of the show and what's good for the show is good for all of us, so please try to be understanding."

"I'll be understanding. But you be understanding if I sneak a look at the prompter again."

"Okay. Where are you headed? Are you going to see your mother?"

"Yes, we're planning to have dinner."

"It doesn't seem like she can be all that sick if they let you have dinner with her."

"I hope not. We won't be sure until the doctors finish checking."

"Well, good luck."

"Thanks. I'll tell her you asked for her," Leigh answered, stepping out of the room.

Neil got up to watch her move through the outer office and spotted Annie Holland standing in front of a hutch of message boxes against the wall. "Come into my office a minute, Annie," he called. "I have Monday's script for you. Don't be picky with the mistakes. We didn't have time to edit it."

Annie followed him to his desk where he began thumbing through a stack of large manila envelopes. "Here you are," he said, looking up to notice a slightly colored puffiness around her eyes.

The cuff of her sweater slipped up as Annie reached for the envelope, revealing an ugly red welt around her wrist.

"Are you all right?" he questioned. "What happened to your wrist?"

"Nothing," she insisted, pulling her cuff back down. "A little accident at home. But it's nothing."

"I hope not." He knew she was lying but didn't want to press her. Neil's mind flashed on her obscene fan letters, but deciding not to bring it up, he glanced at his watch and smiled. "It's time for my coffee break. How 'bout having a cup with me?"

"No," she said, easing toward the door. "I . . . have an appointment. Besides, I don't drink coffee."

"I almost forgot. You're a tea lady, aren't you? What's your appointment? Do you have an interview or something?"

"No, not an interview," Annie hedged. "Not *exactly* an interview. I mean, it's one of those things I'd rather not talk about until it happens."

"Okay," he replied, wishing that Network security had been able to come up with more than the fact that her fan letters had been mailed from New York's Central Post Office. "Whatever it is, I hope it turns out the way you want it to."

After leaving the building, Annie fled self-consciously from a group of autograph seekers outside the main entrance and scurried to the corner where she hailed a taxi.

I shouldn't be afraid of them, she thought, her thin face set in grim determination. *It wouldn't hurt me to give them an autograph. Why can't I let myself be somebody? No one ever asked my mom for her autograph. She never had her picture in a magazine. She couldn't do anything about the life she had, but I can. I just need some help. Just a little constructive help.*

◈ Annie gave her sweater cuff a nervous tug. She was sitting across the desk from Dr. Ralph Brown. "It's a simple procedure to remove that mole on your neck," he said. "It will take only a couple of minutes."

"Good," Annie responded tightly.

"Are you feeling all right, otherwise?" the doctor continued. "Your eyes seem a little red."

Annie stiffened. "I'm fine. That's . . . that's a reaction I get sometimes to my . . . makeup."

"I see." He looked at her chart. "You're an actress, aren't you? It could be that you're more in need of a dermatologist than a plastic surgeon."

"Oh, yes," she replied, glancing toward the door. She wanted to run before he started asking any more questions. "Maybe you're right. I'm sorry if I wasted your time."

"Unless, perhaps, there's something more," he gently urged. "Something else I can help you with?"

"No . . ." she answered, her face beginning to flush. "Except . . . Well, there *is* one thing. You see, I . . ."

The doctor nodded patiently, trying to put her at ease.

"I'm so embarrassed," she strained. "I have this . . . this tattoo thing . . ."

"And you'd like it removed," he assisted. "Where is it?"

"Here," she touched her buttocks, mortified.

"Let's have a look," he said kindly, as he moved from behind his desk. "I'll have the nurse take you to an examining room. And stop worrying. I'm sure we'll be able to handle it."

Annie was lying on her stomach, her face turned to the wall when Dr. Brown came into the examining room. Her mind raced through the list of flimsy excuses she had invented to explain the vulgar stigma on her rear, but she relaxed in grateful relief when the doctor commented with only a noncommittal grunt and assured her it could be removed. She didn't care about the possible scar or the pain. She would be free!

With Zev gone, 'BAD ASS' would be the last connection to her unhappy, degraded past. She would start over—clean and new.

◈ Leigh sat near her mother's hospital bed, patiently waiting as Nancy, not yet free from the influence of the morning's anesthesia, drifted in and out of foggy consciousness.

If only she had told me, Leigh thought as she studied the IV bottle dripping its contents into the vein of Nancy's arm. *But then, Mom never could talk about anything unpleasant. Even events so far back as the trouble between Dad and Jamie; there's no way I could ever get her to tell me about that.*

Her gaze drifted to the bandaged outline of Nancy's breast beneath the bed cover. *The doctor said he was certain the tumor he took out of her breast was benign, but what if it wasn't! What if she had cancer!*

It isn't right for people to keep things like this to themselves. Why is simple communication so darned difficult!

Leigh pushed aside her tray of food that had grown cold, then looked at her mother's sallow face. Nancy's lips moved wordlessly for a moment before she resumed her peaceful breathing.

This relationship I've started with Jamie, I can't talk to Mom about it. My best friend Mindy doesn't understand. And Dad . . . Leigh's mouth settled into a grim line across her face. How can I talk to Dad? No one ever could. Imagine how he'd react if I told him how Jamie's goodnight kiss suddenly made me realize that the man I've fantasized about all my life—the one I've waited to give my heart and everything to— has turned out to be the one and only Jamie Starbuck!

Nancy's eyes fluttered open. "I'm sorry I keep falling asleep," she smiled weakly at her daughter.

"It's good for you," Leigh comforted as Nancy once again nodded off.

When she could see that Nancy was resting easily, Leigh propped her head on the back of the chair and stared at the ceiling. If there was no one else to confide in, she sighed, perhaps she should write to Dear Abby.

Dear Abby: I'm confused. All my life I've thought falling in love was supposed to be fun and make me happy. Where is the fun in lying awake at night thinking about a man whom you are sure feels the same way you do but is too honorable to do anything about it? Where is the happiness in the ache I feel when I lie there imagining what it must be like to be with him in every way, loving him the way I have dreamed about? My work is beginning to suffer. I am having trouble remembering my lines.

No. Leigh interrupted her imaginary letter. She couldn't tell her that. She'd know she was an actress!

Her mouth softened into a wry smile. Think of the scandal! It'll be just like the old days in Hollywood when the stars died for their love.

Okay, Dear Abby, here's the truth: The man I think I am in love with is wonderful in every way except he is married. It can't last. She doesn't care about him enough to be here with him and I'm positive he doesn't miss her a bit. He's older. That doesn't matter. He may be mature, but he looks terrific.

My father hates him. That's because he doesn't really know him. He . . . Leigh paused again and turned to look at her sleeping mother. She didn't have to wonder. She already knew what Dear Abby's answer would be: Dear Confused Actress: Run, don't walk, to your nearest shrink! You are not confused, you are out of your mind!

"Oh Mommy," she groaned as she leaned over to pick a limp green bean from her dinner tray. "Why am I such a fool?"

CHAPTER

16

Jamie was filled with a
sense of well-being as he and Leigh stopped at Sheep Meadow
while walking through Central Park to watch the children
frolicking across the open, snowy expanse.

Damn, it was nice to be with a woman and just have *fun*.
No arguments, no problems, no complaints.

He glanced appreciatively at Leigh's glowing face as she
watched the sledders coursing happily down a gentle slope.

All those idiots with their youth serums and plastic surgery are wasting their time. *This* was the way to stay young:
be happy, have a little fun!

"What are you grinning about?" Leigh asked coquettishly.

"Nothing," he shrugged as he observed two boys on a sled
glide to a stop. "Have you ever ridden one of those things?"

"A sled?" she laughed. "*I'm* not from California. Of course
I've ridden one."

"Want to give it a try?"

"Here? With you?"

"Are you scared?" he teased.

"I'm not if you're not . . ."

"Hey kids," Jamie called to the boys. "Can we take a run
down the hill on your sled?"

"What?" The boys studied them suspiciously.

"I'll give you five bucks," Jamie offered. "We only want one ride and we won't take it out of your sight."

The boys accepted with less interest in the money than the opportunity to see how these two adults would manage on their little sled.

After dragging the sled to the top of the slope, Jamie and Leigh squeezed themselves into position, then with arms and legs flaying the air, went skidding back down the snowy incline.

Their lack of balance and uninhibited laughter left the overloaded sled impossible to steer. It veered away from Jamie's intended course and bounded along, out of control, until it crashed with a tumble into a large drift of soft snow.

As their laughter subsided, Jamie and Leigh found themselves half buried in the snow, face-to-face and wrapped in each other's arms. The chill of the snow disappeared in the sudden passion that sprang upon them. Their arms tightened around each other and their lips blended together in a long, meaningful kiss.

"Hey, you guys," one of the boys shouted. "If you broke my sled, you're going to have to pay."

Jamie and Leigh separated self-consciously and untangled themselves from the sled and debris.

A quick inspection revealed that no damage had been done, and with a five-dollar bonus the boys went contentedly on their way.

A veil of constraint arose between the flustered couple as they brushed off the snow and continued their walk through the park.

Thank God I have an appointment this afternoon with Sam and Devon, Jamie thought, glancing at his watch. *I'm the one who should be responsible in this situation. I'm the one who's supposed to be old and wise enough to control my emotions!*

Leigh was also having troubled thoughts. It occurred to her that perhaps she was no better than Millicent Lipton. Was she conniving to steal another woman's husband, just as Millicent was stealing Russell from her mother? "How's Bucky?" she asked, breaking the tense silence.

"Bucky?" Jamie blinked, the thought of his son reinforcing his discomfort. "Oh, he's . . . ah . . . in the mountains this weekend with some neighbors. I thought I told you."

"That's right, you did. When you were talking about his soccer team making the A.Y.S.O. playoffs. I can understand how difficult it must be for you having to give up coaching your own son's team at such a crucial time. Does Erika help?"

"She offers the typical mother's advice from the sidelines. But even though she's European, soccer isn't a game she really likes or understands."

"But she tries," Leigh continued, feeling more and more conscious of her kinship with Millicent.

"Yeah, she tries," Jamie conceded.

"What did you talk about before? I mean, before Bucky?"

Jamie paused thoughtfully before answering. "I don't know. It's been so long since we . . . just talked. I don't remember."

She wondered if Russell remembered the distant past when he could still communicate with Nancy. *If they don't talk, what's left? Maybe Dad's right to be with Millicent . . .*

"But I've always had a memory like a sieve," he smiled and glanced again to his watch in an effort to divert the conversation away from Erika. "What time is your date to visit Nancy?"

"I still have some time," Leigh responded after a quick look at her own watch.

"I'm glad she's okay," he went on. "Say hello for me, will you?"

"Sure," she answered and then was struck by the recollection of her father's violent reaction when she suggested that another woman may have been one of the causes of his dispute with Jamie. "How well did you know my mother? Were you friends?"

"Friends?" Jamie repeated with a noncommittal shrug. "We always liked each other, but I wouldn't exactly say we were friends." He glanced once again to his watch. "It's almost time for my meeting with the commercial people. We'd better get going."

Leigh pushed aside her nagging doubt and put her arm in his as they resumed walking along the pathway. "And after the meeting, you're having dinner with Sam Allison?" she asked.

"Yeah," Jamie responded, then put aside his feeling of regret at the thought of how long it would be until he could see her again. "I have costume fittings again tomorrow, then the publicity thing at NYU. I guess I won't be able to see you until Monday."

"Monday," she echoed, struggling to maintain her cheerful smile. "I'm having a big day tomorrow, too. I'm helping my friend, Mindy Shrafft, look for a new apartment."

"I had a great time today," Jamie said huskily. "You may not believe this, but I can't remember when I had so much fun."

"Me too," Leigh said, her big eyes glowing with gratitude. "Next time we go sledding, we'll try the expert's slope."

"I don't think we're ready for that yet," he replied guardedly. "Let's take this thing slowly. One step at a time."

◈ Jamie waited in the Ward and McKay Advertising Agency's reception room only long enough to shed his sheepskin coat before a pretty secretary appeared to escort him to Sam Allison's office.

Sam, looking somewhat frazzled, interrupted his phone conversation long enough to wave an introduction between Jamie and Terry Hayden, who had recently been hired to direct the Saddle commercials.

Terry remained hunched over a table strewn with storyboards, discussing a point with two assistants as he casually acknowledged the introduction.

Jamie noticed a resemblance in the way he and Terry were dressed. The difference was that Terry's styled haircut, his small, soft hands, and the pot belly drooping over his belt made his faded denim shirt, jeans, and polished cowboy boots look more like a costume than the apparel of a man in his natural environment.

The discussion ended with the assistants hurrying out of the office.

"Here it is," Terry said, beckoning Jamie over to the table. Sam hung up the phone and amiably stood by Jamie's side as Terry gestured toward the storyboard he held in his hand.

Jamie curiously scanned the series of cartoonlike panels that illustrated the shot-by-shot, second-by-second continuity.

"It's very much like Devon's original idea," Sam commented.

"The shoot will basically be the same wherever we are," Terry explained. "Of course the settings will be different: London, Paris, Rome . . ."

"Madrid, Munich, and Athens," Sam added. "Two cities in each of the three commercials."

Jamie's eyes followed the panels as Terry described the scene. "The whole thing will be shot in a kind of surrealistic fog. You'll come riding this beautiful white horse down one of the famous streets. The camera will see your saddlebags which have been made up to look like the new Saddle Cologne bottles. As you ride by, people along the street and in the sidewalk cafés will stop and stare . . ."

"Like the old 'When E. F. Hutton speaks' campaign," Sam interjected.

"Yeah, except the expressions will be different. The men will have a look of wonder, maybe a slight confusion, but the women will have a look of revelation, as though a great, fantastic truth has finally been exposed to them. The camera will stop on one particularly beautiful girl as she shifts her gaze from you to the boy sitting across from her. The fog will swirl around the Saddle Cologne logo on the saddlebag and in the next cut we'll see her boyfriend riding the horse instead of you. There'll be a tight shot of her smiling dreamily, then a shot of you, back on the horse. From that we'll zoom into a close-up of you smiling and you'll say, 'Put *your* man in the saddle. With Saddle Cologne.' Then you'll ride off into the swirling fog."

"Sounds great," Jamie nodded. "Sure as hell gets the message across!!"

"That's the whole idea," Sam grinned. "They're using sex these days to sell everything from light bulbs to hemorrhoid medicine. We just try to do it with a little class."

"You watch and see," Terry waved his finger in the air. "We'll win some awards with this one!"

"And hopefully, we'll sell some cologne," Devon Rudin cracked from the doorway.

"It can't miss," Terry enthused. "Not the way I plan to shoot it. Hell, everybody gets laid but the horse. It's a cinch!"

"Yeah, a cinch," Devon laughed.

"Terry won a 'Clio' last year," Sam spoke up.

"What's a Clio?" Jamie asked.

"It's the 'Oscar' of television commercials," Sam explained. "It's a big honor."

"We'll all have Clios next year," Devon announced expansively. "This is going to be the best men's toiletry campaign in history! Sam's the best writer, Terry's the best director, you're the best actor, and I'm the best agency exec."

"If enthusiasm counts for anything we will," Sam said.

"Not just enthusiasm," Devon corrected. "We have *talent*, Sam. It's our talent that's going to put us on top, and don't ever think otherwise."

"I won't, Dev."

Devon's expression abruptly changed. "And I'd better remember, Papa Roth is waiting. Jamie, would you mind coming upstairs with me? Papa Roth said he'd like to meet you."

Jamie looked questioningly to Sam who quickly escorted him to the door. "We'll talk later," Sam said. "Terry has a couple of ideas about the costume that I want the three of us to go over."

"I won't keep him long," Devon said. "Papa Roth is only

here long enough to clear up a few things before he leaves for Miami."

Jamie only half listened to Devon's chatter as they made their way up to Rothwell Industries' penthouse headquarters.

The two men paused long enough to be announced, then proceeded through the great, wooden portals into Aaron Roth's office.

"So this is our cowboy," Roth wheezed as he pulled himself to his feet and extended his hand to Jamie.

"It's an honor to meet you, sir," Jamie said, enveloping the tiny hand in his own.

"Thank you," Roth answered, appraising the tall actor while settling back into his chair. "Devon, give the man a cigar," he ordered.

"Yes, sir."

"I've been wanting to talk to you," he continued as he watched Jamie make a selection from his large, walnut humidor. "Do you think you'll be able to save the university?"

"I beg your pardon?" Jamie responded uncertainly.

"Webster," Roth clarified. "What's going to happen? I'm not surprised they're going broke, the way they run things. Jennifer Wells is a fine lady, but she can't be responsible for everything. Do you think the two of you will get married?"

"You're talking about 'Yesterday's Children,' " Jamie voiced incredulously. "Do you really watch the show?"

"Every day," Roth gestured toward a corner sitting area. "Every day I sit right there, turn off the phones, lock the door, and have my lunch while I watch you people do the story. The doctor told me to nap during the day, but for me it's easier and more relaxing to sit here with 'Yesterday's Children.' "

"I'll be damned," Jamie smiled. "The people at the show will be happy to hear that."

"So, tell me. What's going to be happening?" Roth repeated with a flourish of his cigar.

"I wish I could," Jamie said pleasantly. "We're in the middle of a big shake-up right now; new writers, new stories, some new actors coming, some old ones going . . ."

"Who?" Roth demanded anxiously. "Why do they do that? Why are they always changing? It makes me crazy. I get to know someone, to like them, then they kill them. I tell you, it's craziness!" He angrily slapped the desktop with his open palm. "Maybe I should do something."

"Do what, Papa?" Devon asked solicitously.

"I don't know, but *something!* I spend millions every year for their meshuga commercials. They can count. They know they'd better listen to me!" The old man's sagging, round face changed mercurially from anger to anticipated sorrow. "Tell me. Who's going to die? Not that fine lady!"

"No," Jamie comforted. "Not Jennifer. She will never die. I'm afraid it's going to be . . . Dr. Bayard."

The color drained from Papa Roth's face. "Dr. Benjamin Bayard," he whispered as he wiped his face with his handkerchief. "He was the best. A fine man. A fine doctor." He listlessly reached for his intercom switch. "Tell my car it's time to leave for the airport. I'll have to talk to you boys later," he said as Devon helped him into his coat. "Maybe next week."

"I'm going to Europe next week, Papa. To start the commercials for Saddle."

"I know." He gave Devon's arm a weak squeeze. "Don't forget to give a kiss to my sweet Ruth. Tell my little girl her Papa loves her. And my darling grandson, Aaron second, tell him too."

"Yes, Papa. Have a nice vacation in Miami."

"A nice vacation," the old man scoffed. "With news like this, I should have a nice vacation."

Devon returned after walking his father-in-law to the elevator.

"I didn't mean to upset him," Jamie apologized.

"It isn't you. It's just that everybody he's ever cared about is gone, except Ruth and me and little Aaron. I think he's beginning to feel he doesn't have much time left."

"Well, I'm sorry."

"Don't worry about it. If I know him, he'll still be running things long after you and I are gone. Come on," he grinned. "I don't want to spend Saturday night here. Let's get Sam and Terry's problems straightened out and go someplace for a drink. Maybe find a little action."

"I'm having dinner with Sam. If you're not going home, come along with us."

"That's a good idea," Devon grinned. "Between the two of us, maybe we can convince Sam to come out of his shell and have a good time. I know a spot where we can't miss!"

"Ah . . . I'm not really looking for any action. It seems like I . . . have more than I can handle these days."

"You actors," Devon shook his head in admiration. "You really have it made! I never met a bimbo yet who wouldn't lay down for a movie star."

"There are a few around who won't," Jamie smiled amiably. "And believe me, women are just as big a mystery to actors as anybody else."

"Sure," Devon reacted skeptically. "And I believe that like I believe being poor is good for your character."

◈ Nancy smiled in radiant good spirits as Leigh entered her hospital room with a small and artfully arranged bunch of daisies. Her hair was neatly done up with a velvet ribbon and the dressing over her breast operation concealed by a loose, stylish peignoir.

"You look so pretty!" Leigh exclaimed before giving her mother a gentle embrace. "You don't look as though you've been ill at all!"

"Thank the Lord it wasn't as serious as it might have been," Nancy exclaimed as she turned gingerly on her side to face Leigh. "I never believed the tumor was malignant. That's why I didn't mention it to you. But still . . ."

"But, still, you weren't positive," Leigh chided gently, placing her flowers on the bedside cabinet alongside a bouquet of roses. "And you *should* have mentioned it. Has Daddy been here?"

Nancy avoided Leigh's gaze as she shook her head negatively. "The daisies are lovely, dear," she said. "The roses are from your father. He's in Florida. I didn't mention it to him either. All he knows is that I'm here for a checkup."

"Why, Mom?" Leigh's eyes suddenly misted over.

"Oh, honey," Nancy reached for her daughter's hand. "You surely know, even if we didn't tell you, that for some time now our marriage has been more pretense than reality. If my biopsy had shown a malignancy, Russell would be here, but under the circumstances there was no need to disturb him."

"Disturb him?" Leigh cried. "My God, Mom, what has happened between you and Dad? What changed everything?"

"Nothing specific," Nancy answered, unwilling to face the question she had a thousand times asked herself. "People change. You know how it is."

"No, I *don't* know," Leigh insisted. "And it's important that I find out. What happened between you and Daddy is terribly important to me."

"Why honey?" Nancy asked, perceiving the urgency in her daughter's expression. "What is it? Are you . . . Do you think you're falling in love? Are you making a comparison?"

"Maybe." Leigh looked away as she removed her hand from her mother's clasp. "But when I see how people are with one another . . . how their attitudes change . . . how they can become like hostile strangers."

"You're speaking of your father and me?"

"Yes," Leigh frowned. "But you're not the only ones."

"No, we *aren't* very unique, are we?" Nancy smiled sadly. "I used to think we were. I used to think Russell was the most wonderful, most unique man in the world. But he's only human. As I am." She raised her hand to the dressing on her breast. "This cancer scare has made me realize how helplessly human all of us really are."

Leigh shook her head. "You must have loved each other once. That was human wasn't it?"

"Yes, quite human," Nancy nodded. "Unfortunately, the reality is, the Russell I fell in love with no longer exists. I've changed as well. I like to think of it as growth, but nevertheless it's change."

"You mean it's as simple as that?" Leigh puzzled. "You just changed? If it's human nature to change, how does *anyone* stay together?"

"I wish I could tell you," Nancy sighed. "I think most of it is trust . . . Then, going through changes together. Surviving the changes. And having the good sense to learn from your experience."

"But by the time you have the experience, isn't it too late?"

"I hope not," Nancy smiled. "I hope that as long as we keep trying it's *never* too late."

"Experience," Leigh repeated thoughtfully. "Maybe people should try to see where they're going. Have some experience with life on their own, before trying to do it with someone else . . ."

"I wish I could give you an answer," Nancy sighed. "I'm sure what you're saying is part of it . . . but I don't know. Perhaps if I'd taken the time to think. If I hadn't rushed so recklessly into life, things might have worked out differently."

"They still can, Mom." Leigh's eyes were bright with new-found conviction. "All we have to do is apply the lessons we're going to learn from our experience."

Nancy's nod of agreement changed to an expression of uncertainty as she began to wonder if she and Leigh had the same understanding of their conversation.

CHAPTER

"You're in pretty good shape for an old-timer," Terry Hayden remarked as he checked the tailor's last minute adjustments on Jamie's theatrically elegant, cream-colored Western costume.

"Better than you or me," Devon laughed disarmingly, as he patted his extended waistline.

"Me too," Sam agreed.

Jamie nodded stoically, while giving a sideward glance to Terry. "If you don't start taking better care of yourself, you might not live to be an old-timer."

Terry brushed his fingers through his stringy hair. "Live fast, die young, and have a good-looking corpse, that's my motto."

"You're liable to make it," Jamie commented dryly, then spread his arms and admired the costume. "Good job, Louie," he said to the tailor. "You're making a double for this, aren't you?"

"Sure, Mr. Jamie. But I don't need you for no more fittings. I make the double from this one."

Sam and Louie followed Jamie to Sam's adjoining office where he got out of the costume and into his street clothes.

"I appreciate your coming in on Sunday. I wouldn't have

asked, but we want everything to be ready," Sam said after Louie left.

"That's all right," Jamie answered. "I didn't have anything better to do."

"I suppose it'd be different if your wife were here," Sam replied with an edge of melancholy.

"You can say that again," Jamie grunted wryly. "How about yours? Is Cathy back from L.A. yet?"

"No. But since she got that promotion, it's hard to notice if she's in town or not." Sam paused while watching Jamie pull on his boots. "I can't help thinking of what you told me about Leigh's mother. I know she's okay, but it makes me wonder about Cathy. How she would react to losing a breast."

"Yeah," Jamie responded laconically.

"I really don't think Cathy could take it," Sam continued. "She's . . . she's so involved with the way she looks."

"That doesn't make her very unusual," he grinned. "She's still a woman, isn't she?"

"I suppose so."

"Do you ever talk to her? I mean about the show?" Jamie quickly clarified. "Normally I just do my job and let everybody else worry about theirs, but it's hard to ignore all the bullshit going down."

"We don't talk much about the show. She'll be back tonight. Hopefully she'll have some answers tomorrow."

"The studio's become a nuthouse lately," Jamie frowned. "I'm just getting the hang of it. I'd feel pretty bad if the show were to go down the tubes."

"You're not the only one."

"You think it's possible?" Jamie raised his eyebrows. "That 'Yesterday's Children' could be canceled?"

"I wouldn't be surprised at anything that happens at Federated these days," Sam nodded. "Especially with this new scandal brewing. I hear it has everybody at Slippery Rock looking over his shoulder."

"That's what I've heard," Jamie replied with interest. "There's a rumor going around about some of the production managers screwing the network with phony vouchers. But I heard it was only in Sports and Special Projects." Jamie stopped as Sam picked up his ringing telephone.

"Hi, Neil," Sam cheerfully spoke into the receiver. "Yeah. Great! I'll see you at the apartment. And thanks a lot."

Sam stared pensively at Cathy's framed photograph on his desk. "That was Neil Decker," he explained awkwardly. "He's meeting Cathy's plane at Kennedy. He called to tell me what time she . . . I mean, Cathy wasn't sure what time she'd be getting in."

"Like I said before," Jamie began slowly. "Normally, I mind my own business—I know that Cathy doesn't like actors very much, especially if they're taking off for three weeks to make a commercial—but I'd appreciate it if you'd let her know I'd like to help if I can, and that I do care about the show."

"She's not too crazy about husbands who take off for three weeks either," Sam forced a chuckle. "But I'll tell her for you. She isn't herself these days. It's probably the pressure of her new job and everything . . . I know she'll appreciate your support. I'll tell her as soon as I can."

◈ Sam kept an anxious eye on his watch as he worked with Devon and Terry into the early evening.

The arrival of two fresh-faced, young models prompted Terry's flippant departure "to take care of his homework."

Devon and Sam checked and rechecked the last details, then stuffed their briefcases and prepared to leave. Standing on opposite sides of Devon's desk, they peered speculatively into each other's eyes, anxiously pondering the likelihood of an overlooked contingency.

First Sam, then Devon grinned sheepishly. "I think we're ready, partner," Sam said.

"Let's have a drink on it."

Sam looked at his watch. "Just one."

"Of course, just one," Devon replied innocently. "I have a family to get home to. Ruth's having a little farewell dinner for just the two of us."

"You're lucky," Sam signed. "I hope Cathy isn't too worn out from her trip."

"I keep telling you about working wives." Devon's mouth creased into a devilish grin. "Do you want another Quaalude?"

"Naw," Sam shrugged. "That stuff went out with disco music. Besides, it put me to sleep."

"Sleep?" Devon snorted. "And you say *I'm* old-fashioned?"

◈ Sam stopped on his way home and bought a pizza with Cathy's favorite green pepper and pepperoni topping.

After putting the pizza in the oven and taking a quick, invigorating shower, he removed a large suitcase from the closet and began the always difficult task of deciding what to pack.

He was narrowing down the possibilities from the selection strewn across the bed when he heard Cathy's key in the front door. He drew a steadying breath and moved into the living room to greet her.

Sam reacted sympathetically to the fatigue evidenced in Cathy's drawn face as she trudged into the apartment with Neil following closely behind. He hid his disappointment when she went directly to the telephone, brushing aside his welcoming kiss.

While she busied herself speaking with Jim Hennigan, and afterward Vico Fellouris, Sam served three portions of the pizza along with brimming glasses of red wine.

Neil ate voraciously, but Cathy only picked indifferently at a small piece between snatches of conversation before pushing hers aside.

Sam carried his portion to the table where he sat and

talked quietly with Neil until Cathy finished her calls. "Why don't you relax a minute, honey?" he offered. "Nothing is so important that you can't enjoy your food."

"Spare the advice," she snapped. "Neil, I want you to find a copy machine someplace and have the pages ready first thing in the morning."

"You mean, just as they are?"

"Are you going to argue with everything I say?"

"Not me," Neil said, raising his hands in a gesture of surrender. "You want them just as they are, that's the way you'll get them."

"What I want has nothing to do with it." Her expression matched her dark mood. "The Kirkwoods wrote it, Jim approved it, and I don't have the authority to make any changes. I don't know why I was there; they hardly listened to a thing I said. Goddamn writers! They're taking over everything."

Sam and Neil looked tentatively to each other, undecided on how to reply. "Uh . . . If you're interested in some good news," Sam said guardedly, "Leigh Fisk's mother had a tumor removed from her breast that turned out to be benign."

"She's lucky," Cathy replied, taking a long drink of wine. Sam noticed her expression soften into abstract concern as she blankly picked up a slice of pizza, put it to her mouth, then dropped it back on the plate. "I'll send her some flowers."

"It makes you kind of think, doesn't it?" Sam continued. "I mean, what's it all about? What the hell are we working for? Look at you. You're killing yourself and what's it going to get you?"

"I don't know," she sighed wearily.

"Do me a favor," he urged, moving quickly to her side. "While I'm away, think about having a baby. Just think about it. We can talk about it when I get back."

Cathy's eyes opened wide with disbelief. "You're out of your mind," she blurted. "If you want a baby, why don't *you* have it?"

"Let's discuss it later," Sam said with a calming motion of his hand.

"Yeah, discuss it later," Neil tried to lighten the atmosphere. "I don' know nothin' 'bout birthin' babies, Miz Scarlett," he mimicked.

"There's nothing more to discuss," she snapped. "I don't know where you get these stupid ideas. This one is even more stupid than the insanity that made you leave the vice presidency at the network."

"I wasn't a vice president."

"Oh, shut up!"

Sam tensed. "Excuse me Neil. I have to finish packing." His cheeks were burning as he turned to his wife. "If you're late coming to bed . . ." His eyes flashed, but his voice remained calm. "I'll say good night now."

◈ Neil looked up from the work on his desk as he noticed Liz stride through the reception room with a determination he had never seen before. She's read the scene with Jamie, he concluded, then jumped up to follow her into Cathy's office.

"Who's ridiculous idea is that?" he heard Liz demand as he slipped through the doorway.

"I don't know what you're talking about," Cathy brazenly responded.

"I'm talking about this," Liz snapped, and flung her script across Cathy's desk. "Jennifer Wells wouldn't do this; it's totally out of character. My husband hasn't been dead six months and you want to show me in bed with a man I hardly know? We haven't developed any kind of romantic relationship—I haven't even kissed him! *Jennifer Wells doesn't sleep with men she isn't married to!* Everybody in the world knows that except you. And you're the one person who's supposed to know it best!"

"I don't think you understand," Cathy groped, then looked coldly at Neil. "Would you leave us alone, Neil? And close the door."

"Stay where you are, Neil," Liz countermanded. "And there's no need to close the door. Everyone will know soon enough: *I'm not going to do it!*"

Neil looked uncertainly from one woman to the other, then mumbling indistinctly about having something to do, eased out of the office.

"What do you mean, you're not going to do it?" Cathy asked, her confidence slipping.

"I mean I'm not going to tape that script. It will have to be changed!"

"But we're doing it Wednesday. We can't change it!" Cathy gave a conciliatory smile. "I said the same thing to the Kirklands. I said you might think it's bad for Jennifer's image, but Jim Hennigan insisted we do it." She hesitated a moment, not wanting to go too far. "Of course, I can see where it could be good for the show. It could be good for you, too. There'll be some wonderful acting scenes coming up for you—sitting alone, thinking about Spencer, wondering if you did the right thing."

"*I'm not going to do it.*"

Cathy placed the script in front of her and began nervously thumbing through the pages as though they might reveal some solution to the impasse. "Ah . . . I think you should talk to Jim," she said, trying to maintain some kind of poise. "Since it was his idea, I think . . ."

"I realize that it isn't a permanent assignment," Liz interrupted pointedly, "but you *are* the producer of this show, aren't you?"

"Yes, but . . ."

"Then I'm talking to *you*. That's what producers are for, isn't it? To produce whatever is necessary to get the show on the air?"

"Now, Liz, please listen to me," Cathy rose to her feet.

"I'll listen when you bring me a new script," Liz stopped her coldly. "This may be your opportunity to show the network how good you really are."

The image of the hospital room where the teaser would be

performed suddenly popped onto the television monitor in Cathy's office.

"Oh, dress rehearsal is starting," Liz said. "I'd best forget this until we've finished today's show. I wouldn't want to get myself overly upset."

With that, she left the office and Cathy slumped numbly back into her seat.

Sam might be right, she sighed. Having a baby couldn't be any worse than this. She impulsively reached for the telephone, hoping to catch him in time to say good-bye before his departure.

"Yes, it could," she forcefully corrected herself, then replaced the receiver and pensively twisted her wedding ring around her finger. *It's just as well. Now is the time to think of fighting, not giving up.*

◈ After taping, Leigh and Annie met in the hallway and went together to the cast lounge area of the show's outer office, where they began flipping through their packets of fan mail.

"It must be a relief to you, not getting any more of those ugly letters," Leigh observed.

"They just stopped coming," Annie nodded thoughtfully. "Maybe the person who wrote them found something better to do."

"Or found someone else to write to."

"I hope not."

"So do I," Leigh frowned. "Maniacs like that should be in prison—or at least in an asylum."

Annie mumbled a quiet "yes" as she flushed and turned her face away to remove a letter from one of her preopened envelopes.

"Here's one from Hollywood, California!" Leigh squealed. "Isn't that neat! Who ever gets fan mail from Hollywood?"

"I never did," Annie answered.

"Well, I'll take care of that," Stanley said, stepping to the hutch of message boxes on the wall and removing the contents of his. "I'll send you a fan letter as soon as I get there."

"Are you still California dreamin'?" teased Leigh.

"It's more than just a dream," Stanley replied.

"I see," Leigh laughed. "So will you talk to us when you're a movie star?"

"Maybe," Stanley mocked. "If no one is watching. You know how it is with movie stars, they can't be seen talking to soap actors."

"We'll be careful not to embarrass you," Annie joined.

"How about directors?" Leigh raised her voice as Vico came in from the corridor. "Do Hollywood directors speak to soap actors?"

"Hollywood directors speak to anyone they think they can get into bed," Vico responded under a pose of stuffiness. "My policy, however, is to deal with all actors alike. Keeping in mind, of course, that it was an actor who shot Abraham Lincoln."

"How about the actor who took his place?" Stanley taunted.

"Reagan may have been president, but he will never take Lincoln's place." Vico arched his eyebrows, "Never, Stanley. Never."

"Has Jamie come in?" Marnie asked the temporary receptionist as she stepped from the door of her tiny office.

"He isn't coming. He left in a hurry," Leigh explained.

"Hi, girls," she smiled to Leigh and Annie as she moved to place a large envelope in Jamie's box. "It looks like you two have some juicy scenes coming up."

"Really?" Leigh pointed to the collection of unread scripts protruding from the top of her bag. "We haven't had time to read these, so tell us, Marnie, is it really good stuff?"

Marnie nodded affirmatively. "Annie is going to get involved unwittingly in Dr. Bayard's murder. And you're going to get excited because you think your romance with Spencer is getting serious. Then later—while Jamie's away, shooting the commercial—you'll find out Spencer went to bed with Jennifer before he left for Boston. That will give you a chance to really flip out!"

"Jamie is going to sleep with Liz?" Leigh reacted with surprise.

"Didn't you hear them talking about it at rehearsal?" Annie asked.

"No . . . I didn't."

"It seems like Cathy and Mr. Hennigan's trip to the Coast did some good," Marnie went on. "Our writers evidently needed some shaking up."

"Cathy wants you, Marnie," the receptionist called. "And Leigh, you have a visitor at the main entrance."

"That must be Mindy," Leigh said.

"See you, girls," Marnie responded, already moving toward Cathy's door.

"Are you going to see your mother?" Annie asked.

"Yes, but first I'm going with Mindy to look at a few more apartments. We looked all day yesterday and didn't find a thing."

"Stanley's going to California. What about his place? It might still be available."

"That would be perfect," Leigh said enthusiastically. "I wonder if he was going home?"

Annie shrugged. "He didn't say anything."

"Mindy and I will phone him later," Leigh replied as she eyed the envelope Marnie had deposited in Jamie's box. "Thanks for the suggestion."

"I hope it works out for her," Annie said, following Leigh's gaze. "Shall I take that to Jamie? He only lives a block from me . . ."

"I can take it," Leigh insisted more strongly than she intended. Then, realizing she didn't have time, she changed her mind. "All right. Yes, it could be something important." She took the envelope from the box and reluctantly handed it to Annie. "Let's go."

"It must have been an awful experience for your mother,"

Annie reflected as they walked down the hallway. "Discovering the lump in her breast, then having to wait to find out if it was malignant."

"I would have been scared to death," Leigh sighed.

"She never smoked, did she?"

"No, thank God."

"Yeah," Annie nodded somberly. "My Aunt Betty smoked like a fiend. She died of breast cancer before they connected it with smoking."

"Well, Mom's okay," Leigh declared with an involuntary shiver. "She says we learn from *all* our experiences. The awful ones *and* the good ones."

Leigh hesitated as she spotted Jim Hennigan coming from the opposite direction.

"Hi, Mr. Hennigan," the girls smiled.

"Oh. Hello," he nodded through a dark scowl as he continued his pace.

"Talk about awful experiences," Leigh said with a disapproving grimace. "He looks like one that's searching for a place to happen!"

◈ "Just a minute," Liz responded to the knock on her dressing room door. She completed the change from her working costume to her Chanel suit before opening the door. "Why, Mr. Hennigan," she said formally, as he entered. "What a surprise."

"I was in the neighborhood," he answered with forced joviality. "So I thought I'd drop by."

Liz sat at her makeup table, lowered the volume of the Chopin concerto on her tape machine, and began to daub at her makeup.

"I want you to know why we're doing this," he spoke softly.

"*I'm not* doing it," she said firmly.

"Then let me explain why I *want* to do it. Why I feel I *have* to do it. Please."

Liz remained silent.

"First, rating-wise you know we're in trouble," he began patiently. "Now, with ABC dropping our weakest competition and hitting us with 'Dynasty', we could really get killed. We have to do something drastic, especially the first couple of weeks, if we're going to keep our viewers. Our demographic studies show that the viewers who are the biggest consumers of the sponsor's products love these daily reruns of nighttime dramas."

"Don't start again with your demographics," she warned.

"All right. That's not what I'm here to talk about, but until they come up with something better, I can't ignore the ratings, not if I want to keep my job. As long as 'Yesterday's Children' was number one or two, I could afford to leave it alone and concentrate on the other shows I'm responsible for. But right now this network is a weak three and a strong candidate for number four. Daytime is the only programming where Federated has always managed to stay ahead of the other networks. Bottom-rated shows just aren't tolerated."

"We were *always* one or two until you started meddling with those stupid demographics," Liz flashed defensively.

"I don't want to argue with you, Liz, but I didn't start it. It's a policy that was inaugurated before I moved into this spot."

"But she wouldn't do it," Liz shook her head, speaking almost as to herself. "Jennifer wouldn't sleep with him so soon."

"Look," Jim reasoned. "If it's a question of artistic or dramatic integrity, I have an answer for that as well. Playing against character is one of the most common devices since the days of Euripides. It's good and honest drama to put a character in a situation where she does things she wouldn't normally do. It happens every day."

Liz nodded, thinking dimly of her frustrating evening with Eddie Irving.

"We could add a little scene between you and Jamie tomorrow," Jim continued. "A kind of romantic prelude. To make it more believable."

Her emotions were in turmoil as she turned over the cassette in the player.

"Is there some way I can help *you?*" he asked softly. "Maybe there's something you want. Something I can do for you. I'm really up a creek, Liz. If you cooperate, I'll do anything I can to show my appreciation!"

"But I don't think . . ."

"Anything!"

Liz reached to turn off the music. Then in the silence that followed, she blurted, "Fire Neil Decker."

"What?"

"I said, I want you to fire Neil Decker."

"All right," he replied, ignoring his surprise and curiosity. "You've got a deal. Ah . . . When do you want him out of here?"

"When? Whenever the normal time is . . . the usual time when one is given notice. Whatever is fair."

"I'll see that he's given notice the first thing in the morning."

Liz nodded abstractedly. "He mustn't know it came from me. No one must know; not Cathy or anyone!"

"And no one will," Jim assured. "It's *my* decision and I don't have to explain my decisions to those who work for me!"

"Very well, Jim," she looked up with sudden anxiety. "I . . . I . . ."

"*I'd* better get moving," Jim said. "I understand Jamie isn't scheduled tomorrow. We'll have to find him and I'll have to tell Cathy, and Vico too. If you have anything *you* want me to put in . . ."

"No," she shook her head.

"I won't forget this." He smiled, kissed her on the cheek, then hurried out of her dressing room.

Liz sat for a moment, studying her image in the mirror. "Oh, dear God," she cried. "What am I becoming? This isn't like me . . . Jennifer would never do anything so mean and spiteful!"

CHAPTER

18

Liz dropped her scripts on the desk in her small alcove study and was glancing through a list of telephone messages when Fern burst into the room with a letter and some photographs in her hand.

"Teddy isn't coming home for Christmas," she announced with excitement.

"Why not?"

"He says he's going fishing with his father. Look at these pictures."

Liz took the photos showing her strapping son with her ex-husband on the beach in front of Harvey's Malibu home. She was always startled at seeing how much alike they were.

Fern put her finger to a photo of a group on the sundeck. "Harvey must like the blond one. I remember seeing her in last year's pictures."

Liz nodded, also recognizing the girl from previous photos.

"I wonder if Teddy's all right," Fern remarked.

"What are you getting at?"

"Well, you know how unreliable Harvey is. I never trusted him after he deserted you."

How conveniently she has rewritten history, Liz reflected. Harvey didn't want to leave, she forced him out. "Yes, Fern," she said. "I know all about it."

"Well, I've been pretty busy lately with the apartment and your mail and all the little details that take so much energy and time."

"I appreciate how busy you are, but right now . . ."

"So I decided you might agree that I deserve a little trip," Fern plunged ahead. "To California. To see Teddy."

"I'm sure Teddy would like that," Liz said. And so will Harvey, she added to herself. "We'll talk about it at dinner."

"You're a doll!" Fern exclaimed. "Dinner will be ready at seven. Your messages are on the desk. There's nothing that seemed important."

They're all in such a rush to get what they want, Liz mused, remembering Jim Hennigan's exit from her dressing room, while she listened to Fern's hurried footsteps down the hallway.

She opened the taps in her bathtub, peeled off her clothing, then mounted her stationary bicycle and pedaled methodically until the tub was full, all the while attempting to justify her reprisal against Neil.

After closing the taps she stood in front of her full-length mirror and pressed her breasts with the flat of her fingers in a well-practiced self-examination.

Finding nothing out of order, she stepped back to survey her entire body. "Not so bad," she murmured as she pushed up at the flesh which was beginning to show the signs of time and gravity.

She stared for a moment at the photo of Teddy and Harvey, then back into her mirror. "Not so good, either."

Fern's good spirits would not be dampened by Liz's glum distraction as they ate their evening meal.

She prattled on about her impending trip to California and Liz reacted with appropriate responses; but her guilt was beginning to overpower all other thoughts. California. California, she repeated to herself. Good Lord, it's as though California is the answer to the world's prayers! It's all I hear about these days.

She put a morsel of food in her mouth and was chewing it tastelessly when an idea popped into her head. She abruptly excused herself and rushed to the telephone in her bedroom.

She decided to try Jim Hennigan's private office number first.

"Jim," she said when he came on the line. "Jim, listen, I've changed my mind."

"But, Liz," he protested. "I've already . . ."

"Wait a minute," she cut him off. "I'm still going to do it. It's Neil I've changed my mind about."

"I don't understand . . ."

"I've been thinking about it and I've decided that Neil Decker is too clever and talented for the network to lose because of . . . because of me. He wants to be a director and he's going to be a good one some day. You saw the tests he directed."

"Yes, but . . ."

"I don't know how new directors get started, but I'm sure there must be opportunities at Federated's studio in Hollywood."

"I don't know how . . ."

"What about the soap that's done out there? Neil's experienced enough for 'Eternal Spring.' "

"You're asking an awful lot, Liz."

"If you recall, you promised 'anything' for my cooperation. I think what I am suggesting will ultimately be of greater value to the network. Talented directors are becoming an endangered species."

"Dammit Liz, you don't know all the problems I have to deal with up here." Jim curbed his exasperation. "I had to get in early this morning and I still don't know when I'll be able to go home tonight. When I find the time, I'll do what I can."

"That wasn't your attitude in my dressing room this afternoon."

After a moment of silence and an exhausted sigh, Jim tried to sound more gracious. "I wasn't so tired this afternoon. I'll find him a job in Hollywood."

"Thank you, Jim," she said sweetly. "I won't keep you any longer."

Liz swept back into the dining room and resumed her place at the table.

"Shall I warm that up for you?" Fern asked.

"No, it's fine," she answered, attacking her food. "We should think about your clothes," she said between bites. "We'll go shopping this week. You'll need a new wardrobe for California."

◈ Cathy was stunned. She knew the day had been going too well. First Sam and now Neil! How could she replace Neil at a time like this? They were making it impossible for her. Not even George Conley could produce the show under these conditions. He *wouldn't* do it!

"When they asked me to suggest someone for the new director program, I immediately thought of you," Jim Hennigan's voice broke through to her. "How you've been nurturing along Neil's career, giving him those tests to direct so the rest of us would recognize his talent. Then when I looked over his résumé and saw his educational background, plus the little theater he's directed, the choice became obvious. You must be very proud."

"Yes . . . but, I don't know if this is the right time," Cathy floundered. "That is to say . . . is he ready for a move like this? We wouldn't want to push him ahead before he's ready."

"Cathy," Jim smiled patiently. "If the network didn't take chances on people we believe in, where would *you* be today? I think he's ready to fly and I'm going to let you push him out of the nest."

"What do you mean?"

"I mean I'm going to let you tell him. You're responsible for his opportunity; I think it's only fair that you have the pleasure of taking credit for it."

"That's very kind." She forced a smile. "I appreciate your gesture."

"And I told Marnie that it was your idea to move her up to the Associate Producer job."

"When did you talk to Marnie?"

"About an hour ago. I instructed her not to say anything until you make the announcement."

"Oh."

"She's abundantly qualified and I think it's good policy to move people up within the organization whenever possible. Don't you agree?"

"Oh yes," Cathy nodded in something of a daze. "Certainly."

"I'm happy that I'm able to give you some good news to take back to the studio. After all the recent confusion, it should help morale." Jim left the sofa to answer the intercom. "Yes? Yes, I know what time it is," he spoke impatiently to his secretary. "But their investigation isn't any more important than what I have to do. I'll see them in a few minutes."

"What is it?" Cathy asked, noticing his concerned expression as he returned to the sofa.

"Nothing important," he said dismissingly. "A couple of idiots get caught stealing and the network acts as though we have another savings and loan scandal. I can understand the Internal Security people trying to justify their jobs, but they shouldn't interfere when the rest of us are trying to do ours."

His expression changed to an intimate smile as he rested his hand on her leg. "But enough of that. I have some more good news for you."

Please, she thought with a sinking feeling. Not *more* good news.

"You and I are taking the night off. Drinks, a nice dinner someplace, then . . . some morale building of our own."

"That sounds terrific." She tried to sound enthused.

"How's Sam doing?"

"Fine. He'll be gone three or four weeks with his commercial."

"That's too bad," Jim grinned. "I'll pick you up at your place around seven. We'll go somewhere in the neighborhood."

"All right," Cathy answered, cursing herself for revealing Sam's absence from their apartment as she rose from the sofa. "I'd better hurry. I want to be sure there aren't any problems before they start taping the show."

"Did the rehearsals go well?"

"Very well," she shrugged. "I wish I knew what you told Liz. She's been rather quiet, but she couldn't be more cooperative."

"It's all a matter of understanding performers and knowing how to get to them," he explained. "It's a knack that comes with experience. You'll learn."

CHAPTER

Cathy sat at her vanity table mentally cataloging her upcoming day's activities as she applied the final accents to her makeup. *He sure makes himself at home,* she fumed, listening to Jim finish his shower.

"Do you think Sam would mind if I used his razor?" he called from the bathroom.

"I don't think so." *What a question. He thinks nothing of using Sam's wife and his bed, but he has to ask permission to use his razor.*

"How's the coffee coming?"

"Oh, my God, I forgot the coffee! It'll be ready when you come out," she called and rushed into the kitchen. *Have sex with them and get their coffee; even secretaries don't have to do that anymore!*

Cathy had the coffee service on the table and was pouring two cups when Jim appeared wearing Sam's favorite terry-cloth robe.

"I'm not worth a damn 'til that first cup in the morning," he said, remaining on his feet while drinking the coffee.

"Do you want some juice?" she asked, returning to the kitchen and opening the refrigerator.

"Just coffee, thanks."

As she reached for the orange juice she noticed the vitamin capsules Sam brought to her each morning and suffered a momentary feeling of loneliness mixed with guilt.

She quickly washed down one of the capsules and closed her mind along with the refrigerator door.

When she returned, Jim was standing in front of the living room bookcase. "I didn't know Sam won these Emmys."

"They're for local specials he did before coming to New York."

"I was really surprised when he quit." Jim refilled his cup. "I thought he was after my job."

"No. He didn't want to be an executive. He'd rather be creative."

"So now he's vice president in an advertising agency. What's more creative about that?"

"Don't ask me," she answered. "I can't figure it out and I don't have time to try. In fact, I'd better be leaving."

"Don't forget to tell Liz we're sending Sy Cohen, the unit publicist, with her to Norwood University this Saturday." Jim thoughtfully blew at the steam rising from his cup. "It'll make her happy to know we care about her concert."

"Happy," Cathy scoffed. "Yes, we have to keep Liz happy."

"That's right. Because if Liz is happy, we're all happy." He moved closer and slid his hand across her bottom. "And happy people are also cooperative people. Remember that."

"I'll try," she answered, concealing her sarcasm behind a grateful smile.

She glanced at the reflection of her figure in the mirror by the entrance. *This* was all men cared about. They were all so surprised when there was a mind to go with the body. Even her own father wanted her to make money with her body doing those commercials in his rinky-dink TV station in Idaho. She wouldn't have minded if they'd really let her try to sell their tires and chain saws, but to just stand next to them in that tiny bikini while some *man* did the talking. *Not me!* she thought. *Little Cathy has brains. That's why I'm on the production side of the camera. Let the actresses make it with their boobs. You're right, Jim, "happy people are cooperative people." I'm going to be happy because where I'm going, people better cooperate, or else!*

"Two or three soap magazines will be going to the concert too," Jim spoke coming out of the bedroom fully dressed. "Make sure they're good ones because we're picking up their expenses."

"Neil knows more about the fan magazines than anyone," she said. "I'll have him check with publicity this morning."

"Tell him to acquaint Marnie with his contacts in that area. She's never dealt with publicity before."

But she evidently deals very well in cooperation, Cathy thought before nodding her agreement.

Jim picked up his cup, drained the last remaining drops of coffee, and was about to resume speaking when the intercom buzzer sounded. "Who's that?" he snapped anxiously.

"I don't know," she answered, enjoying his alarm as she pressed the answer button. It was Neil. She told him to wait for her downstairs, then breathed a sigh of exaggerated relief. "That was close. The downstairs door is usually open in the morning and he comes right up."

"You leave first," Jim ordered. "I'll follow in the next elevator. I'll . . . I'll call you later at the office."

Jim went ahead to buzz for the elevator as Cathy secured the locks on her apartment door.

She stepped into the elevator, accepted Jim's cautious peck on the check, and maintained her warm smile until his image disappeared behind the sliding doors.

"I'm glad I caught you before you left," Neil said as he deposited Cathy in the taxi he had waiting.

"Why?"

"Why?" he grinned. "Because I'm going to miss our little on-the-way-to-the-studio-morning-chit-chats, that's why. But I'm going to miss your paying for the taxi fare the most."

"What a little shit you are," she smiled reluctantly. "I'm going to miss you too, but for the life of me, I don't know why."

"I know."

"Oh, you do," she scoffed. "Why?"

"Because you trust me," he answered sincerely. "There aren't many men you can trust."

"There aren't *any* men I can trust," she corrected, then softened her expression. "Except you. You're the only man I've ever met who wasn't out for what he could get. And it isn't only because you're gay. Normally I don't trust faggots any more than straight guys."

"Careful with the compliments," he reacted. "You don't want to ruin your image."

"Which image is that?"

"The one you work at so hard. You know, the Joan Crawford, tough businesswoman image."

"I'm not going to ruin it. It's the only image that works. Can you imagine Mary Poppins producing a TV show?"

"No, I guess not," Neil agreed, sensing her odd mood. "Have you ever heard about the rain in Spain?"

"Sure, it's mainly on the plain. So what?"

"According to the morning news, it's not just on the plain, it's all over."

"The Spanish farmers must be very happy," she shrugged disinterestedly.

"Isn't Sam going to be shooting in Spain?"

"I think so. But it's winter. They must have taken into consideration that rain is a fairly common phenomenon in winter. I hear they even get some rain where you're going, in California."

"I just hope they don't run into weather problems. They only have Jamie for three weeks and when you take into account all the moving around they have to do, it's a difficult enough shoot without having to worry about weather on top of everything else."

"Sorry, Neil, maybe it's the Joan Crawford in me, but I can't work up much interest in Sam's problems with the rain in Spain."

"Look, sweetie," Neil twisted in the seat to face Cathy.

"Since you can't fire me anymore for butting into your business, I'm going to try one last time. There's no question that Joan Crawford was successful with her career, but she died a lonely, bitter, old woman. That's not for you, Cathy. If you'd relax a little you could have your career and something good at home as well."

"Like Sam?" she responded coolly. "He's something *good* all right. I trusted Sam. I needed him where he was and he knew it. It was selfish and stupidly shortsighted of him to leave when he did. I don't think I'll ever be able to forgive him."

"He loves you, Cathy," Neil answered simply. "Even though you don't agree with his career decisions, you have to understand that his ultimate goal is to provide a happy life for the two of you. I think he's looking forward to a home, family, PTA—all that stuff."

"Not with me!"

"Only with you! I believe he's written his whole life's scenario with you as his leading lady."

"Then he should stop writing fantasy," she growled. "I don't want a family."

◈ Jamie glowed with the inner satisfaction of accomplishment as he strode from the set of his seduction scene with Liz.

She had come erotically alive under his touch, giving their scene a sexual intensity that he knew would have the network censor biting his nails.

He ducked into the control room to watch as Liz sat mesmerized in the moonlight glimmering through her bedroom window.

She slid out of her bed and floated across the room where she took a hand mirror and studied her disheveled reflection in the eerie light. There was confusion in her face, but there was also a gleam of carnal satisfaction. A teardrop fell, then an enigmatic smile crossed Liz's lips just as the bank of monitors faded to black.

Was it a smile of despair or of fulfillment? Jamie smiled too, because he knew that anyone who saw the powerful scene would certainly tune in again to find out.

Jamie stepped out of the control room to intercept Liz as she came out of the studio.

"We did it," he said proudly. "The scene went like magic. Thanks."

"Thanks?"

Jamie could see by her expression that Liz was still caught up in the mood of her characterization. "For being so good," he explained. "If I never mentioned it before, it's a real pleasure acting with you."

"Thank you, Jamie," she answered, her expression wavering between her sense of accomplishment as an actress and the torn emotions she still carried from their scene. She gave his arm a tentative squeeze. "You're marvelous."

"Liz, you were fantastic!" Cathy flew at Liz, throwing her arms around her. "I've never seen you so good!"

Liz was startled by the abruptness of Cathy's assault. She cast a helpless look to Jamie, then mumbled an embarrassed thanks before fleeing to her dressing room.

"That's a pro," Cathy announced the moment Liz disappeared. "That's what comes from dedication. You'd never see her abandoning the show to earn a few extra pennies."

Jamie's resentment began to rise as he realized her remark was pointed at him. He could live without her praise, but he didn't have to tolerate her abuse!

"Good scene, Jamie," Vico said with a wink as he came out of the control room. "Come on, I'll buy you a drink."

"Thanks Vico, but I have a date with a *lady*," he responded sharply, preparing to turn on Cathy.

Watch your mouth, Jamie, he quickly admonished himself. *You need this job. Don't get screwed up over a stupid broad!*

"I might have time for *one*," he said, looking at his watch, then to Cathy. "And what about you, Madam Producer?" he forced a smile. "Does a friendly drink fit into your schedule?"

"Don't be silly. My schedule barely leaves time for sleep."

"That's too bad," Jamie shrugged, moving away. "Sleep is supposed to do wonders for a person's disposition."

CHAPTER

"This is it!" Leigh trembled, turning away from Jamie's apartment window to at last see him walking up the street.

She darted into the bathroom to study once again the makeup she had tried so hard to get just right. *It was too much*, she moaned. He would hate it, she just knew it, but it was too late to take it off and begin again.

She freshened her lip gloss, sprayed her face with French mineral water, then daubed a touch of Diva behind her ears, between her breasts, and at the back of her knees.

"I'm ready," she declared to her reflection in the mirror. Tonight was the night! No more rehearsals. No more dry runs. No more excuses.

But will he like me? He had been with so many women all over the world.

Her stomach was twisted in knots as she left the bathroom and paused for an instant to look at Jamie's bed. Then she hastened to the kitchen where she opened the refrigerator to gaze upon her special cake.

She smiled in jittery anticipation before returning to the living room where she took a sniff of the pleasantly scented candles strategically placed around the room. She lit the tall, white ones in her mother's solid silver holders, then nervously repositioned the heavy, cut-crystal bowl of Beluga caviar and the fragile, stemmed champagne glasses on the table in front of the sofa.

The sound of the elevator jarred her into an upright position. "He's here!" she gasped.

Almost in a panic, she plumped the sofa pillows for the last time and went to the door where she had left a long, white scarf on the knob.

"Oh, God," she murmured plaintively. "All my life I've been getting ready for tonight. Please, God, don't let me mess it up!"

Jamie put his key in the lock as Leigh pulled it open. "Don't peek," she ordered. She put the soft scarf to his face. "Hold this over your eyes, follow me, and don't argue!"

"Okay," he grinned, allowing Leigh to take his hand and lead him through the living room, into the bedroom where she closed the door.

"The first thing I want you to do is tell me all about your big scene with Liz," she said, surprised at her sudden calm.

"It went all right," he shrugged, pulling the scarf from his eyes and putting his frustration with Cathy behind him. "What smells so good?"

"It's the candles," she sparkled. "But please, don't ask questions. You said this could be *my* night, so just do as I ask."

"All right, but are we going to spend it here in the bedroom?"

"No. But before my evening starts you have to change," she pointed to his dark suit laid out on the bed.

"Aren't you efficient!" he said appreciatively, noticing his shirt, tie, and accessories next to his suit.

"Almost all your other things are already packed. It was easy," Leigh responded.

"You're an angel," he said, genuinely touched. "Give me a minute to check my answering machine and get changed, then I'll be at your command until your chariot turns back into a pumpkin."

"Don't worry," she smiled serenely, as she moved through the door. "My fairy godmother said I can keep it out as late as I want."

Jamie stepped out of his clothing and glanced through his mail while playing back the messages on his machine.

Leigh impatiently peered into the mirror near the bedroom door and once again fluffed her hair and reinspected her makeup.

She listened with vague curiosity, as she overheard Jamie call his agent in Hollywood, Fred Wald.

"I don't mind buying her the car," Leigh heard him speak of his daughter Cheryl. "But does it have to be now? Can't it wait until we get paid from Saddle?

"That's what you said, huh?

"You're a hell of a guy, Fred. You watch my money better than I do. Even when I don't have it.

"Okay, what the hell. If it's that important and Cheryl's found a dealer who'll take a postdated check, we'll buy it. But do me a favor, will you? Talk to her like you did when she called you 'Uncle' Fred. Tell her that her dad would like to hear from her sometimes when she doesn't want something.

"Why *shouldn't* I expect miracles?" Jamie laughed good-naturedly. "That's what you're famous for.

"Jesus Christ, I should have been a dentist!

"Naw . . . She might as well go ahead with it. I don't want Erika's goddamn teeth falling out.

"That's okay. I'll tell her. I'm going to call Bucky in a few minutes anyway."

Leigh was even more attentive to the next turn in Jamie's conversation when she realized he was speaking with Erika.

"Okay, then," he said. "Get him up a few minutes early and have him call me.

"Yes, I know what time it'll be here, but I want to talk to Bucky before I leave.

"Good. And about your teeth, Fred told me the trouble you're having. The Saddle money should be in before the bill comes, so don't worry about it.

"Just do it, Erika." His voice took a firm tone. "There's nothing to discuss.

"What?

"What did *you* tell them?

"Okay, if they ask me in Munich, I'll tell them the same thing: You weren't in Palm Springs that weekend. By the way, I saw the photos. It *could* have been someone else. Why don't we tell them you were here in New York with me? Or is that too outlandish a lie even for the German press?

"Oh, some anonymous fan sent it to me. You know how good news has a way of getting around.

"Yeah, so am I, but let's not start the 'sorry' routine again; I'm already late for dinner.

"Thanks. You too. Don't forget to have Bucky call in the morning."

Leigh gave a startled jump away from the door as Jamie called out to her that he was almost ready.

She arranged herself on the sectional sofa and smoothed away a tiny wrinkle on the white linen tablecloth she had put over the low coffee table in front of her.

"Let our big night begin," Jamie pronounced as he came through the door. "Your wish is my . . ." Jamie stopped, completely taken aback by the living room's elegant transformation.

Leigh stood up, her face beaming, her figure accented in the warm candle glow by her soft-colored, pleated silk dress.

"My God," he gasped. "It's beautiful! You're beautiful! Where did all this come from?"

"I brought it from home," she answered shyly. "Are you surprised?"

"Surprised isn't the word. I'm flabbergasted!"

"I hoped you'd like it."

Jamie took Leigh's hand and gave her a light kiss on the lips. "I don't like it, I *love* it," he smiled, then lifted the bottle from the antique silver ice bucket. "Champagne, caviar, the prettiest girl in New York! What could be better?"

"There's more," she said brightly. "The limo will be downstairs in about half an hour to take us to dinner, then maybe some dancing, if you like; then we'll come back here for something special I have in the refrigerator."

"Sounds like you haven't missed a thing," he said, twisting the cork from the champagne bottle.

"I hope not," she smiled. "I want this evening to be perfect!"

◆ "What a fabulous going-away dinner," Jamie sighed contentedly in the back of the Cadillac limousine. "Le Cote Basque is one of the best, and certainly one of the most romantic restaurants I've ever been to!"

"I'm glad you liked it," Leigh beamed. "I went there a long time ago with my mother and father. The harbor scene on the wall made me think of Italy and mandolins and things."

"Me too," Jamie agreed.

"Did it make you miss Europe?"

"No. When I first came back from Europe I felt a little strange, but now I'm happy to be home."

"I thought you liked it over there."

"I did. Except that even after all those years, I still felt like a foreigner. And after all," he continued, patting her on the knee, "there's a lot to like here."

"I think so too," she agreed happily as the limousine drew to a stop in front of Jamie's apartment.

Before Jamie had a chance to comment, Leigh said goodnight to the driver and sent him away. "There's no sense in making the poor man wait," she explained glibly. "I'll take a taxi when I'm ready to go."

Jamie followed her into the building, then waited dutifully in the hall until she had reset the scene in his apartment.

"What's this?" he smiled curiously, spotting two filled champagne glasses flanking a small cake on the coffee table.

He moved closer to read the inscription on the cake. " 'Bon Voyage, Jamie and Leigh!!' What does that mean?"

"It's my special surprise," she bubbled. "I'm going away too. I'm going to Hollywood for a screen test."

"When did this happen? Why didn't you tell me before?"

"I was saving it for dessert. You remember I told you I played the younger sister on tour with *The Philadelphia Story?* The same director is doing it as a Movie of the Week for Federated and he wants me to test for Tracy Lord."

"The Katherine Hepburn part? Great! When?"

"My agent just told me this afternoon. He has to clear it with Cathy, but they want me sometime next week. I'm not working Thursday and Friday, so it'll probably be then."

"That's fantastic," Jamie said delightedly. "It's a great part and you're perfect for it. Cathy will have to let you do it, won't she?"

"Sure, it's in my contract. They have to give me time off if I get a movie."

Jamie swept the champagne glasses from the table. "Here's to you, star!"

"It's only a test," she cautioned. "I don't have the part yet."

"You'll get it," he answered. "But so we don't jinx it, let's drink to the test."

"And to the Saddle man." She raised her glass. "A *real* star and . . . and the man I'm proud to be with."

She took a nervous breath as she looked at Jamie over the rim of her glass, then put it down. "I, ah . . . I'd appreciate a kiss for luck."

"You've got it," Jamie answered and put his hand on her waist, kissing her lightly on the lips.

As he began to pull away, she flung her arms around his neck, drawing their mouths tightly together, and brushed his tongue with hers.

Jamie's first response was surprise, then tantalizing pleasure mixed with a twinge of conscience.

"This may not lead to the kind of luck you have in mind," he said, regaining his composure. "Kissing like that could lead to all kinds of things."

"Don't you like it?" she challenged. "Don't you . . . like me?"

"Yes, I like it. And I like you, too. I'm just not too sure how much I like myself for liking you the way I do."

"Don't feel that way, Jamie. I know what I'm doing."

"Then you're smarter than I am. I don't know what *I'm* doing."

"*I do!* Really," she said determinedly. "I've been thinking about this for years. Long before I met you."

"Thinking about what?" he asked unsteadily.

"About . . ." Leigh paused, then plunged ahead. "About my first time . . . the first time I make love."

Jamie looked at her, for the moment unable to react. He refilled his glass and flopped on the sofa. "Leigh, I don't know what to say. I mean, if you've waited this long, why me? Why . . ."

"Because you're the first man I ever felt this way about. Because it's an experience I believe I'm ready for."

"Thank you for feeling that way," he struggled. "It's quite an honor, but . . . Well, it's more than an experience. And if I started listing the reasons I'm wrong for you, we could be here all night."

"I've done that already," she continued doggedly. "And it's all right. I don't know if we'll have a future. I don't care. Maybe we can, but the future isn't important. What's important is right now . . . tonight."

Leigh sat next to Jamie and took his hand. "Don't make it more difficult for me, Jamie, but tonight I want to become a woman . . . and I want it to be with you."

He couldn't believe what was happening. Numerous women had come on to him, but never quite like this. "You want me to make love to you," he managed to respond. "I can't say the idea hasn't crossed my mind, but I never thought it would happen like this. As far as becoming a woman, you *are* a woman. The mere sex act won't make you . . ."

"And I love you, Jamie," she interjected simply.

"Yeah." He was breathing erratically, trying to sort through his confusion. "I don't know. Falling in love is easier when you're young—before your emotions get all bruised and screwed up."

"Do you feel *anything* for me?"

Jamie turned, putting his arm around her shoulder. "Anything?" He looked into her eyes. "More than just anything. A lot more."

"A *lot* more?" she asked hopefully.

"A whole lot more," he smiled before covering her mouth with his.

For the first time they kissed without restraint, the floodgates of passion opening up in them.

"What do we do now?" she whispered breathlessly.

"Now?" he smiled, laying aside all of his previous reservations. He scooped her into his powerful arms and carried her toward the bedroom.

"Now, I'm taking you to bed."

It's happening! she silently cried as she felt her body and soul opening to receive the lover she had known only in her dreams.

It's happening!

CHAPTER

21

Leigh awoke from a fitful sleep, reluctant to open her eyes and acknowledge where she was. This wasn't the way she had imagined she would feel with Jamie sleeping by her side. The truth of the matter was she felt guilty.

Why are all my Sunday school lessons going through my head? I'm a modern, liberated woman. What difference does it really make that he's married? If Erika doesn't care enough to protect what's hers, then he's open to whatever comes along.

She sat up and eased out of bed, careful not to wake him.

Guilt wasn't a part of the plan, she continued to tell herself. She grabbed the dress she had brought to wear to the studio and carried it into the bathroom. She loved him and he loved her and that made what they did okay. Yet the guilt continued to nag her.

Oh, God, she sighed to the mirror. *Why can't everything be the way it's supposed to be?*

Now washed and dressed, Leigh was stealthily creeping across the dark bedroom when the early morning stillness was broken by the phone.

Jamie awoke and was well into a transatlantic conversation

163

with Sam before he switched on the light to discover Leigh poised, fully dressed, near the foot of the bed.

The bewilderment was clear in his face as his glance went to the clock, then back to her. "Yeah, Sam. I hear you," he said, seeing the uneasiness in her expression. "I think if it's raining in Paris and we can't be set up to shoot in Rome until Monday, there's no point in my coming over today. I might as well wait until Saturday."

Leigh realized her discomfort must be showing, as Jamie made an effort to nod assuringly between snatches of conversation until the call was finished. "I'm not leaving today," he said after hanging up the phone.

"Why not?" she blurted. "I mean, is something wrong?"

"That's what I was about to ask you," he frowned. "It's five o'clock in the morning. Are you all right? Where were you going?"

"Oh, is it that early?" she feigned surprise. "I must have misread the clock. I was getting ready to go to the studio."

"And you weren't going to say good-bye?" Jamie grinned understandingly. "Are you having second thoughts about last night?"

"No," she insisted. "It happened just the way I hoped. There's nothing to feel guilty about if you love someone . . . Is there?"

"Of course not." He reached out to take her hand. "Nothing at all. *Are* you feeling guilty?"

"No," she lied, then bent over to kiss his cheek. "I love you, Jamie!"

"I love you too," he made himself reply. And smiled. "Hey, since I don't have to leave today, why don't I come by the studio during your lunch break?"

"Would you really like to?" she quizzed intently.

"Yes! I'd love to! I really would."

She kissed him again, fixed them both breakfast, and then went off to the studio, while Jamie stayed in bed until it was time for him to join her.

❖ Having arrived early, Jamie switched on the monitor in the makeup room to watch the balance of the camera rehearsal before Leigh's lunch break.

Although it was too soon to judge, because Leigh and Annie were rehearsing with their scripts in hand, they both seemed to be struggling through the scene. Annie had a bad case of heavy nasal congestion and Leigh was visibly tired.

Jamie remained seated when their scene came to an end. While the cameras were being repositioned for the next scene, Annie came through the door.

It was clear how poorly she felt as she plopped into a chair in front of the makeup table and inspected her feverish reflection. "Hi, Jamie," she sniffed, seeing him through the mirror. "I have a cold."

"Makes it tough to remember lines, doesn't it?"

"Really," she nodded. "I'll feel better when I can go home and get to bed. You must be disappointed about your trip being postponed."

"It's only for a couple of days," he said, watching her try to cover the circles under her eyes. "Listen, I have some chicken stock in my freezer. It's from an old German recipe. If you like, I'll bring some to your apartment."

"You cook?" she turned to look at him.

"Sure I cook," he beamed proudly. "I like to eat and I don't like to go out. So it's cook or starve. The truth is, I enjoy cooking."

"You seem to enjoy a lot of things," Annie said after daubing at her nose with a tissue. "Especially your acting. You were wonderful in that scene yesterday with Liz. Is it really as easy for you as you make it seem?"

"If it seems easy, then I'm a better actor than I thought," Jamie laughed. "No, Annie, it isn't easy. Maybe it's because I spent so many years in film, but since I've been in 'Yesterday's Children' I've had to work harder and I've learned more than I have in years."

"Oh, Annie," Leigh moaned, not seeing Jamie as she came

through the door. "I'm sorry I'm so bad in that scene. I'll be better for taping. I promise!"

"What's the problem?" Jamie spoke.

Leigh's face flushed as she spun around. "Jamie! I didn't know you were here. I . . ."

"It's my fault," Annie interceded. "It's this cold. I can't concentrate. I'm not making contact with her."

"No," Leigh argued, embarrassed to admit that because of her tempestuous night with Jamie, she was simply unprepared. "It's *my* fault. And doubly so because you're sick and I should be helping you!"

"Look," Jamie said, fully aware of Leigh's problem. "It'll do both of you good to relax a few minutes . . . maybe get something to eat, then go back at it with a fresh attitude."

"I couldn't eat anything," Annie protested.

"Sure you can," Leigh seized at the opportunity to spend a few minutes alone with Jamie. "Jamie and I will go down to the commissary and bring something back for all of us. Come on, Jamie," she insisted before anyone could object and led him into the hallway.

"I told her she could have some of the chicken stock in my freezer," Jamie said as they walked. "I can make more when I get back from Europe . . ."

Leigh abruptly took Jamie's arm and pulled him to a stop. "I have to know," she insisted, her eyes bright with anxiety. "Do you still like me? Was I good enough for you? I mean, did it mean as much to you as it did to me?"

"Leigh, honey," Jamie took her hands in his own. "Just for the record, you were terrific. If there's been any change at all since last night, it's that I'm deeper into this thing than I . . . than I thought I would be."

Leigh's eyes suddenly clouded with doubt. "Are you saying it didn't mean that much to you last night? That I was just another . . ."

"No, Leigh. I'm *not* saying that. I'm saying that however strong my feelings for you were last night, they're even stronger today."

"Do you really mean it?" The love and hope that sprang into her eyes almost took away Jamie's breath.

"I mean it," he said as his conscience began to dull his euphoria. "But we do have to remember what you said last night . . . about the future. We're in no position to start hoping for the future."

"I know, Jamie," she replied unconvincingly. "I told you, I thought about that before we began."

"If this isn't some scene for the show," Neil smirked as he approached them, "it certainly should be. You look like something right out of Romeo and Juliet."

Not wishing to embarrass them further, Neil changed the subject. "Jamie, I thought you were on your way to Paris. Don't tell me it's raining there too?"

"Yeah, but how did you know?"

"It was on the news," Neil paused to glance between Leigh and Jamie.

Jamie turned to Leigh, who quickly put on a buoyant smile.

"I think you've helped solve my problem in the scene with Annie," she said. "I'd like to pick up something to eat and get right to work on it."

"You're sure?"

"Positive," she answered, with meaningful assurance.

Neil looked at Jamie as he watched Leigh walk away. "She's a good girl," he said, hoping Jamie might reveal his feelings.

"Yeah," Jamie nodded reflectively. "One of the best."

"Look, Goddammit, I know what I said," Terry blustered while pacing across Devon's suite in the Calvaliere Hilton, overlooking a stupendous view of ancient and modern Rome. "I've shot here three years in a row. The rainy season doesn't start until after the holidays!"

"You must mean the Fourth of July and Labor Day," Devon grumbled.

"You know what I mean, Devon. As your director I'm responsible for a lot of things, but the weather isn't one of them. In spite of what you may have heard, I'm not God."

"No, that's for sure. But when we discussed weather it was you who insisted it wouldn't be a problem. 'Trust me', you said."

"So I was wrong," Terry answered defiantly. "What do you want me to do? Why don't you sue me? Or better yet, why don't you fire me? I don't have to put up with this kind of shit!"

"Wait a minute, you guys," Sam interceded. "Getting excited isn't going t solve anything. It can't be raining everywhere. If it doesn't stop, we'll move on. For Christ sake, our schedule isn't that tight. We can afford a couple of bad weather days." He looked to Luciana Rinaldi, the attractive multilingual production assistant as she hung up the phone. "What did they say?"

"It is not encouraging," she answered regretfully. "There is a stationary mass of clouds covering all Europe. They do not know when it will begin to move, but it could be soon."

"Soon?" Terry snorted. "I know what the Italians mean by soon. It's sometime between later and never!"

"Relax, will you," Sam said.

"I'll relax when I get some coke. Luciana, call Marina's room. See if she's back yet."

"You are speaking of the model from Milano?"

"Yeah," Terry nodded. "She said she knows a dealer here."

"I hope you're being careful with that stuff," Sam cautioned.

"Yeah," Devon agreed. "There's nothing that would get us shut down faster than New York hearing about a cocaine scandal over here."

"You surely remember what happened to Stacy Keach in London," Luciana added.

"He damn near lost his 'Mike Hammer' series over it," Sam joined.

"He's an *actor*, they're always after actors," Terry exclaimed before turning back to Luciana. "Are you going to make the call or not?"

Receiving a confirming nod from Sam, Luciana dialed the model's room. Everyone watched as she listened a moment, then broke the connection and dialed the concierge. She spoke a few words in Italian, then hung up. "I am sorry, Signori, but Marina doesn't answer in her room and she has not been seen in the lobby."

"I hope she wasn't bullshitting," Terry mumbled edgily.

"I am sorry," she repeated, then busily prepared to leave. "If there is nothing more I will stop on my way out and leave a message for Marina to call Signor Terry upon her return."

"What do you mean?" Terry said, moving closer to Luciana. "I thought we were all going out tonight."

"But I . . ." Luciana turned to Devon and Sam. "I must have misunderstood. My family is expecting me tonight."

"Oh, you're married," Terry shrugged.

"No."

"Don't worry about it," Sam interceded. "No one said anything about you having to be with us tonight. We'll get by just fine on our own."

"In that case, I'll say *buona sera*," Luciana nodded, moving to the door.

"I'll go with you down to the lobby," Terry said. "I know Marina wants to come with us. I'll check with the other two broads we brought from Milan. I'm sure they'll want to come too."

"What about the three guys we brought?" Sam asked.

"Who needs more guys?" Terry smirked. "Let's meet in the bar in about an hour, okay?"

Sam and Devon nodded in agreement. "About an hour."

◈ Eddie stood in the background of Liz's dressing room, quietly observing the after-concert accolades being heaped upon her by the roomful of well-wishers. All her past week's pain and anguish seemed to disappear in the shower of compliments.

He was fascinated by the way people generally regarded as VIPs moved closer to her to share in and become a part of her radiated glory.

Shirley Hanna, the network president's wife, and Elliot Harrison, Dean of Norwood University, stood shoulder to shoulder with Liz, shaking hands and accepting compliments for the successful evening.

Sy Cohen, the network publicist, smoothly manipulated the fan magazine photographers into more than adequate coverage of Liz and her fellow actors, Stanley and Joyce, along with shots including Eddie and Liz's record producer, Jack Naterno.

Liz smiled intimately at Eddie and squeezed his arm while the cameras were snapping in their direction, but he felt no real contact. *She doesn't need me,* he thought, becoming more aware of the real distance between them. *This is what makes her happy. She doesn't want me. My music is the only thing I can give her that's any good.*

He smiled shyly and mumbled his thanks as Jack Naterno once again complimented his arrangements; then remembering he hadn't picked up Liz's sheet music from the musicians, he hurried out to the bandstand.

By the time Eddie had the music packed, some of the special guests were already drifting toward the cocktail party at Dean Harrison's house. He started to hurry along with them but paused in thoughtful contemplation at the sight of Jack Naterno talking to some of the musicians ready to board their bus. *Why ruin what I have for something that can never be more than wishful thinking?*

"You got room for one more?" he asked, after making up his mind.

"I thought you were staying here," Jack said. "We booked a room for you at the Norwood Inn."

"No, I have some things to do in the city tomorrow morning. That is, if I can get a ride back."

"Sure," one of the musicians spoke. "There's plenty of room. Get your stuff and climb aboard."

"Thanks," Eddie nodded. "I'll be right back."

◆ Liz sighed contentedly as she watched Elliot Harrison speak with Shirley. With his reserved smile and tall, urbane good looks, he was every bit the way Liz had imagined Spencer Franklyn should have looked before Jamie came into the show.

"I know better than to try and steal her away from your Webster University, Shirley," he smiled. "However, Norwood would move heaven and earth to entice Liz into accepting the chair that's opening up in our drama department. The rapport she has with the students is extraordinary. You saw it in the seminar she conducted this afternoon."

"I've seen it many places, Elliot," Shirley remarked. "And I hope to continue seeing it on Federated Television for many years to come."

"Liz, have you ever thought about teaching?" Elliot asked.

"Never very seriously," Liz smiled graciously. "Sometimes I think teaching at a place like Norwood might be the answer to all my dreams, but how could I ever leave Webster? It seems I've been there all my life."

"I'm not denying Webster is a fine school," Elliot grinned. "With the highest academic standards, but you must admit, our campus is much prettier."

"And your problems more mundane," Shirley added.

"On the surface, perhaps," he conceded. "However, when one digs slightly deeper even Norwood has a touch of soap opera."

"I'm finding that's true of most of the world," Liz said. "I do love it here. It's so peaceful and . . . it's just like a picture postcard fantasy of what a smaller university *should* be."

"And wouldn't Elliot be a perfect leading man," Shirley gushed. "I mean, in the fantasy. I don't believe either of you will be changing schools in reality."

"One can always hope," Elliot said, looking into Liz's luminous eyes. "Some of our most profound realities began as someone's fantasy."

"Yes," Liz said, suddenly realizing Eddie was not in the room. "Yes. That's very true."

CHAPTER

"I don't know why I didn't think of this yesterday at the studio," Jamie said as he took the keys of his Jeep from his living room mantle and handed them to Neil.

"You sure you don't mind?" Neil asked.

"Why should I mind? It's just sitting there."

"It'll only be until I decide what kind of car I want."

"Take your time," Jamie insisted as he made a second pot of morning coffee. "I'm grateful for the way you helped me get started here, Neil. Hell, I wouldn't even have this apartment if it wasn't for you." He poured two cups and offered one to Neil. "And if there's anything else I can do, just ask."

"Well, there *is* something," Neil grinned speculatively.

"Anything except getting involved with Cathy!" Jamie joked. "You've had the patience of a saint with that broad. I don't know how you put up with her as long as you did!"

"She needed me," Neil shrugged. "Women like her always need guys like me . . . someone they can depend on who's not a threat. But I got what I wanted. Because of Cathy, I'm off to Hollywood to become a director. It wasn't such a big price to pay. Anyway, it wasn't Cathy I wanted to ask you about. It's something else. Involving you and *another* producer."

"Another producer?" Jamie repeated warily. "What do you want to know?"

"About you and Leigh's father." Neil was burning with curiosity. "I've been dying to know since the first day you arrived. What's the *real* story about the trouble between you and Russell Fisk?"

"The real story?" Jamie raised his eyebrows. "His version is probably different, but if you're that curious . . ." He refilled his coffee cup. "It goes back to the earlier days of TV, when they were still doing a lot of live, dramatic stuff here in New York. You've heard Vico talk about being a part of it. Russell Fisk was too. He produced some of those shows that only the critics could understand, and somehow he got a reputation for bringing taste and intelligence to the wasteland of television. In those days, the belief in Hollywood was that *anything* coming from New York had to be good; so naturally my old boss, Burt Prinz, hired Fisk to head the TV department at his studio."

Jamie took a sip of coffee, reliving a surge of bitter memories. "I was doing 'Slim Chisholm' then. We were number one when he took over, but he had to make it better . . . more meaningful. He made some other series pilots. He brought Erika from Germany for one of them: 'Mata Hari.' But somewhere the golden boy had lost his wizardry. Everything he touched went right down the toilet . . . including 'Slim Chisholm.'" He paused reflectively. "It was a good show. I was damned proud of it until Russell ruined it with his artsy-fartsy interference. Then, when the people stopped watching, he tried to save it by writing the scripts himself. One day I refused to play a scene the way he had written it. He came on the set, shooting off his mouth," Jamie grinned mischievously. "So I popped him."

"Then what?" Neil queried. "They didn't drop the show because you hit the producer?"

"Probably not. The show was over anyway. It was just a good excuse to get rid of all of us. I went to Europe, Russell to New York, and 'Slim Chisholm' into syndication."

"Sounds like a good story line for 'Yesterday's Children,'" Neil jested.

"Yeah," Jamie reacted good-naturedly. "That's my life all right, just another soap opera."

"Well, thanks for telling me," Neil nodded contentedly. "Can I take you to lunch? If you're not busy, I know a nice restaurant not far from here."

"Thanks," Jamie answered. "But I have to wait for a call from Sam. It looks definite that I'm leaving tomorrow. Anyway, a couple of people are coming over for hot dogs and a Saturday afternoon of football on TV. Why don't you stick around?"

"No, thank you," Neil replied sourly. "Football disgusts me. I'm positive that if it weren't for those macho costumes they wear, they'd never get away with all that hugging and wrestling and ass patting they do. Why they criticize the jiggling booby shows and let them get away with football, I'll never know!"

"I hope you don't find out," Jamie laughed. "At least, not until the season's over!"

◈ "And it's nice to see you," Annie said, trying to maintain a tone of friendly detachment as Zev limped into her studio apartment.

"This is for you," he replied, pressing a bottle of wine into her hands.

"Thank you, but I don't think I should," she answered, sniffing back a trace of nasal congestion. "They say alcohol doesn't mix very well with antihistamine, but I made some tea." She gestured toward a small round table containing her flowered porcelain tea service along with an assortment of fruit and cheese.

"Tea is fine," he said. "Your cold sounds better."

"It is," she answered, seating herself and primly pouring

the tea. "This investigation you were telling me about sounds serious. Is it going to affect you?"

"It might," he said, cutting a wedge of Cheddar with a fork-tipped cheese knife. "They know that when I was with Special Projects I did a few favors for some of the executives. Nothing big. A few airplane tickets for wives and . . . friends. Some presents like luggage and things that went on location budgets. I don't think they'll bother much with me. It's the big guys they want, and a few of the others who were taking cash kickbacks. Those are the ones who'll get reamed."

"I see," she nodded, glancing curiously at the small canvas bag Zev had left near his coat. "How is Albuquerque? Are you happy there?"

"It's all right. Kind of quiet. I haven't met anyone like you there."

"Like me? What do you mean?"

"You know," he shrugged pleasantly. "I mean I haven't met anyone who gets off in the ways you do. But, to tell the truth, I didn't meet many sex freaks like you, even here in New York."

"Please, Zev," she said stiffly. "Don't talk to me like that."

"Oh, come on, Annie," he grinned. "Cut the crap. I know how to talk to you, and I know how to turn you on. You're a no-good, worthless piece of ass who'll eat a mile of shit to be punished because you know that's what you deserve."

"No," she insisted, as a warm tingle teased at her groin.

"No, what?" he bullied. "Shall I leave?"

"No! That isn't what I meant."

"Then watch your mouth. In fact, maybe you should go wash it out with soap. It's too bad soap won't reach the real depths of your dirt."

"I'll do it," she said, her throat tightening with excitement.

"And take off that silly dress. I want to see if your bony, titless body is still as ugly as ever."

"Yes, Zev," as she started to peel off her clothing. "Anything, Zev. I'm still yours, Zev. I'll do anything you say."

◈ "Thank you again for letting me stay, Mrs. Fisk," Mindy said, standing with Nancy and Leigh in the foyer of their apartment house while the doorman helped load Nancy's luggage in the trunk of her hired limousine. "It'll only be for a week or so, until Stanley Gordon leaves for California."

"Nonsense, my dear," Nancy replied. "Stay as long as you like. I hate the thought of Leigh being all alone that big apartment."

"Don't frighten her away, Mom," Leigh smiled. "Mindy will be alone here while I'm in Hollywood."

"I don't mean it isn't safe," Nancy quickly clarified. "It's . . . Well, it's lonely sometimes, that's all."

"I'll be fine," Mindy assured. "The important thing is for you to enjoy your cruise and get well!"

"Sounds like terrific medicine to me," Leigh exclaimed. "Two weeks in the Caribbean sun on the Picard's yacht with nothing to do but rest and have fun with your friends!"

"Your car is ready, Mrs. Fisk," the doorman announced, holding open the door to the street.

Nancy drew her daughter into a warm embrace. "Take care of yourself out there in Hollywood."

"I will, Mom," Leigh returned the embrace.

"And if your father should call . . ."

"I'll tell him you've gone to reap some of the benefits of your experience."

"Don't you dare!" Nancy recoiled, then her expression relaxed as she reconsidered. "All right," she smiled. "Tell him whatever you like."

The girls watched in silence as the limo blended into the midday traffic. Leigh looked at her watch and then, with Mindy close at her heels, darted across Fifth Avenue and began trudging along one of the footpaths traversing Central Park to the West Side.

"Is your mother well enough for this trip?" Mindy asked.

"Physically, yes," Leigh answered. "And emotionally, her doctor says she couldn't do anything better."

"Because of your father?"

Leigh replied with a resigned nod of her head. "He doesn't care who knows about this Lipton woman anymore. Mother has to accept that she's lost him and go on with her life."

"It doesn't seem right."

Leigh suddenly regretted not listening to Russell's attempted explanation the night she caught him with Millicent. "No, it doesn't. But if people don't make each other happy, who's to say they shouldn't get a second chance?"

Mindy cast a sidelong glance to her friend as the frosty ground crunched under their rapid strides. "Is that why we're in such a hurry to get to Jamie's?"

"What are you talking about?"

"In all the years I've known you, this is the first time I've seen you show such an interest in going to see a football game on TV."

"I thought we were going because Stanley will be there. *You're* the one who said you want to talk some more about the apartment," Leigh remarked, her breath turning into puffs of steam in the chilly air. "Besides, I've always been interested in football. There was a time at Princeton when I considered becoming a cheerleader."

"I was at Princeton, too, if you remember," Mindy challenged. "You never thought of anything that didn't have to do with the drama department. With the exception of one or two boys . . ."

"That's not true!" Leigh grew defensive. "And people can change, can't they? You've seen how relationships can stagnate when people don't expand their interests."

"Relationships?" Mindy questioned. "Who's talking about relationships?"

"I don't know *what* we're talking about," Leigh looked away, embarrassed.

"I see," Mindy nodded sympathetically. "What's happening between you and Jamie?" she gently probed. "Is it serious?"

"I don't *know* what's happening," her words tumbled out.

"Except I love him." The rashness of her admission caused her to stop and look to her friend for support. "I haven't talked about this with anyone else, Mindy. It's all so big and complicated. The feeling is as I imagined it to be, but . . . everything else is . . . like I said, complicated."

Mindy resisted the impulse to express her disapproval. "Well, if it gets too complicated, you can always count on me. You know that."

"I know," Leigh responded, linking her arm in Mindy's. "And I appreciate it."

Jamie had never felt much in common with the brash young actor, but he breathed easier knowing Stanley would be present for his first encounter with Mindy Shrafft.

Stanley's ignorance of Jamie's developing affair with Leigh helped relieve the first tense moments as Leigh stood by watching with uncertainty as Mindy and Jamie took each other's measure. The strain quickly passed as Stanley positioned himself next to Mindy and began assaulting her with his insolent charm.

Leigh and Jamie covered their feelings for each other with lighthearted banter, occasional brushing together of their bodies, and stolen looks of desire.

No one paid any real attention to the television as the two college teams began their combat.

At halftime Stanley and Mindy enjoyed a hot dog and a beer, while Leigh was met with repeated busy signals as she tried to phone Annie.

"I hope her line isn't out of order," she grimaced, observing Jamie put a frozen block of his chicken broth on a back burner of his stove.

"If it is," he answered, "we can still take the soup to her. After all, her apartment's only a block away."

"I thought she was better," Stanley interjected. "Didn't she say she would have come today if she wasn't working every day next week?"

"She's probably worried about how she looks," Mindy commented.

"We see her every morning before she goes to makeup,"

Jamie grinned. "She won't care how she looks in front of us."

"You people are all crazy," Mindy shook her head with amusement.

"You just now figured that out?" Stanley laughed. "I thought everyone knew actors are crazy!"

"I'm not surprised, considering the lives you lead," Mindy replied. "It would make me crazy trying to keep the illusion out of real life and vice versa."

"Some of us don't even try," Stanley quipped.

"That's what makes us so fascinating," Jamie agreed. "You can never be sure who you're dealing with."

"Take Liz Barrett, for example," Stanley went on.

"Leigh is example enough for me," Mindy interrupted, then noticed the teams lining up for the second-half kickoff. "And enough of your show business insanity. Let's concentrate on something simple and easy to understand!"

◈ "Her line's still busy," Leigh groaned as Mindy followed her into the bedroom during a commercial break.

"Stanley's kind of cute," Mindy remarked speculatively. "Does he have a girlfriend?"

"No one special," Leigh answered, averting her gaze from Jamie's packed suitcases near the door.

Mindy picked up a postcard from Jamie's night table. She studied the aerial view of North Hollywood, including Cinema Center, Universal and Burbank Studios, before turning it over and discovering it was from Bucky.

"Did you know Jamie's son is a soccer player?" she asked.

"What?"

"Yes, and he must be good," Mindy continued. "He's playing in the East San Fernando Valley championships next Saturday."

"That's *A.Y.S.O.* soccer," Leigh explained, taking the card from Mindy while glancing at the bedroom door. "It's like Little League. He's still a child."

"Why don't you go watch him play?" Mindy quietly gibed. "You'll be out there next weekend."

"Sure," Leigh hissed. "Jamie would just love that. Erika's sure to be there. What would I say? What possible reason could I have for going to that game?"

"You're right," Mindy shrugged innocently. "I don't know what I was thinking about. What possible reason indeed . . ."

"You're not very funny, Mindy," Leigh bristled. "I thought you were going to help me!" She frustratedly snatched the phone and dialed again. "Still busy!"

"She *must* be home," Mindy said. "Why don't you and Jamie just walk over there?"

"What'll you do?"

"Stanley's here," she smiled. "I'll think of something."

"I imagine you will," Leigh's expression softened into a smile. "I can really imagine!"

◈ Zev pushed himself off Annie's spent body and stumbled to the table.

He sat down and nibbled a piece of cheese and chuckled at the sight of Annie's bare bottom sticking up in the air, while her face was buried in the pillows jammed against the headboard and her hands secured to the posts at each side.

"That's right, Bad Ass," he mocked. "Stay on your knees and pray to your great God, Fuck. But it won't do you any good. Just because you took it off doesn't mean I can't put it back!"

Zev took the knife and stabbed another piece of cheese with its forked tip. "So now we're going to play sleepy-time games, huh? You pretend you're asleep until Uncle Zev wakes you up."

Annie's silent immobility rekindled his debauched lust.

He alternated his gaze from the knife in his hand to Annie's rear, then sauntered back to the bed.

He stood looking at her, lightly scratching his own naked posterior with the knife's tip. "I know how to play that game," he smirked, sitting down beside her and gently reforming the tattoo with the knife.

"I'm good at games," he continued, pressing more firmly into her skin. "And I always win!"

Annie's lack of reaction goaded Zev into increasing the pressure until a fine line of blood trailed behind the forked tip. "Always."

"You stupid bitch," he growled when she still didn't respond. "Now, you're going to have to beg." He turned the knife on its side, digging into her skin with all three forked points, pressing harder until the points were lost in her blood.

"What the hell's wrong with you?" he demanded, violently slapping her bloody buttocks, causing her body to collapse in a monsterous heap.

"Talk to me!" Zev grabbed her hair, roughly lifting her face from the pillows and thrust his hand through the mucous still oozing from her nose to pull the tampons from her mouth. "Talk to me, you filthy bitch!"

Zev could barely hear the knocking at the door as he gazed dumbfoundedly into the lifeless stare of Annie's still open eyes. "What are you doing, Annie?" he demanded loudly as the knocking became more insistent.

"Let me in!" Jamie's voice sounded through the door.

"Help me!" Zev began wailing repeatedly as he fumbled with the lock and jerked it open. "Help me!"

Jamied paled, then shoved Leigh to one side, out of view of the naked, blood-spattered figure in front of him.

"It's her fault!" Zev howled, pointing at Annie with the knife as Jamie moved toward him.

"My God," Jamie gasped as he saw Annie's battered corpse on the bed. His revulsion snapped the last vestiges of Zev's sanity. "I told you I didn't do it," he cried and ran hysterically out the door, his bad leg impairing his frantic escape.

Leigh screamed at the sight of Annie's bloodied body, then fainted when the corpse twisted awkwardly over the edge of the bed. Jamie quickly checked to see if Leigh was all right, then dashed after Zev, who was down the stairs and lurching into the street.

Jamie caught up with him after a few yards but pulled back when Zev turned to defend himself with the bloodied knife.

"Put it down!" Jamie tried to reason through Zev's cloud of crazed panic.

The gathering crowd drove Zev into a frenzy. He began to babble wildly about a game he and Annie were playing. Suddenly he lunged at Jamie, cutting through the arm of his coat with the knife.

"All right, you crazy bastard," Jamie shouted as he parried the next slash with his injured arm. Before Zev could strike again, Jamie hammered his huge fist into Zev's startled face.

The swelling crowd drew in closer as Zev collapsed into a grotesque scramble of naked skin and blood.

Jamie fought back the urge to vomit as he stood unsteadily over the unconscious murderer. Then remembering Leigh, he ran back into Annie's building.

◈ "Thanks for questioning Jamie and Leigh in the apartment rather than at the station," Sy Cohen, the network publicist, said with a deferential smile. The stocky detective in charge of the case was making his final notes before leaving Jamie's apartment.

"No trouble," the detective replied. "We want to keep things as quiet as possible. And in a case like this, where celebrities are involved, it ain't always easy."

"How well I know!" Sy agreed, covering his eagerness for the detective to depart. "You can rest assured we'll do all we can to cooperate."

"Thank you, Mr. Cohen. I know where to contact all of

you. I'm sorry to delay your trip, Mr. Starbuck. We'll get your detailed statement first thing Monday morning, then you can be on your way."

"Under the circumstances," Jamie shrugged, "I don't think one more day will make a lot of difference."

Sy looked to Leigh who was sitting next to Mindy on the sofa, struggling to control her intermittent sobs. "Miss Fisk, Mr. Gordon and I will be available to you most of the day Monday at the Federated Studio," he said.

"It's just routine," the detective smiled comfortingly to Leigh as he buttoned his coat.

Jamie escorted him to the elevator and said good-bye. As he returned to the apartment Sy met him outside.

"It won't be long until the press is in on this," Sy breathed furtively. "I appreciate that you're under a strain, but I'll have to know what's going on here."

"Going on?"

"Between you and Leigh. The press will want to know how you're connected. Why did you go to Annie's together? What's Stanley's involvement . . . and this other girl, Mindy Shrafft?"

Jamie suddenly realized the possible implications of their innocent afternoon of watching television. "Jesus Christ, Sy, there's nothing going on between anybody! We're all friends who were sitting around watching football and who took some chicken soup to another friend who was sick with a cold. That's all there was to it! How can the press make anything out of that?"

"Come on, Jamie," Sy replied impatiently. "You're not one of those kids in there. You know damn good and well what they can make out of it!"

CHAPTER

 "She's on her way," Marnie
said, coming into Cathy's office.

"Barbara Lloyd?" Cathy asked.

"She's the one Neil hoped we'd get," Marnie affirmed. "She
has a similar look to Annie and she's supposed to be quick
with dialogue."

"What about Leigh? Does it look like she'll be able to get
through it today?"

"Neil says he *thinks* so."

"If she can't, we close down," Cathy said, a metallic edge in
her voice. "We have the show taped four days ahead. After all
that's happened, I don't want to go on with substitutes for
both of them."

"I think Dave and I have it worked out," Neil said, charging
into the office with a script in his hand.

"I wish Vico were directing today," Cathy sighed. "Dave
Pardo is good, but Vico's so much better under pressure."

"Dave's doing fine," Neil assured. "We figured a way to cut
in some flashbacks so that Leigh and Annie—I mean Barbara—will have about half as much to do. Dave has also reset
his plan for the cameras so they'll be on the other actors most

of the time. If you approve, I really don't think we're going to have any problems."

His attention turned to Sy Cohen hurrying through the outer office. "At least, no problems with the taping."

"You're going to have to say something to the press, Cathy," Sy insisted.

"But I don't know what to say!"

"I have it all written for you here," he said, laying a type-written statement in front of her. "The lawyers have already okayed it."

"Has Hennigan okayed it?"

"Don't worry about Hennigan," Sy smiled. "Once the law-yers take over, anyone else's opinion doesn't much matter."

"I'd still like to hear from my superior about this," she replied defensively. "I've been trying to reach him all morning."

"Look, you do what you want to do, honey," Sy responded patiently. "But I'm sitting on a powder keg—maybe the biggest thing that's happened in daytime since I've been here—and I'm not going to blow it. If you don't want to give this state-ment to the press—then I'm going to Liz. She's been around long enough to know what has to be done."

"No," she reacted, her cheeks burning with embarrass-ment at being chastised in front of Neil and Marnie. "I'll do it. Where do you want me to go?"

"Just come with me," Sy said, ignoring her discomfort. "And don't worry, they don't want to eat you. They only want to do their jobs, the same way you and I do."

"Do you want me to come along?" Neil asked.

"No," she stiffened. "Of course not. You stay with Dave and make those changes. I'll look at the flashbacks later."

"That's what I expected you to say," he winked support-ively. "But I thought I'd ask."

"So after you've read the statement and they start asking questions," Sy instructed as he led Cathy toward a small room where the press was assembled, "keep as much as possible on the subject of Annie—her career, her background, the positive things. It's all right to be horrified about Zev." He paused. "Has anyone told you that it was Zev who wrote those letters to Annie?"

Cathy recoiled with shock. "Zev!?"

Sy responded with a small, fatigued nod, then continued, "Whatever you do, try *not* to talk about the other people. This scandal is juicy enough in itself to divert the media's attention away from the others."

"What others?" Cathy asked bewildered.

"Leigh and Jamie. Maybe there's something going on between them and maybe not. But we don't want anyone to get the idea that the sweet, young ingenue from 'Yesterday's Children' might have gone to Annie's for more than chicken soup."

"But that's ridiculous," Cathy protested.

"Sure it is," Sy stopped before opening the door. "I think so too. On the other hand, if someone had told you a couple of days ago that Zev Brahms was capable of such a horrible crime, it wouldn't have seemed any less ridiculous. Would it?"

Cathy began sorting through the possibilities Sy had planted in her mind as she followed him through the door and reacted with a start at the sight of Jamie waiting alone in the room.

"I'm glad you could make it," Sy said, shaking Jamie's hand.

"I thought it over and you're right," Jamie replied. "It could be made to look strange if I leave the country without saying anything. It's better if I talk to them now."

"It went all right with the police?"

"They were swell," Jamie nodded. "In fact, one of the detectives who watches the show is waiting to drive me to the airport."

"Then we'll make this as brief as we can." Sy reached for the door to the conference room. "Wait here a minute. I'll get things started, then come get you."

Cathy sat uneasily, her mind a confusion of the personal and professional troubles in her life, until she found herself staring at Jamie. All at once her problems had a focus. Somehow this man was at the center of everything: Annie's death, Sam's commercial, Liz's worries, and Leigh's corruption. "What is it with actors like you?" she blurted. "Is it part of your hairy-chested, stud image to put a stain on everything around you?"

"What?" Jamie laughed with a mixture of surprise and irritation. "I don't know what's eating you, Cathy. But whatever it is, you can't spend the rest of your life taking it out on everyone else. We're all doing our best for this show. Everybody! Even Annie, sick as she was the last day I saw her here, was more concerned about the show than her own condition. Lighten up, Cathy! You may be cute, but you're sometimes a king-size pain in the ass!"

Cathy blanched with anger. "If you think I'm a pain in the ass now," she hissed, "just wait till . . ."

"Okay," Sy said, coming through the door. "They're ready. Just relax and keep your head. Everything will be fine."

The crowd of television, radio, and print newspeople made Cathy forget her anger for a while. She and Jamie followed Sy to a raised podium at one end of the room.

After being introduced, Cathy was about to begin reading her prepared statement when a pretty newswoman interrupted. "Tell me, Ms. Allison, how does it feel to have a genuine hero in your show? You must be very proud."

"Proud?" Cathy repeated vaguely, looking to Sy for support.

"Yes," the woman went on. "The alleged murderer was armed with a knife when Jamie chased him."

"He stabbed you before you got him down, didn't he?" another newsperson addressed Jamie.

"Well," he began, also surprised by this line of questioning. "Yeah. He nicked my arm a couple of times, but nothing serious."

"So with one blow you knocked him out," the woman moved closer.

"Yeah," Jamie nodded dubiously. "I guess so. It all happened so fast, I . . ."

"This isn't the first producer you've knocked out with one punch, is it?" an unidentified voice came from the crowd.

Cathy glanced at Sy, then stepped forward before Jamie could answer. "We're very proud," she smiled. "We're proud of his bravery. And we're proud to have him in 'Yesterday's Children.'"

"How would you feel if they used this for a story line in the show?" a TV reporter asked, as Jamie smiled his appreciation at Cathy for coming to his rescue.

"I'd prefer we forget it as soon as possible," he said. "Annie Holland deserves better than to only be remembered by this tragedy."

Sy stood by contentedly through the rest of the questioning. At the end of Cathy's prepared statement, Sy remained behind while Cathy and Jamie stepped out of the conference room.

"I wish I could figure you," Jamie said when they reached the hallway. "You can be pretty decent if you want to be."

"Maybe," she replied indifferently. "But life isn't a popularity contest. Some of us don't need the public's praise and approval."

Perplexed, Jamie watched Cathy hurry away from him down the corridor. *Why did she run?* he wondered. He hated to admit it, but he found her fascinating.

◈ "He hasn't returned my calls all day," Cathy complained into her phone to Jim Hennigan's secretary. "I got us through the show. I took care of the press, but there are *some* things I need help with."

"I'm sorry, Cathy," the secretary explained. "Things have been just as chaotic over here. Mr. Hennigan hasn't been able to return any of his calls. He's hardly been in the office since early this morning."

"Well, I hope what he's doing is important," Cathy huffed. "Because . . ."

"It is, Cathy," she interrupted. "You'd understand if I could tell you."

"All right. Just have him call me."

Cathy's irritation was set aside as Marnie came into the office.

"With everything that's going on, I don't know what made me think of this," Marnie began reflectively. "While I was watching the taping it occurred to me that the long-story has Stanley being wrongfully accused and convicted of Doc Bayard's murder, right?"

"That's right, but why bring that up now?"

"Well, when Stanley goes to prison, what happens to Joyce? I mean, don't you think it might be inviting unnecessary trouble to have the first black female lawyer on television *lose* her first important case? I was working on a documentary about the feminist movement before I started with you and it seems this is the kind of issue they really get excited about."

Cathy eased slowly back in her chair. After all that had happened, her mind was slow to grasp the significance of this new question.

"But they couldn't," she said haltingly. "No one thought about it *that* way. It's meant to be a breakthrough. Having a black woman as a lawyer is a step forward. Even the publicity department loved the idea."

"Well, I could be wrong," Marnie offered.

"Yes, but you might *not* be. I'll talk to Jim about it."

"Which brings me to another point," Marnie continued. "I overheard Stanley talking about moving to the Coast. His contract is up this week, isn't it?"

Cathy suddenly realized what Marnie was getting at. "Hasn't anyone extended his contract? He *can't* leave now!"

"I talked to Casting. It's their job, but no one told them anything about it."

"Oh, shit," Cathy groaned. "What else can go wrong today? Tell Stanley I want to see him right away."

"He's gone home. They're all gone."

"Why didn't someone tell me this before?" Cathy demanded hostilely.

"Who was supposed to know?"

"Well, I can't think of everything! Where's Neil? He's not a director yet; as long as he's still drawing his salary here, he'd better stay on the job!"

◈ "How's Leigh?" Stanley asked. He and Mindy were in the kitchen of the Fisk apartment. They had with them a takeout package of hot roasted chicken and french fries.

"She's all right," Mindy answered. "Her mother called from Nassau. Leigh convinced her that she didn't have to come back. She's in her room studying her script for tomorrow's show."

"Has Jamie called?"

"Not yet. He said he would before his plane leaves."

"I would never have guessed about them," Stanley grunted as he opened the refrigerator and took a beer.

"You're not going to say anything?" Mindy demanded apprehensively.

"And give that bastard press something else to write about?" he responded firmly. "Hell, no! It's bad enough what they're writing about Annie."

"It's disgusting."

"What's really disgusting is the goddamn network," Stanley continued angrily. "You know how they acknowledged her death? Her whole existence with 'Yesterday's Children' was summed up in the notice they put at the beginning of the show we taped today: *'Because of unforeseen circumstances the role of Carol Browne will be played by Barbara Lloyd.'* That shows you how much respect they have for actors!"

"I'm beginning to see it's not as glamorous as it appears from the outside."

Stanley nodded grimly. " 'The hardest way in the world to make an easy living'—that's what Jamie says."

"Really," Mindy agreed, then turned her attention to the package of food. "I'll go see if Leigh's ready to eat."

"You go ahead. I'll eat later," Leigh responded to Mindy's invitation from behind her bedroom door.

Leigh returned to her bed and tried to focus her mind on her script. "It's no use," she moaned as her eye followed each change of the numbers on her digital clock. She was totally mystified by what had happened. Zev had always seemed so sweet and helpful. Now to realize that it was Zev who had written those letters. It was all too much.

Leigh gave up on her script and sat staring at the clock. Each changing minute seemed like an hour until the phone rang.

She knew immediately that it was Jamie and almost burst into tears before he spoke. "Oh, Jamie," she gulped, hearing his voice.

"Hi, honey," he returned. "I'm at the airport and they've just announced that my flight is ready to board.Now if the weather cooperates I might be able to shoot this commercial and get back. Are you all right?"

"I'm still a little shook up, but I'm all right."

"I wish I could be there."

"Did you call Sam?" she asked, bringing her own voice under control. "What did he say? Are you going to Rome or Athens?"

"I'm meeting the others in Rome and we're flying together to Athens."

"I've always wanted to see Athens," Leigh said. "But you've been everywhere. It won't be anything new for you."

"New?" Jamie reacted warmly. "It's *always* new. Especially when you realize Athens is where it all started! The first actors, the first playwrights, they all worked in the world's first theater, and it's still there, at the base of the Acropolis."

"It must be beautiful."

"It will be if it doesn't rain," Jamie said with a smile. "Did they send the script for your screen test?"

"I don't know," she replied with a start. "I forgot to check the mail. It doesn't matter though. I've always wanted to play that part as long as I can remember. I know it backward."

"You'll be great," he assured. "I'll try to call you Wednesday at this same time. If I can't, I'll call you Friday in Los Angeles. Do you know where you'll be staying?"

"The Beverly Hills Hotel."

"Okay. Well, I just wanted to tell you I miss you already, and let you know old Sophocles, Aristophanes, and those other show-biz types around Athens will be joining with me to cheer you on!"

With every word from Jamie her self-confidence and humor returned. "Even Zorba?"

"Sure," Jamie laughed. "Even the greatest Greek of them all!"

"I love you, Jamie."

"Yeah," Jamie's voice sobered. "I love you too."

CHAPTER

"Why does the network only make minority problems in Daytime?" Jim complained to Cathy. She had been waiting for him with coffee and the morning reports when he arrived in his office. "Why isn't there a problem in Nighttime? They're loaded with black shows; *all* black shows! Cosby was number one for how many years?"

"What happens if we let Joyce win her case?" Cathy asked.

"I don't know," he growled. "But we have to risk it. The network won't put up with any more bad press. According to the papers I read on the way in this morning, Federated's production department is run by a bunch of perverts who spend their time victimizing our innocent, sex-crazed talent. A couple of them have even tried to tie it together with the network's rumored kickback scandal. I've never seen our dignified Mr. William Hanna so nervous as he was yesterday. After he sees today's papers, he'll *really* flip his lid!"

"Mr. Hanna's on his way down!" Jim's secretary announced as she appeared in the door.

"Down *here?*" Jim bolted upright in his chair.

"He'll be here any second."

"Oh, shit," he said, rising to his feet. "You'd better wait outside, Cathy."

"Maybe I should go back to the studio."

"No, wait. I want to talk to you about this situation with Stanley Gordon. Hanna won't stay long. He never does."

"Good morning, Mr. Hanna," Cathy beamed as the network president brushed past her in Jim's outer office.

"Good morning, good morning," he responded automatically without breaking his stride.

Cathy nervously leafed through a magazine. Fifteen minutes passed. Then she called Neil at the studio to check on the progress of the morning rehearsal. She cut Neil off at the sound of the opening door and smiled prettily as Hanna walked grimly out of the office.

She went into Jim's office again. The moment she saw Jim's gloomy face, she realized there was trouble afoot.

"Now," she ventured, sliding back into the chair in front of his desk. "About Stanley Gordon . . ."

"I don't have time for that now," he answered, crestfallen.

"Don't tell me something *else* has happened."

"Nothing that will affect you very much. I just resigned."

"Resigned?" she repeated incredulously. "Resigned from what?"

"From my exalted executive position at the Federated Television Network. I gave them two hours' notice. I'll be out of here by lunchtime."

"But why, Jim?" Cathy demanded.

"*Somebody* has to be the scapegoat for this mess," he smiled ironically. "At least I've got a choice: my head or my resignation."

"But that isn't fair! What are you going to do? What am *I* going to do?"

Jim's smile broadened. "My guess is that very soon *you'll* start worrying about whether my successor will be as supportive of you as I have been. As for myself, I suppose I'll start worrying about another job. Maybe Sam wasn't so foolish after all. What was the name of the advertising agency he went to? I might send him a résumé."

Cathy was speechless. What would happen to her with Jim gone?

◈ "Yes, I've already heard," Marnie said bitterly. Cathy had called for her and Neil to meet with her in Cathy's office. "And it isn't fair," Marnie continued. "I was working for Mr. Hennigan in Special Projects while the whole business was going on. I know how minimally he was involved. Mr. Hanna must know too. Damn that Zev Brahms! This stupid business might have blown over if he hadn't forced it into the open."

"What are you talking about?" Cathy asked probingly.

Marnie glanced from Cathy to Neil, then shook her head negatively. "I'll tell you this much. It wasn't because of his wife's health that Zev was transferred to Albuquerque."

"Then why?" Cathy persisted.

"Obviously to keep him quiet," Neil intervened for Marnie. "But they don't have to worry about that now," he continued. "I hear he hasn't said a word since they locked him up. He just sits there in his rubber room over at Bellevue, staring off into space."

"The sonofabitch is probably faking," Cathy growled.

"I don't know," Neil replied. "I talked to one of the medical reporters in the newsroom and he thinks that rather than accept what he did, Zev's mind has disconnected itself from reality and has gone off to the land of makebelieve."

"I only have a minute," Liz came bustling through. "I should be at rehearsal, but I thought if you haven't heard . . ."

"Heard what?" Cathy clipped.

"About Pam Godfrey," Liz stretched her moment of suspense. "About Pam leaving CBS and coming over here to take Jim Hennigan's place."

"Pam Godfrey?" Cathy repeated, dubious.

"She was one of the vice presidents in Daytime programming," Marnie spoke. "But I always got the impression her function was more as a doctor of their sick shows than a regular executive."

"Maybe she can cure *our* problems," Liz said, glancing hopefully from face to face. "Maybe she'll have courage enough to go against the computers and calculators and those stupid demographics. Maybe a strong woman is what this network needs. A strong, *intelligent* woman, who'll listen and remember the values that made us so successful in the first place!"

Neil could see the antagonism Liz had unwittingly provoked in Cathy. "Or someone like me," he minced lightly. "Then they'd have the best of both worlds. But it'll never happen. There's no one here with enough courage to make a decision like that."

"Decisions concerning *who* runs the network and *how* they run it are made at Slippery Rock," Cathy pointed her resentment at Neil. "When they feel they need our help, I'm sure they'll ask for it!"

"I was only kidding," Neil smiled and gestured appeasingly with his hands. "Besides, who in their right mind would want to leave the new job I have in California?"

"I thought you'd like to know," Liz began an uncomfortable retreat. "I . . . ah . . . They need me in rehearsal. We'll talk more later."

Cathy went through the motions of shuffling some papers on her desk as Liz hurried off. "Now," she said more calmly. "Now that we know who's replacing Jim, we have to make her aware of the potential problem our wonderful writers have put us into by forcing the first black woman lawyer in Daytime to lose her first important case."

"And Stanley's contract," Marnie spoke up. "It's already Tuesday and his contract's up on Friday."

"He's planning to leave for the Coast next Monday or

Tuesday," Neil added. "If my new job didn't begin so soon, I was thinking of driving out there with him."

"Stop reminding me of that new job!" Cathy moaned, displaying her appreciation for Neil's deflecting her anger away from Liz. "When I think this is your last week too, I . . ."

"Remember the image, Cathy," Neil grinned. "Don't spoil it by saying anything nice."

"I won't," she grimaced. "What I was going to say is, since you and Stanley are on such . . . intimate terms, I want you to talk to him first. I can extend his contract another two weeks on my own authority. I hate to do it, but once he's out there in Hollywood we'll never get him back, and there's no doubt that somehow it'll all end up being my fault."

"He's off today," Neil said, moving to the door. "I'll try to call him at home."

"Do you have any ideas about what to do with Joyce?" Cathy asked Marnie after Neil had left.

"I've been thinking about it," she responded. "I'm sure that the black and feminist pressure groups will come down on us if she loses the trial. On the other hand, if we take her off the case and replace her with a *man* who loses it, they'll cry cop-out."

"You know why they don't have these problems in Nighttime?" Cathy challenged, then continued without waiting for an answer. "Because of Bill Cosby and their other black stars. They know how to use their black power."

"If you say so," Marnie responded dryly. "But I'm afraid the only answer to our problem is to leave her on the case and let her win it. I don't see any other logical way out. If it's important to get rid of Stanley, we'll have to find some other way."

"I'll think about it," Cathy sighed as Neil came back into the room.

"Stanley's meeting me at Kerry's later this afternoon," Neil said.

"Be sure to come back here, after," Cathy replied.

"Fifteen minutes," a male voice came through the intercom from the studio.

"I should get down there before they start taping," Neil said thoughtfully. "I want to stay as close to Leigh as I can. She isn't too steady today."

"Go ahead," Cathy nodded.

"I'll stay with her through the taping and, if there's time, I'll take her home before I meet Stanley."

"Okay," Cathy responded. "But don't be late. This meeting with Stanley's important!"

"I know," Neil answered, pausing at the door. "And so is Leigh."

◈ "How's it going, cutie?" Neil smiled a greeting as he caught Leigh in the hallway on her way to the studio.

"Oh, all right," she answered, the strain on her emotions showing clearly through her expression. "It's just so strange. Barbara's sweet. She's a good actress. A lot like Annie in many ways, but . . ."

"You know, I've been thinking," Neil began with a mischievous grin. "I'll be leaving the show in a few days and I'm still waiting for you to keep your promise."

"What promise is that?"

"You promised to fill me in on the real scoop of what happened between Jamie and your father. Didn't you even swear something on your grandfather's Bible?"

"Oh," she blinked thoughtfully. "I asked, but . . . I don't think I ever got the whole story. Everyone admits that they didn't get along personally or professionally, but I suspect there was more. Somehow, I think there was a woman involved."

Neil raised a savvy eyebrow and announced, "It was a model."

"A model?"

"Yeah, I got the whole story. The reason Jamie and your

father had their fight was because they were both in love with this model. He was gorgeous! He called himself Butch Cassidy. A real outlaw!"

"What?" Leigh reacted with disbelief, then catching the glint in Neil's eyes, she realized he was pulling her leg. "You're terrible, Neil! You think that just because you're a pervert, everybody else in the world has to be one too."

"I'd go straight if you'd give me a tumble," he smirked.

"I'm going to miss you, Neil."

"I'm going to miss you too, cutie. But you're the only thing around here that's worth missing."

"Even if I read my lines off the prompter?" she grinned.

"Screw the prompter."

"Really?"

"Really."

Leigh eased away from Neil and moved to the studio door, a taunting smile pulling at her lips. "I didn't know we had gay prompters."

"Screw you too," Neil laughed, then blew her a kiss and headed for the control room.

❖ Cathy paused to read the raised metallic letters spelling Pam Godfrey's name already in place on the door to Jim Hennigan's former office.

She straightened the skirt of her most conservative gray flannel suit, took a breath, and pushed through the door.

After being admitted to Pam's inner office by her secretary, Cathy could feel herself being appraised as she approached her superior's desk.

Pam was softer, more feminine, than she had expected. Although in her mid-forties, she displayed a slim figure dressed in a silk blouse and skirt, accented with fine gold chains and bracelets. Her eyes behind large, rounded, and rimless glasses revealed nothing of the determined personality for which she was famous throughout the television industry.

"First of all," Pam said after their initial greetings, "I want to tell you that although I'm planning many changes, your position as producer of 'Yesterday's Children' is, for the time being, secure."

"Thank you," Cathy reacted in a manner which she hoped projected the image of a pleasant, well-organized executive. "I know you haven't had time to acquaint yourself with all our little problems, so I thought I'd bring up a few of those which I consider most urgent."

"All right," Pam leaned forward, displaying her undivided interest. "Let's hear them."

Cathy referred to her neatly typed notes, then explained the anticipated problems involved with Joyce losing her court case, and the possible solutions she had worked out with Marnie.

When she finished, Pam nodded judiciously. "That's one of the things I reviewed last night with Jim. I've decided to leave things as they are."

"But the consequences," Cathy insisted, feeling she hadn't stated the problem clearly enough. "With all the negative publicity we've been getting . . ."

"I don't believe in bowing to pressure groups," Pam explained calmly. "The story line was acceptable when it was conceived and for my purposes, it's still acceptable. What's the next problem?"

"Well . . ." Cathy shuffled through her papers, still unconvinced she had conveyed the gravity of the situation. "As long as you understand. Jim thought it might turn into an unnecessary confrontation with . . ."

"Jim's gone," Pam reminded Cathy. "I've been given carte blanche to run this division in any way I see fit. That was the major consideration in my accepting this job and that's the way it's going to be. We're not going to bother the writers with any further plot changes. You said you had some other problem?"

"Yes," Cathy uncomfortably returned to her notes. "Because of the script changes that Jim initiated, someone inadvertently allowed Stanley Gordon's contract to lapse."

"Stanley Gordon?"

"The actor who plays Ned Carson, the one the black girl defends in court."

"Oh, yes."

"Even without changing the story line, we need him at least another two weeks. To replace him with another actor this soon after the Annie Holland incident might be so disturbing to the audience that . . ."

"What's the problem?" Pam cut in.

Cathy got right to the point. "His contract demands. He wants a $25,000 bonus, movies-of-the-week guarantees, a Nighttime pilot."

"When's his current contract up?"

"Friday. The day after tomorrow."

"Replace him. Tell casting to set up the interviews for tomorrow."

"But . . ."

"Anything else?"

"Yes," Cathy nervously checked her notes. "My associate producer is leaving at the end of the week. The production assistant is moving into his job, so I need a new production assistant."

"Do you have someone in mind?"

"Well, not . . . anyone in particular."

"Advance someone from within your staff. It will be good for morale. Anything else?"

"Ah . . . no," Cathy struggled to maintain her composure. "Nothing I can't deal with."

"Good."

Cathy began stuffing her notes into her briefcase. "I won't keep you any longer."

"Jim told me how closely you worked together," Pam said, rising to escort Cathy to the door. "I'm hoping you and I will have the same rapport."

"I'm sure we will," Cathy managed to smile. "Jim was . . .
is a fine man."

"Yes," Pam agreed. "I heard this morning he might be going
to Chicago to head the Special Projects Division of one of the
new cable networks."

"*Head* the division?" Cathy repeated, unable to hide her
surprise.

"You know how it is with old television executives," Pam
laughed. "They never die, they just change companies. It was
nice meeting you, Cathy. As soon as things settle down here a
bit, we'll have dinner."

CHAPTER

Jamie jumped out of bed in response to his wake-up call and dashed to his hotel room window to peer contentedly into the crystal blue, cloudless Athenian sky. He quickly showered and shaved, then climbed into his handcrafted cowboy costume.

When he descended to the lobby, Sam and Luciana were already seeing off Giorgio and his camera crew, while Demetri Lambros, the Greek production manager, attended to his team in the parking lot. After being informed that the makeup would be done on location, Jamie went into the hotel coffee shop where he joined two of the bleary-eyed models, their hair in fat plastic rollers, for a light breakfast. Finding little in the way of interesting conversation with the girls, who were still numb from their night on the town with Terry and Devon, Jamie wandered back to the lobby.

"You might as well stay here where it is comfortable," Luciana suggested.

"Yeah," Sam agreed. "We'll send a car for you as soon as we're set up."

"It'd be better if I spend some time with the horse," Jamie countered. "He's liable to be a little frisky after all those days he was cooped up in Rome. I'd feel better if I could work him out some, get to know him before I risk breaking both our necks on that cobblestone street."

"Sure," Sam nodded approvingly. "Come on with us."

The quaint little street where they planned to shoot was being gaily decorated with colorful bunting, while some of the extras dressed in traditional Greek costumes sat talking at the table along the sidewalk.

Giorgio stood to one side displaying the stoic patience of his ancestors as he watched Terry in high-strung agitation, darting to and fro with his portable viewfinder, trying to decide on his first camera angle.

Sam went to Devon, who was attempting to hide his colossal hangover behind a bluster of activity, while Luciana spoke to Demetri about Jamie's wish to rehearse with the horse. Finding the horse was still enroute, Jamie went back to the car where he took a paperback novel from his bag and settled down to pass the idle time.

After awhile, he looked up to see Terry stomping angrily toward the car. Terry jerked the door open and flopped onto the seat next to Jamie, pulling a vial of cocaine from his pocket. "Fucking amateurs," he growled as he scooped into the white powder with a small spoon attached to the vial's lid and snorted two generous portions up his nostrils. "If there's anything I hate, it's working with amateurs! Want a toot?" he asked offering the vial to Jamie.

"No, thanks," Jamie replied.

"I'm going to quit one of these days myself," Terry rattled on. "You know, I put nearly two hundred thousand dollars up my nose this year. And the fucking bimbos! It used to be they'd put out for a bit part in a commercial, or even an extra part, but now they're all coke-whores. They won't so much as *think* of getting it on if you don't have drugs for them." He gestured toward the model seated at one of the sidewalk tables in an exhausted stupor. "That Marina, for example. What a space cadet! She has a nose like a vacuum cleaner. I dumped her on Devon, and did she fuck his head up for him!"

"That's great," Jamie said sarcastically. "And what about the horse? Do you have him doped up too?"

"The horse? What about the horse? Where *is* that goddamn horse, anyway?"

"The last I heard, he's on the way."

"My ass, on the way. He's supposed to *be* here! How am I supposed to get set up without the horse?"

"What was the problem before?"

"The fucking dolly track. I have about a two-hundred-foot traveling shot and they only brought eight feet of dolly track. That Wop cameraman says he can do it with a zoom lens, but what the hell is he going to zoom in on if we don't have the horse?"

"Well . . ." Before Jamie could continue, Terry was out of the car and storming back to the set.

Jamie placed the paperback into his bag and stepped out of the car to watch Terry yelling about the horse.

"We don't need the horse right away," Sam reasoned. "Why don't we start with Jamie's point-of-view of the girl and boy at the table as he rides by?"

"With eight feet of track?" Terry protested. "The camera will have to travel more than eight feet to get that shot."

"Perhaps if we use the camera car," Luciana suggested.

Terry's resentment over his inability to seduce Luciana suddenly surfaced. "Oh, so now *you're* a director too. Why is it that every cocksucker within ten miles of a movie camera thinks they're a director? Okay, sweetheart, you set up the shot. I'm taking a walk."

"Wait a minute," Sam ordered, his face reddening with anger.

Terry defiantly walked away from Sam and Jamie got in step beside him, placing his arm around Terry's thin shoulders. Terry tried to shrug Jamie's arm away, but Jamie just held on tighter.

"I don't know about you," Jamie spoke firmly, "but I want to get this thing over with and get out of here. It's no secret that stuff you're sticking up your nose knocks the hell out of your nerves, but if you don't want to look like the biggest amateur around, you'll try to control it."

"Fuck you, too, cowboy," Terry snapped, trying unsuccessfully to twist out of Jamie's tenacious grasp. "Don't play hero with me!"

"And after you have your nerves under control, you might give a thought to your choice of words. Some people, especially ladies, object to being called cocksuckers . . . at least in public."

"People that sensitive shouldn't be in show business," Terry modified his aggression.

"Some people don't have our experience and sophistication. They don't understand the way we show-people talk. My point is, *I* understand you don't mean it when you tell *me* to go fuck myself, but some people might take offense; they might even react violently."

"Are you trying to threaten me?"

"Hell, no," Jamie smiled, releasing his grip on Terry's shoulder. "What actor in his right mind would ever get his director pissed off at him?"

"You're probably right." Terry waxed calmer by the second. "It's this cheap coke. They've cut it with some kind of speed and I'm so wired I'm about to pop. But I'm afraid if I come down, I'm liable to crash."

"Maybe crashing's not such a bad idea, but let's get through the day first, okay?"

"Yeah. Come on, let's have a little toot and get back to work."

"You go ahead," Jamie replied amiably. "I'm trying to follow President Bush's advice."

"What's that?"

"You know, 'get high on life.' Isn't that what he said?"

Terry glared at Jamie, then turned sourly away, "Who gives a fuck what George Bush says?"

With nothing to do until the horse arrived, Jamie accepted

a ride back to the hotel with Devon. While Devon went to bed, Jamie took a refreshing swim in the hotel pool, had a rub-down, and was sitting in the lobby finishing a cheerful postcard to Leigh when Sam and Luciana came frantically through the entrance.

"What's up?" Jamie said, rising to meet them.

"Demetri has left us," Luciana answered.

"Yeah," Sam explained. "That goddamn Terry did it again. There's some mixup over permits and Demetri's people haven't been able to get the horse out of customs. He was about to straighten it out with a cousin of his in the Ministry when Terry heard about it and climbed all over him."

"The things he said were terrible," Luciana grimaced.

"I can imagine," Jamie frowned.

"So Demetri quit. I thought he was going to kill Terry, but instead he just walked away. If he talks to his cousin now, that horse will die of old age before we get him out of customs."

"Then we'll have to get another horse. They have white horses in Greece."

"How?" Sam asked. "Demetri's the one with the connections here in Greece. We don't know anyone else!"

"Let me make some phone calls," Jamie said speculatively. "I told you I made a couple of movies here. Maybe I can find someone who'll help."

"That'd be a lifesaver." Relief entered Sam's face. "We're getting down to where we don't have any more time to lose."

"Then you'd better get some tranquilizers into Terry and get him to bed. He's just going to get worse if he doesn't get some rest."

"I don't know," Sam sighed wearily. "It's like we're jinxed. We finally get some decent weather and now this."

Luciana looked at Sam's worn expression. "You, too, have need of some rest, Sam. You'll become ill if you don't see to your health."

Sam shook his head. "The only thing that'll help my health is getting this job finished."

CHAPTER

Leigh felt the sensation of being a continuing part of television history as the taxi drove her through the gates of the Burt Prinz Studios.

She studied the administration building. She hadn't seen it in the many years since Russell was the head of the studio's television department. She looked nostalgically down the row of huge sound stages where she vaguely remembered first watching Jamie film his "Slim Chisholm" TV series.

Upon entering the makeup building, she was struck by the gallery of photographs featuring the studio's current and past television stars which lined the long hallway. Make room for Leigh Fisk, she excitedly thought as she went down the hall. Her picture would hang there too, someday!

After being made up, Leigh continued on to the videotaping stage, stopping at the door to look at the call sheet and count the names of eight other girls testing for her role. A quick appraisal of the competition raised her confidence when she recognized none of the girls as an exceptional talent.

While awaiting her turn, which according to the call sheet was last, Leigh sat in her tiny dressing room mentally projecting herself into the character she was to portray. Her concentration was interrupted by the sound of a knock at the door. Thinking her turn had finally come, she took a deep breath and opened it to find George Conley.

"George," she cried, happy to see a familiar face.

"Hello, Leigh," he said, then paused as each of them put aside the impulse to speak of Annie. "I heard you were testing today," he went on, "so I thought I'd better come over and wish you luck. Not that you'll need it."

"George, it's great to see you! Is this where you're working now?"

"Yeah. I'll tell you about that later. I've talked to some of the studio people and they're pretty high on you for this part. The producer, Rob Weber, has the final word about who gets it, but I know he liked the tapes he saw from 'Yesterday's Children.' When are you going back to New York?"

"My reservation is for Sunday morning."

"Good. Tomorrow night I'm taking you to a very important party at Tanya Prinz's house. He smiled enigmatically. "Old Burt Prinz's daughter-in-law. She's the head of television here now. But that's another story for later."

"Why, thank you, George," she bubbled. "That would be terrific."

"It's my pleasure. I put you into television, so I feel kind of responsible for what happens to your career. I have to get back to the office. I'll call you in the morning. Where are you staying?"

"The Beverly Hills Hotel."

"Don't worry about a thing," he said, giving her an encouraging hug. "You're the only girl testing who's ever been in a soap, and everyone knows soap actors are the best in the business. Break a leg," he winked, then left, closing the door behind him.

When Leigh was called to the stage she ran through the scene a few times with the actor who was already signed to play the role of her fiancé. The director made some suggestions and adjustments, then the taping began.

After a couple of takes, Rob Weber, a medium-sized man with a thin, hawklike face, came onto the set. He put his arm

around Leigh, complimenting her performance. He then suggested that she try a different approach to the scene. He asked
her to try a more zany interpretation, one with more comedic
abandon.

Leigh nodded her understanding, then was startled at the
touch of Rob's hand grazing lightly over her backside as he
removed it from her waist.

She quickly got back into character as the countdown to
taping began. She played the scene with such skill that the
young man acting with her almost broke up with laughter.

"I'm not supposed to say anything," he whispered when it
was over, "but of all the girls, you're the best, by far. I hope you
get the part."

"Excellent," the director complimented, coming to the set
with Rob.

Rob walked with her to the dressing room, asking her
impressions of the script and the rest of the cast. He suggested
they meet later at the hotel where they could continue their
discussion over a drink in the Polo Lounge.

◈ Leigh walked into the Polo
Lounge of the Beverly Hills Hotel and immediately spotted
Rob in a booth facing the bar. She identified herself to the
maître d', explaining she might be receiving a phone call, then
joined Rob in his booth.

"Something wrong?" he asked, signaling to the waiter.

"No," she answered, trying to brighten up. "I went to the
drugstore and missed a call from Europe. He left a message
that if he doesn't try again soon, he will in the morning."

"I see," Rob nodded, then looked up at the waiter, poised
for their order. Leigh asked for a glass of white wine and Rob a
martini. "Boyfriend?" Rob asked.

"What?"

"The call from Europe."

"Oh," Leigh hesitated, finding the term *boyfriend* some-what inappropriate for Jamie. "Yes."

"That's too bad." Rob smiled pleasantly.

"Why?"

"Well, sometimes a boyfriend can be a hindrance for a girl starting out in this town."

"Really?" Leigh returned his smile. "How?"

"Oh, social demands, for example. Publicity. Promotion. Younger men tend to become jealous, overly possessive, when their girlfriends get into the limelight and have to fulfill social obligations without them."

"I wouldn't worry about that," Leigh replied with a small laugh, thinking of Jamie's reaction to Rob's appraisal of their relationship.

"Good," he grinned, completely misinterpreting her meaning. "Very good!"

He looked speculatively at Leigh while the waiter placed their order on the table. "Yeah," he said, "a girl who knows where she's going can really get ahead in this town."

"That's why I've worked so hard," she agreed. "It's a diffi-cult profession and one can easily be distracted if one isn't totally dedicated." Leigh's attention was caught in uncertain recognition by a beautiful, casually dressed woman with pulled-back, naturally blonde hair who was speaking famil-iarly with the maître d' at his station near the entrance.

The woman reluctantly accepted the meaning of the maître d's negative gesture, made an exploratory tour of the room, then departed.

"Do you know her?" Rob asked.

"I thought so. I'm not sure."

"She's that German singer, Erika Norden, who used to go with Tony Mitchell. That's who she's probably looking for."

"Used to?" Leigh asked, masking her shock and surprise at being confronted with the reality of Jamie's wife.

"That's his story. She acts like she hasn't gotten the mes-sage yet."

"Oh?" She was still stunned from having seen Jamie's wife.

"Getting back to what I was saying," he resumed. "The way I see it, the choice is between you and Kate Miller."

"Who?" Erika's image still clouded her consciousness. "Oh, yes. The dark-haired girl with the big green eyes."

"Yeah. The network's been pushing her on me from the beginning, but I think I could change their minds if I made a serious effort. A lot has to do with charisma, with personal feelings. I mean, if I'm going to take a chance on my future with an actress, especially a new actress, she has to take a chance on me too. You understand?"

Leigh put Erika out of her mind as her head nodded slowly. "I think I'm beginning to, Mr. Weber."

"This business is built on emotion," he went on. "For it to be successful, emotions have to be in tune to be shared. All the great movies have been collaborations between men and women who had something going for them off camera as well as on."

"Like Melanie Griffith and Don Johnson," she said, resentful over the direction he was clearly heading.

"Yeah, I guess so. This isn't exactly a Melanie Griffith part, but it could make you just as big a star . . . if we worked together."

"Working together is what it's all about, isn't it?" she answered, trying to humor him away from his obvious goal. "That's what they taught us in acting school. For a production to be successful, everybody has to work together."

"That's right," he smiled complacently. "Say, what are you doing for dinner? There's this great little restaurant on the beach near my place in Malibu."

"Oh, I can't. I'm having dinner with my aunt. She's driving in from Santa Barbara to meet me. She should be here any time now."

"That's too bad. How about tomorrow?"

"Oh, darn. I'm busy tomorrow, too. And I'm leaving Sunday morning. I have a show to do on Monday."

"Well, maybe next time," his smile vanished as he began thinking of another partner for the evening. "When you come back."

"If I come back," she answered with friendly decorum. "We shall definitely see each other."

◈ "There's only one thing that could make this going-away party better," Neil cried, glass in hand, leaning unsteadily on the tightly packed, familiar corner table at Kerry's. "That would be if I could take you all to Hollywood with me!"

"Hear, hear," the crowd at the table erupted in agreement.

"And if Leigh was here . . . but she's *already* in Hollywood."

"And let's hope she never has to come back!" Stanley added loudly.

"Of course, she has to come back," Liz protested. "We need *some* of our familiar faces. Don't we, Cathy?"

"Oh, yes," Cathy agreed. "We're not letting go of our Leigh. There's been enough change around here lately."

"That's no lie," Stanley snorted sarcastically as Chris Knight, a young, part-time actor and full-time waiter approached the table.

"How about a round on the house?" Chris offered, lowering his ladened tray to the table and wiping his hands on his apron. "The boss says 'bon voyage'!"

"Thanks, boss!" Neil raised his glass toward the bar. "As long as I'm thanking, here's to *my* boss!" He toasted Cathy. "Thanks for the job I'm leaving and thanks for the job I'm going to!"

"You deserve it," Cathy said.

"And more," Liz concurred, with the secret satisfaction that she would soon have Eddie to herself.

"And to Marnie," Neil went on, "who's taking my job. I want to thank Marnie for also taking my shit. You're a real pal!"

"So are you," Marnie provocatively got to her feet. "I'd really show you if I could."

"He wouldn't know what to do with it," Vico cracked.

"I'd know what to do with *your* worn-out Greek ass," Neil returned, then grinned at Marnie. "You can show me anything you got, honey. Anytime you want."

Marnie remained on her feet, her expression displaying an alcohol-dulled vacuity. "What the hell," she mumbled. "It's a going-away party, so why not? I wasn't going to say anything yet, but you and Stanley aren't the only ones leaving."

"What?" Cathy gasped apprehensively.

"I'm going too. To Chicago. I'll be a full producer, doing my own shows on that new cable network . . . with Jim Hennigan."

"Hey, great!"

"Wow!"

"When did this happen?" Cathy managed to speak through her shock. "Why didn't you say anything?"

"I was going to," Marnie shrugged sheepishly. "Next week when things had calmed down some."

"Next week, huh?" Cathy voiced, her spirits collapsing into a well of vulnerability.

"Atta girl, Marnie," Stanley needled. "It's almost like graduation day. We've gotten our education at Webster University and we're going off into the real world. How about it, Cathy? Are you going to give us some words of wisdom about our responsibility to the future?"

"No," Cathy reacted with cool civility. "I don't have any . . . I mean, if something's to be said . . . it should come from Liz."

"Yeah, tell us, Liz!"

"Give us a speech!"

"I don't have a speech," Liz said, taking a reflective sip of her vodka before putting it down. "But I will say, I think of you all as my family. Neil, Stanley, Marnie, if we've been an influence on your lives, if you're taking something with you that will help in your careers, then we who are remaining are proud and happy for you. Speaking just for myself, I love you and I hope you stay in contact with me."

"That was beautiful," Neil exclaimed, working his way to Liz's side. "Let's have a drink to the greatest lady in show business!"

Liz reacted shyly as the table exploded with cheers.

Neil gave her a squeeze, then turned to Eddie. "What about you, maestro? Don't you have something to say?"

Eddie shot Neil an embarrassed glare, then raised his glass to Liz, uncomfortably avoiding her eyes. "The greatest lady in show business," he repeated. "The first person to give me a break. The album she let me do for her proves what I can do . . . and I'm grateful. It gives me a chance to show the world."

"Damn, you're long-winded," Neil interrupted. "You shouldn't be writing music. You should be writing soaps!"

Eddie's face reddened. "What I'm trying to say is," he stammered, "I'm going with Neil."

Liz's face turned white as she looked to Neil. "What's that?" she was barely able to speak.

"Oh, for Christ's sake," Vico groaned. "Not another faggot wedding?"

"Why not?" Neil smiled, half in jest. "How else are we ever going to control AIDS if people won't make commitments?"

"God bless monogamy," Stanley chuckled.

"To the happy couple," Chris toasted with a glass from his tray.

A taste of sour bile rose from Liz's stomach. She attempted a smile, then determinedly got to her feet. "You'll have to excuse me. I . . . I'm expected at home."

◈ *How could she have been so stupid!* Liz castigated herself as she stamped into her empty apartment. She went straight to her kitchen freezer, took out a bottle of Polish vodka, and filled a small water glass.

It was bad enough for a woman of her age to lose her head over a boy like Eddie, but to lose it over such a blatant little fairy! No wonder everything was falling apart in her life.

She should have known she'd be punished for sacrificing all of her principles. She had spent a lifetime building a respectable reputation, then she threw it all away; all in one day for some tawdry sex with that conniving little . . .

"AIDS," Liz exclaimed with fear and anger. She gulped down a large portion of her vodka, then slumped forlornly into a chair at the kitchen table, her eyes filling with bitter tears.

She should have known better. Fern was right. Damn her! Why did she have to be right again? Why did Liz have to be so alone that she missed her?

But she was always alone, she thought, tipping the glass to her lips. It was because she was alone so much that occasionally she was so stupid. That's why Jennifer got into trouble too. Since their husband died, they had both become lonely and frustrated. Jamie's smooth line of talk would never have worked if they weren't so lonely. Well, it wouldn't happen again! When Jamie came back, he would have to take his smooth talking somewhere else!

Liz pulled herself erect at the jangle of the telephone, then with deliberate control reached over and answered it.

"Teddy!" she cried with delight, recognizing her son's voice. "How are you, darling? I thought you were going to call yesterday . . . I mean, the day before."

"I did, Mom. I left a message with the service. We want you to come out here for Christmas."

"Christmas?"

"Grandma already said it's okay with her. Ever since she found out Dad's remarried, her whole attitude toward him has changed."

"Your father has remarried?" she took another hefty gulp of vodka.

"Yeah. You'll like her. She's really hot."

"How nice for her. Let me speak with your grandmother."

"Teddy's right," Fern's voice boomed. "Let's spend Christmas here!"

"With Harvey's *hot* new bride?" Liz replied caustically.

"She's a nice little girl, actually," Fern reacted. "You've seen her in those pictures on the beach that Teddy sent."

"Not that skinny blonde?" Liz's eyes began to tear again. "She's young enough to be . . ." She stopped with a futile shake of her head.

"That's the one," Fern verified. "But she's sweet. And she's good company for Teddy. She's almost like having another . . ."

"Mother!" Liz interrupted sharply. "If you say she's like having another grandchild, I'm hanging up! What does that make *me*? No, Fern. I'm not spending *my* Christmas playing mother to my husband's wife! I can think of much better things to do!"

"Are you drunk?" Fern countered.

"Mother," Liz brushed a tear from her cheek. "I am not drunk, yet . . . If you hang on the line a while, I probably will be . . . but not yet."

"Then stop it right now and go to bed," Fern ordered.

"I'm sorry, Mother," Liz repented.

"Call me in the morning when you can act like a human being. And don't drink anymore!"

"Good night, Mother."

"And don't drink anymore," Liz mimicked to the silent telephone, only to be startled half out of her wits when the phone's bell responded almost as a warning. "Hello," she answered tentatively.

"Liz," a man's voice sounded enthusiastically. "It's Elliot Harrison."

"Who?"

"From Norwood University."

"Oh, Elliot," she sat a little straighter and smiled at the phone. "Naturally it's you. I was concentrating on something else . . . My script for tomorrow; I was thinking about my lines."

"You're working on Saturday?"

"I mean Monday . . . Didn't I say Monday? That's what I meant . . . Monday."

"I apologize for the late hour. I've been calling all day to invite you to dinner tonight. I told your answering service I'm in the city for the weekend and I hoped to see you."

Liz looked at the clock, noticing it was only 7:30. "That's a wonderful idea," she said, but when she got to her feet she realized she was in no condition to go anywhere. "But I've already made other plans. I've been so busy I forgot to check the service. Call me tomorrow, Elliot. Good-bye."

Liz disconnected the line with her finger, keeping the receiver to her ear. Dean Elliot Harrison. Another good-looking, smooth talker. Well, she wasn't falling for *that* again. She released the disconnect button on the phone and dialed her answering service.

"This is Liz Barrett . . . No, hold the messages until tomorrow," she instructed, closing one eye to gauge the remaining contents of the vodka bottle. "And answer my phone . . . I plan to be out for the rest of the evening."

CHAPTER

"Ooh," Liz groaned, nei-
ther sober enough to feel sick nor intoxicated enough to feel
well. "Why do I do this?"

She rolled out of bed and shuffled on bare feet, down the
hall to the kitchen. Coffee, she thought. A cup of coffee would
make it better.

She move sluggishly, attempting not to offend her sensitive
ears with unnecessary noise while she turned on her automatic coffeemaker, then paused to drain the last of the vodka
bottle standing on the table.

"This may be what I *really* need," Liz sighed, opening the
freezer and taking out a fresh bottle.

"Dr. Bayard's cure-all for delicate ladies," she quoted Karl
Herbert, after downing a full measure of the frozen vodka.
"Dear, dear Dr. Bayard," she voiced, proceeding, glass in hand,
toward the living room.

"Gone forever. Died in Webster Memorial Hospital and
gone to his little Deer Creek Theater in the sky. Or was it 'The
Man Who Came to Dinner' he was going to?

No matter. She shrugged. Karl was a good actor and he
would be a great teacher. Any aspiring actress who's lucky

enough to be accepted at the little Deer Creek Theater would be honored to know she was studying with the man who . . . who . . ." A whimsical giggle escaped Liz's lips. "The man who came to dinner."

A large basket of cut flowers caught her attention as she passed through the foyer.

"Fern? Juanita?" she called for her mother, then the house-keeper, before realizing neither was in the apartment.

"Sorry about last night. How about next week?" the card said, and it was signed, Elliot Harrison.

"Elliot Harrison," she read the name again. She dimly remembered speaking to him the previous night. She seemed to recall having been a bit rude to him. What had he wanted? Ah, yes . . . dinner—and probably a lot more afterward. Men were all alike. Well, she wasn't interested in Mr. Elliot Harrison. Intellectual men of his ilk never have successful relationships with women like . . . with women in show business. Look at Marilyn Monroe and Arthur Miller. Look at . . .

Liz steadied herself by leaning on a table. There must be some men out there worthy of a woman of her quality. But with the state of her head and stomach at the moment, men, any man, was of minimal importance.

Liz stepped over to her desk and fumbled through her phonebook.

I'll just call Mr. Dean of Norwood University and tell him Madam Liz of Webster University is occupied. Should I find time in my calendar, perhaps I'll grant him an audience sometime next week.

◈ Leigh forgot for a moment where she was as she reached for the ringing telephone. "Jamie! I've been thinking about you all night," she said, shaking off her sleepiness.

"I've been thinking about you too," he anwered huskily. "I'd tell you what I've been thinking, but they have laws against talking like that on the telephone."

"Where are you?" she asked, contently brushing her hand over her suddenly erect nipples. "You sound so near."

"I'm nearer than I was yesterday," Jamie chuckled. "But not as near as I'd like to be. I'm in Madrid."

"Then you've finished in Athens?"

"Well, you might say that we're finished in Athens, but we didn't shoot anything."

"Oh, no," Leigh responded sympathetically. "Not again!"

"The original comedy of errors," he sighed. "The director's a coke freak, the horse got stuck in customs, and the Greek production manager quit. By the time we got a new production manager and found another horse, the storm front that's been tracking us all over Europe finally caught us in Athens. It's already passed Madrid, so unless it decides to turn around and come back, we should be finished with our weather problems. How did your test go?"

"All right, I think," she said, her feelings of sensuality ebbing away. "Everyone *said* they liked it. The actor I tested with told me I was the best of all the girls, but who can tell?"

"I don't know the other girls, but I'm sure he's right. If they have any brains, you'll get it."

"I hope so. I wish you were here, Jamie. The waiting would be so much easier."

"So do I. I wish I was there with you in the hotel, right now. Afterward we could get dressed and drive over to watch Bucky play in his championship game."

"Yes, that would be fun," she reacted as she recalled the tight desperation in Erika's face. "I saw your . . ." Leigh began, then decided not to mention Erika.

"What did you see?"

"I saw . . . George Conley. He's taking me to a party at Tanya Prinz's house."

"Good old Tanya," Jamie laughed. "I heard she has a big job at the studio now. Say hello for me."

"George says she's the daughter-in-law of the original Burt Prinz. Where's her husband?"

"That's a long story. Burt Junior lives in Rome. After they got married, Tanya went to Hollywood to meet Burt's mother and sister, Judy. They liked Tanya so well that they moved her in with them. Then, shortly afterward, they put her in charge of the studio."

"Just like that?"

"Just like that," he smiled. "It's one of the better-known, typical Hollywood success stories."

"I don't know," Leigh smiled ruefully. "Hollywood may be too much for me."

"Or vice versa," he laughed gently. "Listen, I'll call you Monday in New York. Cross your fingers that nothing else goes wrong for us. I want to finish and come home."

"Home?" she questioned timidly.

"To New York," he answered. "To you."

CHAPTER

Leigh parked her rental car on the street bordering the tree-lined North Hollywood Public Park. She tilted the mirror to confirm once again that the bandana over her hair and the large sunglasses on her nose were enough to conceal her identity.

I hope I'm not making a mistake, she thought as she trudged across the grassy field toward a group of family and friends cheering a small boys' soccer game.

As she neared, the first person she sought to identify was Erika and when she did, she prudently moved to become a part of the group of parents on the opposite side of the field.

The stiffness Erika displayed the night before was replaced by a wild enthusiasm and there was no mistaking the object of her attention. She followed Bucky's every move with the vigilance of a mother eagle.

Leigh felt a guarded sense of pride as she recognized Jamie's looks and movements in his young son, but she also felt like an intruder. She hadn't expected to find such an obvious bond of affection between Erika and Bucky.

She slowly began to realize that her vision of Bucky's potential need for her, and of the necessity for her to become a surrogate wife and mother, were merely wishful thinking.

She frowned. Jamie wanted to be with her . . . of that she was certain. But it would break his heart to give up Bucky.

Leigh looked to the other side of the field, observing Erika's intensity as she followed her son's every move. Nor would Erika ever give Bucky up without a battle.

The eruption of screams and shouts from the audience of parents turned Leigh's head in the direction of a tangle of young bodies in a pileup on the field. One by one, the exuberant boys extricated themselves from the heap until a single body remained lying motionless on the ground.

"Bucky!" Erika shrieked, dashing onto the field.

"Bucky!" Leigh echoed, starting to run from the other side, then catching herself before Erika could notice.

Bucky began to stir as one of the coaches helped him to regain his breath and was quickly back on his feet, filled with embarrassment at his mother's hysterical outburst.

"I can't stand this," Leigh whispered to herself. "I don't belong here. I shouldn't have come!"

◈ In spite of George Conley's extravagant praise of her newly blossomed, womanly beauty, Leigh was still feeling like a misfit as she strolled with him near the swimming pool of the Prinz mansion.

"So that's what I'm doing," he explained. "The network has been desperate for someone to come up with a nighttime soap opera, so I figured it was a natural opportunity for a person who was familiar with the formula. I presented the idea, they went for it, and we're going into production almost immediately with a commitment for thirteen episodes."

"Isn't that unusual?" Leigh asked. "I mean, for the network to do a series without first shooting a pilot?"

"A little," George agreed. "But with the bad publicity that's been surfacing and the firm hold Federated has on the bottom of the nighttime ratings, they're willing to try the unusual."

"Fort Worth," she repeated the title.

"Yeah, but don't mention any of this to *anyone!* They don't want to announce it until we go into production."

"My lips are sealed," Leigh smiled earnestly. "I swear."

"That's the girl who's playing the part I would have liked you to do," George indicated across the pool to a pretty girl with a figure similar to Leigh's. "The series she was in has been dropped, but the network is high on her so I have to use her."

"She's good," Leigh allowed.

"She's okay. I wish I could use more soap people, but I'm stuck with this archaic mentality that believes the only names which mean anything are nighttime names."

"Well," Leigh responded good-naturedly, "so long as I'm in 'Yesterday's Children,' I couldn't do it anyway."

"Yeah," George shook his head, then looked up with a smile at the graceful, full-bodied woman walking toward them. "Our hostess," he said under his breath.

"You won't believe this," Tanya greeted her. "But I saw you on the soap opera show with Jamie Starbuck only a few days ago. I was home with the flu and decided to see what it is you people are doing that causes so much attention in the press. It was quite interesting."

"Thank you," Leigh replied graciously. "I told Jamie I was coming here tonight. He asked me to give you his best."

"Is Jamie in town?"

"No. He's in Europe, making a commercial. We spoke by phone."

"I see," Tanya smiled knowingly. "It was interesting to see Jamie playing a heavy for a change. The way he talked that woman into bed showed a side of him I've never seen before— at least, not on the screen."

"Yes," Leigh giggled, masking her embarrassment. "The funny thing is, it wasn't written that way. It just kind of came out."

"It's about time the real Jamie came out," Tanya grinned. "It might overcome his old, Slim Chisholm image." She glanced at a group of people walking out of the house, then put out her hand to Leigh. "I understand you tested for *The Phila-delphia Story*. I don't have a say in the casting, but I can wish you good luck. Perhaps we can speak again later."

"What's this about Jamie Starbuck?" George asked Leigh in an accusatory manner, as Tanya moved away.

"Nothing," she reacted defensively. "We're very close friends, that's all. After all, I've known him since I was a little girl."

Sure," he said skeptically. "But whatever he does wouldn't surprise me—considering the way his wife's been chasing after Tony Mitchell."

"Yes, I heard about that. Doesn't *anything* go on in Holly-wood without everyone knowing about it?"

"Not much," he laughed. "It's like living in a fish bowl. For example, everyone knows Tony's chosen another girl for his TV specials, just as they knew that's the reason she was chasing Tony in the first place."

Leigh's gaze swept coolly over the party guests. "Does Erika know?"

"If she doesn't, she will," George shrugged. "It'll be in all the papers on Monday."

"Terrific," Leigh replied, her heart filling with compassion for Erika. "Really terrif . . ." The words died in her throat as her eye caught Kate Miller, with her arms draped intimately around Rob Weber's neck, in the group talking to Tanya. "This whole experience has been a really terrific education for me."

"Well, how about it, Bucky boy," Jamie spoke warmly into the phone while stretched out on the bed in his hotel room. "How'd we do?"

"It wasn't fair, Dad." The long-distance call from California made twelve-year-old Bucky sound even younger. "We'd have won if the coach didn't take me out of the game."

"Took you out? What for?"

"Aw, Dad, it was nothing. I got the breath knocked out of me, that's all. If Mom hadn't made such a big deal out of it, Coach would have let me play to the end. *You* would have!"

"Maybe I would and maybe I wouldn't."

"I *know* you would have, Dad. You should have been here!"

"I wanted to be . . . But, there's always next season. Maybe next season we can be in. . ." Jamie stopped as he thought about Leigh, then Erika. Where the hell are we going to be next season? Where are *any* of us going to be? "In New York or maybe even back home in the Valley," he went on assuredly.

"That's what I was hoping," Bucky shouted enthusiastically. "But Mom says we might go back to Germany."

"Germany? What is she talking about? We can't go back to Germany."

"See, Mom? Dad says we're *not* going to Germany!"

Erika was obviously standing by, and knowing her as well as Jamie did, he knew she wouldn't stand for any insolence from Bucky very long. Sure enough, she was on the line the next second. "Wait a moment, Jamie. I'm sending Bucky to his room until he can speak with some respect."

"Forgive me," she said when she returned. "I know Bucky's upset, but we cannot stay here any longer. I am taking Bucky and going home."

"Going home?" Jamie repeated, angry and confused. "What the hell are you talking about? You *are* home!"

"Not any longer," she answered, controlling her hysteria. "They are laughing at me here. This is not my home. It's my *prison*. I'm going back to Germany, where I'll be judged by what I can do instead of by my mistakes!"

"What mistakes? What have you done now? Goddamn it, Erika, I'm not going to play your guessing games. If you don't tell me what you're talking about, I'm hanging up."

"Tony Mitchell took another singer for his TV shows."

"So?"

"You don't understand, Jamie. I was *with* him. I made a fool of myself for that job . . . and at the last minute he gave it to someone else. It will be in the papers tomorrow. I'll never be able to show my face in Hollywood again."

"Oh, bullshit," Jamie replied before realizing that with Erika he had best demonstrate some restraint. "What I mean is, why should Bucky have to suffer? Why does he have to go to Germany because of us? Erika, things are tough enough on this commercial we're shooting. Wait until I'm finished before you nail me with these heavy decisions."

"I'm not sure I *can* wait," she said, full of remorse. "I'm so embarrassed!"

"For Christ's sake, Erika!" he ranted. "Think how embarrassed you'll be if the commercial doesn't turn out? Think how we're going to pay your dentist. And suppose you go to Germany. What are you going to live on when you get there?"

"I don't know. I hadn't thought about it . . ."

"Then *do* think about it!" Jamie took a breath and tried to compose himself. "Just take it easy. I'll be back in about two weeks. We'll figure out something then. Okay?"

"Okay, Jamie," she relented. "I'm sorry to be such a problem . . . Is everything well for you, there?"

"Well?" Jamie humphed ironically. "Everything's fine. Couldn't be better."

◈ Devon took a breath of cold, fresh air from the second-floor balcony of Terry's suite in the Hotel Emperatriz, down the street from the Hilton. Then with a slight shiver, he stepped back into the room. "It's cold, but it's clear," he said contentedly. "Not a cloud in the sky."

"And the weather man says there aren't any in sight," Terry concurred, holding the coke spoon for Yvonne, the tallest of the three models, before putting it to his own nose. "It's going to be smooth sailing from here on in. I never thought we really needed three weeks for this shoot in the first place."

"That's not what you said in New York," Devon reminded him while accepting a glass of champagne from Marina. "And I thought you said you were going to lay off the cocaine. We don't want any more scenes like we had in Athens."

"Don't sweat it." He made light of the incident with a wave of his hand. "If that dumb fucking Greek had done his job, there wouldn't have been any scenes. It's different with this guy, Carlos, we have working for us here. He's on the ball. Even the goddamn horse is ready to go to work."

"I just want you to be rested."

"I said, don't sweat it," Terry insisted. "When the coke we have is gone, there ain't no more. You heard Carlos; I couldn't get any more if I wanted it. And as far as being rested," Terry grinned at Yvonne as he reached to grip her buttocks. "Who wouldn't sleep after a session with this ambitious sex machine?"

"Just the same," Devon said, holding his glass to Marina

for a refill, "tomorrow we're getting a new start. I don't want to take any chances on screwing it up. Especially when you think of how much money we've already spent for nothing."

"Oh, shit," Terry groaned. "If you can't forget business for a while and enjoy yourself, why don't you go over to the Hilton with those other two stiffs? Yvonne, get me a glass of champagne . . . and close the terrace door. The fucking racket is driving me nuts. Don't they have laws here about blowing their car horns at night?"

"The door *is* closed, Terry," Yvonne scowled.

"I told them I didn't want a room so close to the street." Terry stormed out onto the terrace and looked down to see two honking cars blocking each other's way.

"Knock it off, you fucking assholes," Terry yelled.

Both drivers looked up. The driver of the second car put it in reverse, then made his way around the stalled one, still blaring his horn. The stalled driver showed his contempt with a staccato of loud honking in return.

"I said knock it off, you dumb motherfucker," Terry screamed.

The driver looked angrily at Terry, yelled something in Spanish, and continued blowing his horn while making a rude gesture with his other hand.

"I'll show the sonofabitch," Terry threatened, reentering the room and snatching the champagne bottle from its bucket, carrying it by its neck back to the balcony. "I told you to shut up," he shrieked, brandishing the bottle over his head.

"Terry, get a hold of yourself," Devon exclaimed, rushing after him. But Terry had already thrown the heavy bottle, which landed with a loud *thump* in the middle of the car's hood.

"Oh, shit," Devon groaned as the man leaped from his car, howling in Spanish and beckoning wildly for Terry to come down to the street.

"Fuck you, asshole," Terry howled at the top of his voice. And before Devon could react, he ran out of the door and down to meet the challenge.

Devon and the two girls gaped in disbelief as they watched Terry, two flights down, flailing his fists at the man. The driver ducked, then caught Terry on the shoulder with a vicious blow from a tire iron he had concealed at his side.

"Stop it!" Devon yelled, then ran for help as the girls stood screaming in panic.

The girls' cries seemed to bring the man to his senses. He stopped hitting Terry and looked at them, suddenly scared. He jumped into his car and sped away, just as Devon and a handful of hotel guests emerged onto the street and ran to Terry's battered body.

◈ Carlos Riva, the Spanish production manager, arrived at the hotel almost as soon as the ambulance. He moved with cool efficiency, making certain there were no traces of illegal drugs in Terry's suite, and coached Devon and the girls regarding what to tell the police.

He also sent Jamie, who had come with Sam, back to the Hilton, explaining that if the Spanish police recognized him, the affair might be blown into unmanageable proportions.

Carlos exercized his maximum Latin charm, assisting the senior detective through the language barrier while unobtrusively guiding Devon, Sam, Luciana, and the models toward the proper responses to his questions.

When he had finished with the others, the detective spoke sternly for a few minute with Carlos, then took his men and departed.

"You must leave the country as soon as possible," Carlos explained to Sam and Devon.

"What do you mean?" Devon protested. "We didn't do anything."

"That is true. But it is also true that it is possible for the police to lock you up as material witnesses."

"They can't do that," Devon continued. "There must be laws!"

"There are laws. And Spanish law gives wide, and at times, undefined authority to the police. You must leave."

"What about Terry?" Sam asked.

"Terry is more difficult. The most serious of his wounds and broken bones will be tended to immediately. Then if he is gone within forty-eight hours and payment is made to the proper authority, he will be free to leave as well."

"How much?" Devon questioned skeptically.

"I won't know until morning. You may be certain it will be costly. They are of the opinion that all film people are very rich."

"Oh, shit," Devon shook his head. "What happens if we don't pay? Suppose we get a lawyer and fight it?"

"Once the forty-eight hours have passed, it is quite possible for Terry to sit for a year before they so much as charge him with anything. No, in these situations it is always best to pay and be finished with it."

"Someone will have to stay," Sam spoke. "To arrange for the payment and get Terry out of here when he can be moved."

"I will do it," Luciana offered.

"No," Sam replied. "It has to be me or Devon. It's our responsibility."

"Where shall we go?" Devon despaired.

"The weather is clear in Paris," Luciana said. "The permits are still valid and that's where we have the reserve horse. We could be ready to shoot in a day."

"There is a flight to Paris late tonight," Carlos remembered. "One of the airlines coming from Africa makes a stopover here."

"What about a director?" Devon worried.

Sam's eyes narrowed in thoughtful speculation. "Jamie and I can do it. I know what we want and Jamie knows how to get it. Terry's probably better, but we should be able to do almost as well."

"Then *you* should go to Paris and I'll stay and take care of things here," Devon decided. "Since the bribe money is going to have to come from New York, it'll probably go faster if I'm here to handle it."

"So," Luciana managed a tight smile. "Our original plan was to begin in Paris and that is precisely what we are doing . . . except for the slight delay."

CHAPTER

31

It was so strange without Neil beside her, Leigh thought as she left the rehearsal hall and slowly walked toward Cathy's office. She wondered if their planes passed each other in the sky yesterday.

It was almost like a different show . . . Jamie wasn't there. Stanley was gone. Marnie was leaving. And Annie . . .

Suppose she had gotten really close to Annie . . . or Zev Brahms? Leigh shuddered at that frightening thought. Maybe it was smarter not to get too close to the people you work with.

Erika would have been wise to stay away from Tony Mitchell. It'll probably be the same for Kate Miller. If my test is better, it won't matter a bit how close she got to Rob Weber Saturday night.

She smiled grimly to herself as she stepped into the office to see Marnie searching through a stack of papers on her desk.

"Welcome back, Leigh," Marnie looked up with a preoccupied smile. "How was Hollywood?"

"I'll know when they decide on my test," she replied pleasantly. "I came up here to say hello to Cathy from George Conley."

"She's awfully busy," Marnie shook her head. "And Chris Knight's in with her now."

"I can come back later," Leigh said and turned to leave as Cathy's voice came over the intercom, demanding the whereabouts of a list of potential replacements for Neil and Marnie.

"It's with those other papers I brought in a minute ago," Marnie explained while waving good-bye to Leigh.

"You won't regret giving me this chance," Chris spoke exuberantly as he opened Cathy's door and began backing out. "I've been working a long time to be ready. I won't let you down!"

"I don't expect you to," Cathy said condescendingly. "And keep in mind, although it's a small role today, if you do well enough there's no telling how important it may become."

"That's what I'm counting on," he grinned. "Except for Thursday, when I do my first show for you, I'll be finishing out the week at Kerry's, so if you have time, stop in and I'll buy you a drink."

"Thank you," she answered with a dismissing wave of her hand as she located Marnie's list among the papers on her desk.

Cathy buzzed Marnie on the intercom; then, after receiving no answer, she buzzed the secretary in the outer office. "Where's Marnie?" she barked.

"I'm right here," Marnie's voice was tight with urgency as she came hurriedly through the doorway.

Cathy raised her eyebrows inquisitively.

"It's just been confirmed," Marnie almost whispered. "William Hanna resigned this morning!"

"Hanna resigned . . . ?" Cathy reacted uncertainly.

"They're announcing it's because of his health, but it really has something to do with the production manager scandal."

"I don't see how that can affect us," Cathy spoke deliberately. "I mean, the president of the whole network doesn't concern himself with the day-to-day operation of one soap opera . . . does he? I'd better call Pam Godfrey!"

◈ "You have absolutely no-
thing to worry about," Pam's voice came through the phone
with cheerful assurance. "It won't concern us in any way."

"I didn't think so," Cathy answered calmly. "I actually
called to discuss some other developments that have come up
and just thought I'd mention it."

"There are a few things I'd like to discuss with you, too,
but I'm awfully busy right now. Why don't we have that
dinner we talked about, this Thursday night?"

"Thursday?" Cathy repeated with unexpected pleasure.

"Yes. Are you free?"

"Oh, yes! And if I wasn't, I certainly would make myself
free. Thursday night then . . . it's definite?"

"It's date."

"A date," Cathy repeated with quiet exhilaration as she
hung up the phone. "A very important date!"

"Excuse me, dear," Liz spoke, leaning tentatively in the
doorway.

"Is something the matter, Liz?" Cathy reacted with a sense
of cool confidence.

"I was talking with Karen Moore. Don't you think she
might be the best choice to become your new assistant?"

"Why do you ask?"

"You mentioned you'd like me to recommend someone.
I've thought about it and she seems to be the best qualified."

"She may *seem* to be, but she isn't," Cathy replied
brusquely.

"Oh," Liz retreated. "It's so easy to be mistaken about
things these days. Except for you and me, there's almost no
one to depend on anymore."

"You and me?"

"Yes. I remember your original concept of this business
between Jamie and me. You visioned it as a beautiful, tender
love story involving two honorable, sensitive people. Look
what they've done to us: I'm becoming a silly old fool and
Jamie a heartless Lothario. I can do something about the

scenes I'm in, but that scene today between the Fosters—
when they talked about me the way they did—it's disgusting.
We have to do something about it."

"What do you suggest?"

"We can go to Pam Godfrey together. She'll listen to the
two of us. She'll have to!"

"She has it in her contract that she doesn't have to listen to
anybody."

"How do you know?"

"She told me."

"She *has* to listen to me. I'm Jennifer Wells!"

"She told me you've been calling," Cathy lied. "She said to
ask you if it was about anything that I could take care of."

"No," Liz wrung her hands. "We have to do it together. It's
that director, Dave Pardo. His camera work is terrible. He has
no sense of timing. He's trying to make me do things no self-
respecting woman would *ever* do—I want him fired."

"He's only doing what he's told."

"By whom?"

"By me," Cathy forged ahead. "It's what Pam wants. She
likes the way Dave directs. In fact, except for one thing, she's
very satisfied with the show."

"What are you talking about?" Liz insisted, pursing her
lips. "What is it she doesn't like?"

"Well, I've covered for you as best I can," Cathy answered
smoothly. "I've told her about all the strain you've been under
. . . She isn't very happy about your resistance to playing
Jennifer the way she's being written. I'm supposed to talk to
you about it."

"*She* doesn't like the way I've been playing Jennifer!" Liz
shrieked. "What can she know? I've been Jennifer Wells all my
life. I *am* Jennifer Wells! Who could know Jennifer Wells better
than I?"

"Well," Cathy replied condescendingly, "as you said before,
it is easy to be mistaken about things these days."

"Then *tell* her that! Tell her she's mistaken!"

"If you really want me to, I'll try. But if you don't mind, I'll wait until Thursday night when we're having dinner. She'll be in a more relaxed mood then."

"You're . . . having dinner with her?"

"We're working very closely."

"Good," Liz replied uncertainly. "Maybe you shouldn't mention Dave Pardo. Maybe you should just talk about Jamie. He doesn't have to be bad to me when he comes back from Boston. Even if he doesn't get the money for the college, he could ask me to marry him. I've been alone long enough. A wedding would be good. Tell her, *everybody* loves a wedding. You know, Cathy. It was your idea."

"I'll see what I can do, but you have to cooperate as well."

"I don't appear again until Thursday," Liz gushed. "But I'll do everything I can to make it easier for you. It's another week-and-a-half until Jamie comes back. We can arrange it by then if we really try."

"I'll do my best, but don't be disappointed if it takes a little more time. It isn't easy to change Pam's mind."

Liz's eyes glistened as she reached across the desk to clasp Cathy's hands. "You're a good friend, Cathy. I appreciate what you're trying to do . . . for me and the show. You *should* be our producer. You deserve it because you honestly care!"

CHAPTER

The Eiffel Tower glimmered in a swirling mist over Jamie's shoulder as he expertly rode his prancing white stallion up to the motion-picture camera and smiled into the lens. "Put *your* man in the saddle," he urged sexily. "With Saddle Cologne!"

"Cut!" Sam cried, looking to Giorgio for confirmation of no problems with the camera. "And print!" he continued after receiving Giorgio's nod of approval. "We got it, Jamie! Goddammit, we got it! One more day like today and we'll be finished in Paris and off to the next location."

Jamie was filled with a sense of well-being as he relaxed in the back of the company Mercedes sedan for the return journey to the Georges V Hotel.

It's going to be okay, he thought. *Sam has a good head on his shoulders. And if the weather holds, between the two of us we can finish easily in two weeks, even without Terry . . .*

We could just as well do without Devon too, for that matter. It's too bad both of them don't go back to New York, instead of sending Terry with a nurse.

Jamie looked out of the car window as it crossed the Pont Alexandre III over the Seine and smiled to himself at the sight of the barge traffic on the river. *Someday I'll have to take*

Leigh on that boat with the dinner cruise through Paris at night.

Jamie's thoughts wandered back to the last time he had made that cruise—back when things were still good with Erika. That was the night she swore she got pregnant with Bucky.

What an exciting time that was. In those days his career was going great guns. He was Number One in Erika's life and she wasn't so career-obsessed. Those were the happiest times of his life. What a pity they had to end!

Leigh's youthful image again came to his mind. Would the relationship he was starting with her end the same way it had with Erika? God, he hoped not!

Sam, Luciana, and Giorgio were still on the sidewalk in front of the luxurious, world-renowned hotel talking with the French production manager when Jamie drove up.

Sam, filled with the exuberance of their first successful day of shooting, clapped Jamie on the back and invited everyone inside to continue their discussion over a drink in the fashionable Georges V bar.

Stopping along the way to pick up his messages, Sam felt a stab of anxiety. Two urgent messages were waiting for him to immediately call Aaron Roth in New York. *Now* what's wrong! he worried. He tried to mask his concern and told the others to go ahead into the bar while he returned some phone calls.

"Sam," Papa Roth's voice came quickly on the line from Rothwell Industries' executive suite. "Devon and your bum director are on their way to New York. I want you and the cowboy to come back too."

"But Mr. Roth," Sam quickly protested. "It's going to be okay. We got a good day's work done today. We had some problems, but it's going to be okay."

"You had some problems, all right," Roth said. "I heard all about your problems from the man who runs our manufacturing plant in Spain. I try to run a clean business. These kind of problems I don't need."

"But the problems are behind us, Mr. Roth."

"Sure the problems are behind you, Sammy. They're on their way home. How did you get mixed up with such a troublemaker in the first place?"

"Terry Hayden is supposed to be the best commercial director in the business. He's won all the top prizes."

"That broken head of his is a wonderful prize," Roth commented dryly. "And while we're talking about prizes, don't leave out my daughter's husband. That's a prize if I ever saw one!"

"Devon's been trying, Mr. Roth," Sam argued respectfully. "He's really been working hard, both on the commercial *and* on keeping Terry under control. He . . ."

"Some control. Devon can't even control his own putz! How can he be expected to control that oversexed dope fiend?"

"I don't know what you've heard . . ."

"I heard it all," Roth cut in. "When I have to pay $100,000 bribes, I make sure I know what I'm paying for."

"But like I said," Sam pressed. "That's all behind us. We started late, but we *have* started and we can finish in the time we planned. And think of the money we've spent; if we stop now, it'll all be wasted."

"I've thought about the money. I've also thought about this Hayden idiot. You and Devon said you took him because he's the best. Who's going to take such a genius's place?"

"Well," Sam hesitated, then proceeded with confidence. "Jamie and I are going to do it. I have two Emmies for TV specials I wrote and directed, and Jamie . . ."

"Jamie's a cowboy and you're an executive," Roth interrupted. "If you didn't need a director, you wouldn't have hired one. I trust you, Sammy, but I've made up my mind. The money you've spent, we'll find a way to write off. And as for the campaign, I've been turning it around in my mind and I ask myself: What're you doing in Europe? Saddle's American, isn't it? And the people we want to sell it to, they're also American. Why take an American cowboy to Paris when we want to sell American cologne to Americans? I like the cowboy, but I think I'd believe him more if he were here, out in the Old West, instead of clopping down some foreign street like a fruitcake. I'm no genius, but that's what I've been thinking."

"But we only have Jamie for another two weeks. There's liable to be a problem getting him free again from 'Yesterday's Children.' "

"I said I like the cowboy, but if he isn't available when we want, we'll get another one. There's lots of cowboys."

"He'll have to be paid . . ."

"How much do you have to pay someone for a job that didn't get done? Don't worry about it, Sammy."

Sam paused, unsuccessfully searching for an intelligent argument to Papa Roth's reasoning.

"And another thing," Roth continued. "My Ruth doesn't like the idea of her husband gallivanting around the world like a jet-setter. A little hanky-panky don't hurt anybody, but Devon's mind works better when he stays closer to home. You understand what I'm saying, don't you, Sammy?"

"Well . . ."

"Good. Come see me as soon as you get back. I'll tell you about the new setup."

"Yes, sir," Sam almost whispered. "But what about . . ." he attempted a final protest, then stopped when he realized the phone connection had already been broken.

New setup? Sam mused bitterly while leaving his room to carry the news to his coworkers in the bar. He was no genius either, but he knew what *that* meant!

◈ Luciana had just finished settling the financial accounts with the Italian camera crew and was chatting with Giorgio about their travel arrangements when Sam came into the hotel lobby from the street entrance.

"Jamie's flight departed without problems?" she asked, after excusing herself from the Italians.

"He'll be in New York in time for dinner," he answered.

"Just as you will be, tomorrow," Luciana spoke with a flicker of regret. "Have you notified your wife?"

"No." Sam was deliberately vague. "I hadn't thought of it. I mean . . . there's no real reason until I know exactly what time I'll be arriving."

"Certainly," she nodded, trying to hide her satisfaction. "I am so sorry it is all ending this way. Yours is a greater loss than mine, but still, I had put many of my own ambitions into this project. I have much to learn from your techniques and experience in television advertising. I had even hoped—at my own expense, of course—to go to New York and follow the campaign to its conclusion."

"If we haven't already reached the conclusion," Sam replied flatly.

"Oh, no. I'm sure you'll continue," she encouraged. "Your concept is sound. There is no reason it cannot be realized as well, or possibly better, in America. You must not lose confidence in your ability, Sam. You are marvelously talented."

"Thanks for the support," Sam smiled, reflecting on how little he received from Cathy. "Look, everything's pretty well wrapped up. We haven't done a damn thing but work and worry about the weather since we started this thing. Let's take some time off and see the sights."

"Tres bon, Monsieur," Luciana brightened. "Where shall we begin?"

"It may sound touristy, but I'd like to check the view from the top of the Eiffel Tower. What do you say?"

"I say, *allons*—let's go. I have visited Paris more times than I remember and I have never been to the Eiffel Tower."

Sam's thoughts were more on the woman at his side than the crisply defined panorama of the great city spread out below their historic vantage point.

Her interest in her work, her career, seemed the same as

Cathy's, but she didn't seem to be so devoured by it. For some reason, he had the impression Luciana could have a career and a personal life and be successful at both. While for Cathy, her personal life—especially her marriage to Sam—was nothing more than an impediment to her career.

"I don't like to intrude on your thoughts," Luciana spoke softly. "But you seem so pensive . . ."

"I was just thinking about how much help you've been, and . . . well, I don't know what's going to happen when I get back to New York. I don't know if we're continuing with this campaign or something else, or if I even have a job . . . And my personal life is just as uncertain."

Luciana followed his gaze as he looked down the Seine to the model of the Statue of Liberty on Pont de Grenelle.

"What I'm getting at is, *if* we go ahead with Saddle . . . and everything else works out . . . and *if* you're still available and still interested I'd really like for you to come to the States and work with us . . ."

Luciana's excitement flashed in her dark eyes. "I *am* interested, Sam. And you can rely upon my being available."

CHAPTER

Jamie maneuvered his two bulky bags and heavy coat out of the elevator and down the short hall to the door of his apartment. He dropped everything on the floor and was reaching for his key when the door swung open and Leigh flew into his arms.

Jamie reacted with a start, but before he could express his surprise, his words were smothered in a long, passionate kiss. His arms automatically engulfed her willing body in a tight embrace as their mouths and tongues mingled hungrily.

"We'd better get inside," Jamie urged hoarsely, still holding her close. "I wouldn't want to embarrass you in public."

"We aren't doing anything wrong," she teased.

"Not yet," he grinned hungrily, "but we will be in a minute."

Jamie pushed his bags into the apartment with his foot, slammed the door, and once again took Leigh in his arms.

"Oh, Jamie, it's been so long," she gasped between greedy kisses.

"Too long," he agreed, gently sliding his hand over the roundness of her bottom.

Leigh's whole body seemed to shiver at his touch. "You may think I'm terrible, but let's not wait," her voice quavered.

"I'd never think you're terrible," he kissed her again, "and we've already waited long enough."

◈ They lay together—Leigh holding Jamie inside her long after the ardor of their lovemaking had been spent—gazing into each other's eyes, quietly exchanging the tender endearments they had saved for this moment. After a while, Jamie rolled to one side and, keeping one arm around her, drifted into a peaceful sleep.

Leigh nestled close to Jamie and dozed off, feeling snug and secure in the comfort of his presence.

She was lying on her back, sleeping peacefully, when the phone rang.

Jamie reached groggily for the phone as Leigh peered at the softly illuminated bedside clock to see it was a little after six A.M.

Jamie bolted to an upright position upon realizing that he was speaking with Erika.

"Oh, my God," he exclaimed after hanging up the phone.

"What is it?"

"Erika. She's here."

"Here?"

"She's at the airport, but she's coming here."

"Here? To this apartment?"

Leigh gasped, looking to the chair where she had placed her clothing. "Why is she coming here?"

"I don't know. I didn't ask . . ." Jamie turned suddenly to Leigh. "I was half-asleep. I didn't think . . ."

"I have to go," she cried, feeling self-consciously aware of her nakedness as she leapt out of bed and grabbed her clothes on her way to the bathroom.

"I'm sorry, honey, I feel rotten about this," Jamie apologized as Leigh returned to gather her few remaining articles and toss them into her bag.

"I do too," she answered, bitter and humiliated. "I feel worse than rotten. I feel—cheap!"

"There's no reason to."

"Maybe not," Leigh sighed. "But that's the way I feel."

"I don't know why she's here, but she won't stay. She made that abundantly clear before I ever met you," Jamie explained soothingly. "This doesn't have to change anything."

"Things have already changed! I don't know why, Jamie, but the whole world seems changed in the last few weeks. *Nothing* is simple and uncomplicated anymore."

Jamie moved to comfort her, but stopped as both their heads turned toward the sound of the elevator arriving at his floor.

"It couldn't be her," he said, shaking off his apprehension. "She couldn't be here this soon."

Leigh waited until she heard a neighboring door close before she moved to open Jamie's. "I'm sorry, Jamie," she said huskily. "Maybe I'm reacting like a child. It's probably because this is all so new to me and it's happening so fast. Call me later. I'll be better when I've had some time to think."

◈ Jamie had just finished remaking his bed when he looked down to the street from his apartment window to recognize Erika's slim, long legs as they unfolded from the open taxi door. He could feel his heart throbbing in his chest as he watched beautiful Erika pay the driver, pause for a moment to gaze up at the facade of his apartment building, and then disappear inside the building's foyer with a small suitcase. In another minute the apartment bell rang from downstairs.

He gulped the cold remains from his coffee cup and pushed the button releasing the downstairs door lock.

At least Bucky isn't with her, he thought as he went to refill his cup.

The strain of her emotions showed through the smile on her classically chiseled features as Erika stepped hesitantly into the apartment, apologizing for her unexpected visit.

"Not even I knew I was coming until last night," she explained, noting Jamie's uncertainty about where to put her suitcase. He was also going out of his way to be polite. "But I've been obsessed with only one thought since you called to tell me the filming of your commercial was canceled: What is going to happen to us?"

"I've been thinking about that myself," Jamie responded, disconcerted by her directi.ess.

"And I knew that whatever we had to say would be better said face-to-face. So when I heard on the television it was the last day for the special half-price airline flights, I asked Mrs. Gannon to stay with Bucky, packed my bag, and went to the airport. I don't know exactly what I want to say, but I knew the time has come to say something."

"You must be tired," Jamie stalled. "Do you want to take a shower or have some food?"

"Yes, but not now," she answered, not to be dissuaded. "Now, if you don't mind, I'd like to talk about what I am going to do with the rest of my life. What am I—or we—going to do about our son? And what about us?"

"What do *you* want?"

"I'm asking *you.* I know about your pride. I know how my thing with Tony Mitchell must have hurt you. And I'm profoundly sorry. If you want a divorce . . . I'll understand."

Look, Erika," Jamie spoke slowly, trying to form his thoughts. "It isn't just Tony Mitchell . . ."

"There haven't been any others," she asserted. "There have been times when I let you think there were, but that was only because of . . . of what you were doing."

Jamie's eyes reflected his skepticism as he looked at Erika while drinking from his cup.

"You don't have to believe me, but it is the truth."

"If I do or I don't, that isn't what I was talking about."

"Then what is?" she asked softly.

"Lots of things."

"Tell me."

"A lot of little things," he faltered. "Which may sound stupid when you talk about them individually, but when you add them up . . ."

Jamie decided to plunge ahead, knowing full well she wouldn't let up without an answer. "Like your goddamn attitude. You never gave a shit about 'Slim Chisholm,' or anything else I ever did. And out of all those pictures I made while we were in Europe, I can't remember *one* that you had anything good to say about."

"That isn't true."

"All right, then, which one?"

"What about that first film you made in France, *La Chasse?* I told you many times how I loved it."

"Okay," he conceded. "So out of more than thirty films you liked *one*. And how about 'Yesterday's Children'? You haven't said a single word about it. Being married to a soap actor may be embarrassing to you and your hotshot Polo Lounge crowd of superstars, but surprising as it may sound, there are still people in this world who think Jamie Starbuck is important!"

"What about the way you've regarded *my* career?" Erika retorted, her eyes flashing. "How much encouragement have you given to me? You've *had* a career. You've been a big star in films *and* television. You know what it's like. What's wrong with my wanting a little taste of it too? *You're* the one who's had nothing good to say, Jamie. Perhaps I wasn't very good in 'Mata Hari,' but that was *years* ago. I've learned a great deal since then. How do you think it felt to me when everything I tried was 'stupid' and 'a waste of time' to my big-star husband? Perhaps I haven't fawned over your successes, but what support have you given me in my failures? Don't you understand how embarrassed and hurt I was by 'Mata Hari'? And how much I've sacrificed all these years for another chance? I appreciate that it hasn't been easy for *you*, but in spite of everything, you've had the satisfaction of knowing you've *been* there. What kind of satisfaction do you think I get from knowing all my sacrifices—my pride, my husband, my hopes for a normal family—have all been for nothing? Have you ever taken the time to think about that, Jamie?"

Jamie took a heavy breath and shook his head pensively. "No. I guess I haven't."

"Then what makes you think it would be different with a *new* wife?" Erika drove her point home. "This young girl you're with. Is her career any less 'stupid' or 'a waste of time' than mine was? Or is she so much in love with you, she's willing to give it up?"

"Look, Erika," Jamie shrugged confusedly. "This is pretty heavy stuff for so early in the morning. I can't give you any clear answers without some time to think about it."

"Very well," she replied, gripping her hands tightly in her lap. "And while you're thinking, consider that I've already thought about it and I've realized that I *am*. If it's not too late."

"You are, what?"

Erika gazed into his eyes. "Willing to give it up . . . To forget show business and start a new career . . . at home, with you and Bucky."

"Dammit, Erika," Jamie spoke, getting to his feet and pacing aimlessly around the room. "Why didn't this happen five years ago . . . or even five months?"

"I understand, Jamie," she conceded with a forced smile.

"I wish *I* did," he reacted perplexedly. "Look, you're probably tired. Why don't you go in the bedroom and get some sleep? I think I'll go to the Y and run or something. You've hit me with so much that I really need a few hours to sort it out."

"Yes, I am tired. I was too nervous to sleep on the plane."

Erika stood by the window, watching until Jamie walked out of sight down the street. She leaned her head against the sill, exhausted, uncertain—but grateful that he had agreed to think about what she had said.

◈ Leigh walked the streets for what seemed like hours until she found herself in front of the apartment Mindy had sublet from Stanley.

She rang the bell, then glanced at her watch to reason that Mindy must have already gone to work. Not wishing to go home, Leigh rummaged through her bag for Mindy's extra key and let herself in. She curled up in a corner of the sofa, studying the phone, wondering if Jamie had tried to call her. When she could no longer stand not knowing, she dialed her answering service.

There was no word from Jamie but there was a message from her agent and one from Neil. He had arrived in town last night and could be reached this morning at Slippery Rock.

It was too early to call the agency, so she dialed the number Neil had left instead. "Neil," she cried happily when Federated TV's switchboard operator finally located his extension number.

"Hi, cutie. How are you?"

"I'm okay," she allowed. "Why are you back in New York so soon?"

"I'm here with George Conley. I'm going to be directing some episodes of 'Fort Worth' and he brought me with him to help with some casting problems." Neil lowered his voice and raised his hand to the telephone's mouthpiece. "The main reason I came was to help Eddie finish packing and hurry his butt out to California. I'll tell you everything when I see you."

"I'm dying to see you too, Neil," she said with more significance than she intended. "When can I?"

"Are you all right?" he asked, discerning the tension in her voice. "I hope you aren't too upset about *Philadelphia Story.* I don't think you'd like the new script, anyhow."

"New script?" She was at once apprehensive.

"Yeah, it's the pits. The original's a classic. They're nuts to try and modernize it. You may be disappointed now, but when you see it on the tube, I know you'll be glad you didn't do it."

Leigh tried to think of a lighthearted response but could answer only with silence.

"Leigh? Oh, shit," Neil groaned. "Don't tell me you didn't know!"

"No . . . I . . . When did you find out?"

"Yesterday . . . before we left. It's in this morning's *Variety.*"

"It said I didn't get the part?"

"Not exactly. *Variety* merely mentioned that Kate Miller did."

"Oh. There was a message from my agent, but I haven't called him back yet." Leigh slowly shook her head as she remembered how brazenly Kate Miller had courted Rob Weber at Tanya Prinz's party. "I thought she might get the part. She worked hard enough for it."

"I saw the tests," Neil argued. "Yours was much better!"

"That isn't what I meant," Leigh reacted glumly.

"I know," he agreed. "But remember what I said. You wouldn't want to do it anyway. The new script is so much different from the original, they could call it the Palm Springs story!"

"Really?"

"Trust me, cutie. Listen, I have to go. Are you working tomorrow?"

"No."

"Let's meet for an early lunch and talk about everything."

"Yes, we'll talk," she answered, delaying her tears until she hung up the phone.

◈ Jamie let himself into the apartment and crept softly to the bedroom door where he could see that Erika was still asleep.

He looked from his watch to the telephone. He had to call Leigh. She must be waiting to hear from him, but what should he say? He glanced toward the bedroom. There was a lot of painful truth in what Erika had said. She was so much like Leigh when they had started out together—fresh, wholesome, perky, and sexy as hell. A young, blonde Teutonic goddess. And when Erika was Leigh's age she had the spirit of a thoroughbred. Not even those terrible reviews of "Mata Hari" could bring her down for very long. Her vulnerability to criticism came later, when she realized no one would forget those reviews.

It was one of the facts of show business; so often the only performance you're remembered by is the worst one you've ever given.

The more he thought about the two women, the sharper was the realization that in Leigh he perceived Erika as she was during their early years together. Was he unconsciously trying to relive his life through Leigh, using her to turn back the clock to the time when he was young, vital, and successful?"

Jamie found himself gazing at Leigh's apron, which was still draped across the back of the chair where she dropped it. But in spite of everything he felt he still loved Leigh. Or did he? Could it be that what he was feeling was an infatuation with his *own past?*

Jamie walked to the window, unnerved by the thoughts that were jarring his consciousness. "Aw hell," he groaned unhappily. "Don't tell me I'm just another middle-aged fool who's chasing his lost youth."

◈ Feeling the unconscious need of a warm rejuvenating soak in her own bathtub, Leigh's aimless wandering brought her home. She let herself into the apartment and was immediately struck by the sound of voices from the living room. She stopped when she heard the voices moving in her direction.

"Mom!" she cried, as Nancy, followed by two unfamiliar men, stepped into the foyer. "You're here!"

"Leigh, darling," she replied, taking her daughter in her arms. "I was going to call you, but Professor Winston and his son, Stephen, offered me a ride in their foundation's jet, so here I am."

Leigh took notice of the men whose casual dress and tanned, weathered skin suggested a preference for the outdoors. She politely offered her hand to the robust, bearded professor and his tall, studiously handsome son, then returned her attention to Nancy. "I thought you were still on your cruise."

"I decided I'd rather be here," she smiled and placed her arm around Leigh's waist.

Leigh ignored Stephen's shy but obvious interest in her as his father said good-bye to Nancy and confirmed their appointment for lunch later that week.

After the men left, Nancy led Leigh into the living room and sat beside her on the sofa.

She clasped her daughter's hands in her own and gazed at her with fond affection. "There was a conversation we had while I was in the hospital that won't stop picking at my mind," she began softly. "It was about *experience*. From what I've heard, you've been having more than your share recently."

Leigh dropped her gaze to her hands, which were tightly entwined in her mother's. "What have you heard?"

"More than I cared to, and probably less than I should know about," Nancy smiled. "I think it's time for us to have an honest talk."

"All right, Mother . . ." Leigh's expression was gloomy but determined as she looked up into Nancy's eyes. "But I also have something running around my mind that I'd like to have an honest talk about."

"What's that, dear?"

"The problem between Dad and Jamie."

"Very well," Nancy sighed. "I'll tell you whatever you want to know . . . But first, I want to hear about *you*."

◈ Cathy and Marnie sat making notes while watching dress rehearsal on the monitor in Cathy's office.

"It isn't working," Cathy contemplated a scene between Joyce and Bruce Parsa, the actor who replaced Stanley, as it came to an end. "What do you think is wrong?"

"I don't know," Marnie answered. "Joyce seems unsure of herself, as though she hasn't learned her lines."

"That isn't like Joyce. Make a note to ask Vico," Cathy instructed, as the television screen dissolved from blackness to a large, soulful image of Liz's face.

Liz's expression of grief was uncomfortably real. Now the previously taped seduction scene with Jamie was gradually superimposed over her close-up.

"Damn her," Cathy growled when at the end of the scene Liz began weeping wretchedly. "She's not supposed to cry. She's supposed to be happy when she thinks of Jamie!"

"I heard Vico explain that to her during rehearsal this morning."

"Just because she's the best whiner in television she thinks she can get away with it," Cathy snapped. "I'll have to talk to her again. She doesn't realize things have to change around here."

"We're a little long," Marnie said as the rehearsal ended and she consulted her stopwatch. "We may have to make some cuts."

"I'd like to start with Liz's throat," Cathy turned away from the television. "You've talked to the hairdresser, haven't you?"

"Yes. She's staying to do you right after taping."

"Good," Cathy replied, then reached to pick up her buzzing intercom line. "Who?" she paled. "Yes, of course, have her come in."

She took a deep breath to compose herself. "We'll finish later, Marnie. Pam Godfrey's here."

Pam returned Marnie's greeting, then looked with quiet appraisal around the small office.

"This *is* a pleasure," Cathy gushed, closing the door behind Marnie.

"Not really," Pam replied, taking the seat in front of Cathy's desk. "In fact, it's quite difficult."

"What?" Cathy asked, her elation suddenly vanishing. "What is it?"

"I just this minute came from a programming meeting with our new president." Pam's gaze went from a photograph on the wall of the current cast to her neatly manicured hands in her lap. " 'Yesterday's Children' has been dropped from the network's daytime schedule."

"Dropped?" Cathy echoed in utter dismay and disbelief. "That doesn't make sense! I realize things have been bad, but not *that* bad. Not bad enough to drop us! Why, Pam? Tell me why?"

"First of all," Pam answered supportively, "it has nothing to do with you. You and everyone connected with the show have been marvelous. The recent problems, the bad publicity and everything were only minor considerations. The main problem is your half-hour format. When 'Yesterday's Children' began, *all* the shows were half-hour: 'The Guiding Light,' 'General Hospital.' Then one by one, they changed to full hours. The bottom line: an hour show is cheaper to produce than two separate half-hour shows, and the viewers seem to get more involved in them."

"That's no reason to drop 'Yesterday's Children.' We could become an hour show!"

"I know," Pam admitted patiently. "But we had to make a choice. It was between you and 'Eternal Spring.' And what it got right down to was studio space. An hour show needs almost twice as much studio space, which we simply don't have here in New York. 'Eternal Spring' is done out on the Coast where we do have the space."

Cathy stood slowly shaking her head despairingly, watching her dreams of personal grandeur go up in smoke. "It doesn't seem fair . . . all the work and effort. And it's all discarded because of *space?* I'm sorry, Pam," she apologized, falling into her chair.

"I understand," Pam nodded. "I'm sorry too."

"How long do we have? How many more shows to wrap things up?"

"Well," Pam hedged. "The hour version of 'Eternal Spring' will start a week from Monday. With today's show, we'll have enough 'Yesterday's Children' to carry us through next Friday, so . . ."

"You're not saying today's is the last show we tape?"

"I'm afraid I am."

"But you can't," Cathy protested. "We have scripts, contracts!"

"They'll be paid off, or if they're willing to relocate, two or three of the actors as well as a few of the staff, like Vico Fellouris, will be offered contracts with 'Eternal Spring.' "

"What about me?" Cathy asked, overcoming her reticence.

"We'll talk about that tonight at dinner," Pam smiled vaguely. "I have a thought that might be interesting for you."

CHAPTER

34

"One day!" Chris Knight squawked as he walked away from the group Cathy had called together on the set after taping. "I had a running part on a Daytime serial for *one day.* How is that going to look on my résumé?"

"I only had *two* days," Bruce Parsa said, falling in step with Chris. "But at least it was work which, with this show folding, there'll be even less of here in New York."

"Jesus, you're right," Chris exclaimed with a jolt. "I'd better get over to Kerry's before they give my job to someone else. I'm going to be needing it."

"Wait a minute," Joyce called, coming up behind. "If you're going to Kerry's, I'll come too and buy you boys a drink. I hate losing the show, but I've been here long enough that they have to pay off my contract, so I'm celebrating. For the first time in years, this girl can afford to go home for Christmas!"

Liz maintained her facade of the reliable mother of 'Yesterday's Children' as the longtime regulars in the cast and crew expressed their shock and sadness.

"What a rotten business," Vico growled. "They take a part of history and just throw it away like an old script. We were the last show in Daytime with any class. Who else tried to

259

shoot from start to finish, like in the good old days of live television?" He put his arm around Liz's shoulder. "Come on, honey. Let's go where they're honest about cheating us. Let's go to Kerry's."

"No, thank you, dear," she smiled with a fragile serenity. "I have an engagement for dinner later. I think I'll stay here for a while."

Liz accepted a tearful embrace from the wardrobe mistress, brushed aside Sy Cohen's request for a meeting with the press, and stoically walked away as Cathy repeated Pam's proposal that she keep Jennifer Wells's character alive in 'Eternal Spring.'

There's no Webster University in California, she thought, as she sat looking at herself in her dressing room mirror. There's *nothing* in California. All my friends, my colleagues, my students, they were all here. All here at Webster.

She changed her clothes and freshened her makeup, consciously avoiding the lifetime of mementos displayed around the dressing room's walls.

Perhaps Shirley Hanna and Elliot Harrison were right. Perhaps she should transfer to Norwood University. Teaching was what she had always felt she should be doing.

Liz glanced in the mirror to give herself a sly smile. *I'm glad I accepted this dinner with Elliot tonight. It could be the perfect opportunity. And the best part is, I'll be able to get away from that lecherous Jamie Starbuck.*

◈ Nancy returned from the kitchen carrying tea service for two on a silver tray. She moved with a false composure, trying not to display the anguish she felt for her only child. *This isn't what I had hoped and planned for her,* she thought. *I wanted Leigh's life to be a joyful, painless experience. I wanted . . .* Leigh's expectant expression gave her pause. *I definitely* did not *want to tell her about Russell and . . .*

"Thanks, Mom," Leigh voiced as she watched Nancy set down the tray and begin to pour the tea.

After an uneasy moment, Leigh cleared her throat, then forged ahead with a resolve that Nancy knew would not be put aside. "Now it's my turn . . . Was it another woman?"

Nancy raised her hand to the back of her neck, as though trying to rub away an ancient pain. "Not entirely . . ."

"Erika?"

"Yes . . . partially."

"You promised to tell me."

"I will. That's what I'm doing . . ." Nancy sagged down onto the sofa and gave a slow stir to the tea in her cup. "Yes, he was having an affair with Erika. It had been going on for some time. If I'd been stronger, if I'd confronted him then, in the beginning, we might have . . ."

Nancy stopped stirring, but her gaze remained on the spoon in her cup. "By the time he broke up with Erika—or rather when she left him for Jamie—it was too late. You see, like it or not, marriage is based on trust. And we no longer trusted each other."

"Each other?" Leigh asked. "Why didn't he trust *you?* You didn't do anything."

"No, but he thought I did." She lifted the cup to her lips and took a slow, tasteless sip. "In the beginning I let him believe it out of revenge. Then, as time passed, the truth became irrelevant."

"I don't understand. How can the truth become irrelevant?"

"The damage had been done. The truth became irrelevant when it didn't matter any longer."

Leigh frowned in confusion. "You said he didn't trust you because he thought you did something. What?"

The color rose slightly to Nancy's cheek as she replaced the cup in its saucer and turned to her daughter. "He thought I was having an affair with Jamie too."

Leigh's eye widened and she sprang suddenly erect in the sofa. *"You?"*

"It wasn't true of course, but . . ." Nancy glanced away,

embarrassed. "Let me see. How can I explain? Your father began life with everything possible—except the chance of ever equaling the accomplishments of *his* father and grandfather. That's probably what led him to television. He was part of a group that came right out of Princeton and became an immediate sensation by bringing important literary works to live television."

Leigh waited impatiently for Nancy to get to the part she did not already know.

"As a member of that dynamic young group, he could do no wrong. But when he accepted the offer to go to Hollywood— on his own—things changed."

Leigh's expression made it clear to Nancy that she would not be able to avoid the issue by talking around it.

"The studio system. The networks," she continued. "The entire concept of life out there was completely foreign to him."

"Where did you fit in?"

"Where did I fit in?" Nancy echoed. "I don't know if I ever did. We married immediately after graduation. I was interested in fabric design, but you came along, and Russell's career demanded so much of our time . . .

He wasn't prepared for failure. No Fisk in living memory had ever failed at anything, least of all your father."

"I don't handle it very well myself," Leigh nodded with dry irony.

Nancy went on, almost as though she hadn't heard Leigh's comment. "He kept it all inside, pretending that he was right and would be vindicated as soon as the public had time to understand his vision. Justifying that vision took over his life. So . . . I had to find my own. I had you, and tennis, and I revived my interest in the fabric business. 'Mata Hari' was Russell's creation and his last desperate hope."

Nancy took her cup and drifted to the carved marble mantlepiece over the dark, empty fireplace, where she stood with her back to Leigh. "Unfortunately, he became trapped in the mystique he created around his leading lady. Erika was an exotic, foreign beauty who completely captured his imagination."

She turned, lifted her chin, then continued flatly. "I didn't discover they were sleeping together until later. At first I wouldn't believe it . . . Then I tried to ignore it. Then I had to prove it for myself.

"One night I drove by her house and saw his little green MG parked in front. He was with her. I couldn't believe it when I saw him through the window, but I didn't know what to do . . . I drove around until I got control of myself. And then I went home."

Nancy paused reflectively. "I pretended to be asleep when he came home late that night, and when he left early the next morning."

She paused again. "I suffered through the next day, blaming myself . . . until my self-pity slowly turned into anger. Then, that night I went back to her house. His car was nowhere in sight, but by that time I was so furious that I was certain he had hidden it, parked it somewhere up the street. I sat for an hour or two, staring at the shaded bedroom window. Then I must have lost my mind, because I jumped out of my car, forced my way into the house, and flew into the bedroom where I discovered Erika and *Jamie* sitting on her bed playing cards."

Leigh made a move to leave the sofa and come to her mother's side, but Nancy stopped her with a restraining motion of her hand. "No," she said. "Stay there until I finish."

Leigh sat back down and Nancy resumed telling her burdensome story. "You can imagine how shocked and humiliated I was. I collapsed in a flood of tears. Erika and Jamie tried to comfort me, but I was so mortified that I couldn't move. I was clearly in no condition to drive, so they insisted that Jamie take me home, which he did . . .

Jamie walked with me to our front door. He held me a moment until I was steady enough to go inside, and then he left. We didn't notice, but your father had come home just in time to see us at the door."

"Oh, no," Leigh gasped.

"Oh, yes," Nancy nodded bleakly. "Oh, *yes!* I was lying across the bed when Russell burst into our room. My disheveled appearance and his own feelings of guilt must have confirmed his worst suspicions: He knew Jamie was sleeping with his mistress, and now he believed that he was also sleeping with his wife!"

"Mom, that's terrible!"

"Perhaps," she replied, maintaining her cool but fragile facade. "But I refused to respond to his accusations. He could think what he wanted. Letting him live with his imagination was the most effective revenge of all."

"And you never told him the truth?"

"No. I thought about it, but I'd let too much time go by. It was too late. As I said, it had become irrelevant."

"And now me, his daughter," Leigh cried as she swiftly rose from the sofa and moved to Nancy's side. "No wonder Dad hates Jamie so much!"

"And Jamie hates your father because of 'Slim Chisholm.' Jamie *was* Slim Chisholm. He would have been happy to play that role for the rest of his life."

"Jamie doesn't hate . . ."

"Don't be so sure," Nancy gently interrupted. "It's part of our defensive mechanism to block those emotions. They're too painful to live with for very long."

◈ Elliot Harrison's evening with Liz was definitely not going well. Although her shock over the show being canceled was understandable, he had to struggle to find the sense in her fragmented conversation.

"You drink vodka, do you not?" he asked as they were seated at their table in the Plaza Hotel's busy Oak Bar.

"No. Gin and lemon soda," she reacted with a crooked smile. "That's Dr. Bayard's tonic for delicate ladies."

"I don't believe I know Dr. Bayard."

"No," she responded sadly. "How could you? He left before . . ."

"Oh," Elliot nodded knowingly, then turned as the waiter arrived.

"You're Jennifer Wells, aren't you?" the waiter beamed. "I watch you every day before I come to work. That's pretty hot stuff you're getting into with that Spencer guy."

"It isn't at all as it appears," Liz reacted stiffly. "He has quite a surprise coming."

"My money's on you," the waiter winked before leaving. "Keep up the good work."

"I can only imagine how difficult it must be for you," Elliot put a comforting hand on her arm. "After all those years."

"It's been such a responsibility," she concurred. "You have no idea how everyone depends on me. Even in my personal life I've had to set an example they could rely on. That's why when Spencer returns from Boston, things are going to be entirely different."

"Oh? Are they going to resolve that situation? I thought I understood your housekeeper to say how unhappy she is because the stories aren't to be concluded."

"This one is."

Elliot breathed a wary sigh. "I see. Look, if you're not feeling well," he spoke solicitously, "we can discuss your coming to Norwood another night."

"Discuss *what?*" she reacted sharply.

"Nothing important." He tried to sooth her by lightly patting her arm as the waiter set down their drinks.

"Is this all part of some plan to ruin Webster?" she shrilled, jerking away her arm.

"No," he smiled nervously at the waiter, who discreetly ducked away from the table. "It's just a mistake. Perhaps we should go home." He was actually alarmed. He couldn't tell if she was drunk or having a nervous breakdown, or both. Nevertheless, she was coming apart before his very eyes.

Liz eyed Elliot suspiciously as she took a drink from her

glass, then abruptly put it down and pushed it to one side. Her eyes appeared to glaze as she continued to stare at him. "No, you don't, Spencer Franklyn! That's how you did it last time. All your liquor and romantic talk! You almost destroyed me, Spencer! You're not going to do it again!"

Conversation at the surrounding tables stopped as Elliot got to his feet and gently tried to lift Liz from her chair.

"Take your hands off me!" she screamed, pulling free from his grasp. "You think you're so great! You think you're such a fantastic lover! You didn't seduce me. I seduced you! I did it for the school! I'd do anything for the school and you're not going to take it away from me!"

Elliot looked helplessly to the onlookers for assistance, but no one moved. "We don't need you!" She stumbled away, surrendering totally to her hysteria. "We don't need your money or your demographics or your studio space or *anything!*"

A path opened through the tittering crowd as Liz staggered toward the door with Elliot protectively following as closely as possible.

"He raped me," she cried to the spectators. "He said it was for the ratings, but it was really for that little queer. You all know I wouldn't do anything like that!"

As she turned to flee out the door she was confronted by a large, uniformed policeman.

She peered intently into his face, then with an agonizing cry for help, she collapsed into his arms.

◈ *She's everything I've always wanted to be,* Cathy reflected as she sat across the table from Pam Godfrey, dawdling over her after-dinner coffee in the posh atmosphere of Le Cygne restaurant. *She's attractive, but not so much that she can't get along with women as well as men. She's intelligent, graceful, successful. She's only about ten years older than I am and she has it all!*

"So you see," Pam's voice penetrated Cathy's thoughts. "It will help if we can blend Liz's character into the 'Eternal Spring' story line, even if it's only for the first few months. It'll help the audience to identify with the expanded time slot and lighten their criticism over the cancellation, especially if we continue this romance we've started between her and Jamie Starbuck."

"She isn't too happy about that romance," Cathy let out. "I think it embarrasses her, probably because she's played the part too long. She was telling me she thought they should get married."

"That might not be a bad idea," Pam sparked. "A 'Yesterday's Children' wedding on 'Eternal Spring.' Leigh Fisk can be the bridesmaid; then we can ease her into a love affair with young Ron Joy from 'Eternal Spring.' It would be a perfect marriage all around. It's a terrific idea, Cathy. Thanks a bunch."

"Well," she replied modestly, "you're the one who really worked it out."

"*You're* married, aren't you?" Pam smoothly changed the subject.

"Yes," Cathy faltered. "But . . . well . . ."

"You're married, 'but', 'well'," Pam laughed. "I know the condition exactly. I was in a similar circumstance while I was still in college. Fortunately, he was drafted into the army before we were actually married so we were spared the agony of divorce."

"That was the only time?"

"And it was enough," Pam nodded. "The mystique of wedded bliss has eluded me ever since. I'm too ambitious and singleminded to complicate my life with a man."

"I'm beginning to feel the same way," Cathy confessed ruefully. "We get along, but he wants a *Ladies Home Journal* kind of wife, not one whose career is just as important as his.

Not one who doesn't want children. After all, raising children didn't seem to do very much for Joan Crawford."

"Isn't that the truth," Pam sniffed. "You give them your life's blood and they turn on you. No, I'm happy the way I am. Where is your husband? What does he do?"

"He is in advertising. They're in Europe now, shooting a commercial."

"I'm sure you realize I've been watching you," Pam said, reaching across the table to take Cathy's hand. "And testing you. I don't know how you feel, but I think you would do very well on the executive side of the business. In many ways it's far more creative than production."

Cathy did not know how to react to Pam's firm handclasp. "Well . . . to tell the truth, my real ambition has been to become part of the executive staff at Federated. It's been my goal since . . ."

"How would you like to work for me?" Pam interrupted. "As my assistant? It isn't the most important job at Slippery Rock, but it's how I started at CBS."

"I hope you're not kidding," Cathy gushed. "Because I can't think of *anything* I'd rather do!"

"Then it's settled," Pam answered, boldly pressing her knee against Cathy's thigh. "What do you say we go somewhere and have a bottle of champagne to celebrate?"

Oh, my God! Cathy thought with ironic dismay. *How far ahead do I have to get in this business before I can begin screwing who and when I want to??*

CHAPTER

35

Sam stepped out of the Pan Am customs section of JFK Airport to be immediately accosted by Aaron Roth's uniformed chauffeur.

The chauffeur explained that Mr. Roth had originally hoped for Sam to come by the office on his way home, but because of the plane's late arrival he would appreciate Sam stopping a few minutes at his Manhattan apartment.

Sam expressed his regrets to the chauffeur for making him wait the more than three hours the plane was late, then settled into silent speculation as the long black limousine sped through the winter's night.

"Come in," Papa Roth waved his big cigar, gesturing for Sam to follow as he padded on slippered feet to his study.

He guided Sam to an old leather chair in front of the marble fireplace, sitting down opposite him. "The girl is bringing some chicken and a little wine. I thought you might be hungry."

"Thank you, sir," Sam responded. "It's been a while since I've eaten."

"Have you talked to your wife?"

"No. I called from the airport, but she wasn't home."

"Working women," Roth grumbled. "They're *never* home.

And they're never satisfied. That's why I don't have them around."

Sam nodded in cautious agreement, impatient to hear why he had been summoned.

"Then you haven't heard the news," Roth continued. "They take away all an old man's pleasures. First my favorite food, then my brandy. Lately they've been after my cigars . . ." He paused to savor a long puff. "And the bimbos . . ." Ha! That's so long ago I don't even remember."

"And now," his pudgy face sagged. "They've taken away my favorite television. 'Yesterday's Children' is going off the television."

"What? When did you hear that?"

"A few hours ago. Devon's happy because now the cowboy will be free to make your commercials, and you'll be happy because your wife'll be home where she belongs. *I'm* the only one who's not happy. Me and the other poor schmucks who have our lunch every day while we watch the story. It makes you wonder what's left to live for."

"Cathy must be a basket case," Sam breathed heavily.

"If it wasn't for Devon, I think I'd join Sarah in my grave right now. But Sarah would never let me rest, knowing I'd left our little Ruth at his mercy. I have to arrange things first, that's why I wanted to see you . . ."

Roth stopped as an elderly housekeeper brought in the bland supper she had prepared. She served each of the men on a small table next to their chairs and before leaving she cautioned Sam not to let Mr. Roth sneak any of his wine.

The blandness of the food did nothing to improve the old man's disposition and it took some minutes for him to return to the subject in discussion. "Devon's a good boy," he spoke slowly. "The trouble is, sometimes when he gets out of town he forgets to mind his business. Chasing the bimbos is okay after business is done. Even I did that—and nobody loved his wife more than me. But it has to be *after* the business is done. This advertising company. These commercials. There's too much traveling. Too many temptations for a man like Devon.

So I've decided to take him out of that—keep him here, next to me—train him to take over when I'm gone. You're a good man, Sam. I believe you could have finished the Saddle commercials over there. I believe you can run the agency *and* the Saddle campaign by *yourself.* What do you think?"

"Well," Sam hesitated while trying to decide what he actually did think. "I believe I should discuss it first with Devon."

"It was Devon who *put* the idea to me. He says there's no one better for the job."

"Devon said that?" Sam felt a sudden flow of affection for Devon.

"And when I told him about 'Yesterday's Children,' he suggested you hire the cowboy to work for Saddle, full time. Kind of like Cary Grant did some years ago for Faberge. Be a permanent representative of the company in addition to doing the commercials."

"Full time," Sam ruminated. "That means he'd have to give up acting."

"He'd still be acting. We're all actors, Sammy. He'll just be acting on a different stage, without a camera."

"There's no doubt that it's a good idea," Sam nodded. "I know from experience what a help he was to me. The question is, does he want to change careers at this point in his life?"

"You won't know until you talk to him."

"That's right," Sam agreed. "And as for myself, I'd like to talk to Devon before I make up my mind."

"He lives around the corner. Why don't you talk to him now? I'm getting too old to have much patience waiting for decisions."

"Do you think he's home?"

"He's home and waiting for you."

"You know something, Mr. Roth," Sam said. "Working for you would probably be the greatest learning experience a man could have."

"Call me Papa. And take a cigar from the humidor over there."

◈ Sam slumped with fatigue as the elevator carried him up to his floor, where he wearily pushed his suitcases to his apartment door.

The light in the kitchen was the only one he noticed as he stepped through the entry. Then, deciding to discover whether Cathy was asleep or still out, he left the door propped open with his luggage and crept quietly toward the bedroom.

Moans of sexual delight filtered from the bedroom before he made out the figures of two glistening bodies passionately entangled on his bed. Rather than rage, his first impulse was to silently retrace his steps back to the front door and flee into the night. He felt humiliated, rejected, betrayed. Then the anger hit him like a bursting dam. Some bastard was screwing *his* wife in *his* bed!

He dropped his suitcase on the floor, slammed the door, and stomped back into the bedroom.

"Who the hell is *that?*" he yelled at the sight of Pam Godfrey's unmistakably feminine figure as she dashed into the bathroom.

"That . . . that's my friend," Cathy stammered, fearfully pulling the bedsheet up under her chin. "She's sleeping over . . . What's wrong with having a friend sleep over? I didn't know you were coming home! Why didn't you call?"

"Don't try to give me that crap, Cathy," Sam's voice cracked in full fury now. "It won't work this time! I saw you two in action! Jesus Christ! I knew something was wrong between us, but I didn't think it was because you're a goddamn dyke!"

"I'm not!" Cathy cried. "You don't understand . . ."

"I understand what I saw and I'll be damned if I'm going to put up with it!"

Sam strode to the bathroom door. "Come out, you sonofabitch! Come out before I bust the door down and drag you out!"

"Stop it!" Cathy screamed. "You don't know who that is. You can't treat her like this!"

"I can't?" Sam challenged. "Just watch me!"

"Wait," Pam's voice sounded from behind the door. "There's no need for violence. I'm coming out."

Sam controlled himself as Pam cautiously opened the door. When he saw she had wrapped herself in his favorite bathrobe, he nearly went mad with anger. "You may be man enough to fuck my wife, but you're not man enough to wear my clothes," he bellowed as he seized Pam by the lapels of his robe and dragged her to the front door.

He roughly jerked her around, stripped her out of the robe, and shoved her into the hallway, locking the door behind her.

"You can't do that!" Cathy beseeched as she scrambled out of the bedroom. "That's Pam Godfrey. She's a vice president! Don't you understand, Sam? You just can't treat her like that. What will happen to me?"

"Are you crazy?" Sam demanded. "I'm standing here so out of my mind that I could kill you and you're worried what *she* might do? She must be vice president of the whole *world*, for Christ's sake! What's wrong with you?"

"Please, Sam, please! Don't leave her out there with nothing to cover her body. No one will understand. It will be the end of all of us!"

"Wait a minute," Sam demanded. "How about if I give you a choice? How about if I give you a chance to stay here and maybe save our marriage—or take some clothes and go with her?"

"Can't I just take her something now, while we're talking?"

"If you go out that door, you're not coming back. Not ever!"

Cathy's indecisiveness lasted only for an instant before she broke for the bedroom to hastily retrieve the clothing she and Pam had discarded on their way to bed.

"I'll send for the rest of it," she called on her way to the door.

"You won't have to," he answered, moving to the window and pulling it open. "Your things will be in the street by the time you get there!"

CHAPTER

I'm never getting back to sleep, Jamie thought as he lay in the predawn darkness. He was still on European time. *It's 5:00 A.M. here so it must be 11:00 A.M. there. No wonder I can't sleep.*

A sanitation truck passing noisily in the street caused Erika to stir and move closer to Jamie.

With all that was on his mind, it was a miracle that he could sleep at all!

Oh, well, at least the money situation wasn't so bleak. It was quite a blow last night when Fred told him the show had been dropped. But things looked better when he pointed out that because he was available to finish the Saddle commercials, they would have to pay the full contract, whether they used him or not.

Then there was the possibility of keeping the Spencer Franklyn character alive opposite Liz's Jennifer Wells in 'Eternal Spring.' It would be perfect. They'd shoot in L.A. He could be home! *But what home?*

He wondered if it were true that Erika hadn't been sleeping around as much as he had thought. Was it possible she pretended only to make him jealous? If that were true, she was a better actress than she ever got credit for! *But she wasn't acting last night,* he reflected on his lovemaking with Erika a few hours earlier. *Last night was as good as it ever was . . .*

The warmth of Erika's presence ironically made him think of Leigh. *It's just as good with Leigh,* he reasoned unsurely. *And not only because she's young! She's warm and alive! She would never pretend in bed!* He glanced ruefully at his sleeping wife. *But neither would Erika when she was Leigh's age.*

Jamie rolled quietly out of bed, picked up his clothes, and scuffed out of the bedroom toward the kitchen.

He measured the proper amounts of coffee and water into the automatic machine, then decided not to turn it on until he returned from the Columbus Avenue newsstand with his morning paper.

The crisp winter air quickened Jamie's gait and sharpened his awareness of the tempting breakfast aromas wafting from the corner coffee shop.

It was nearly 8:00 when he returned to the apartment. The coffee was made and a radio was playing in the bedroom.

"Erika?" he called, tossing the paper on the table.

"Jamie," she replied, anxiously coming into the room. "Where have you been?"

"I went to get the paper and . . ."

"Sam Allison phoned," she interrupted. "He said to have you call him at the office as soon as you returned."

"At the office?" Jamie glanced at the clock. "I guess I'm not the only one with jet lag."

Erika set a fresh cup of coffee at Jamie's side as he dialed the direct number to Sam's office, then kissed him on the forehead and disappeared into the bedroom as Sam came on the line.

◆ "Hi cutie," Neil beamed after locating Leigh's table in the popular Dailey's Dandelion.

"Oh, Neil," she gushed, rising to give him an effusive hug. "I'm so glad to see you!"

Neil returned her embrace, then stepped back, glancing impishly from side to side. "You have to control yourself, honey," he cracked. "I'm practically a married man. We don't want people to talk!"

"Hollywood has made you more disgusting than ever," she chided as she returned to her chair.

"And I haven't directed my first show yet," he joked. "Wait till I'm a success, then I'll really be disgusting."

"No fooling, Neil," she smiled. "How are you doing out there?"

"No fooling? It's great. I've already been assigned to direct the third show of the series, and until the script is ready I'm working with George in production. I guess it hasn't been so great for you, though," he continued more seriously. "Losing the part in the movie and having 'Yesterday's Children' canceled all in the same week."

"You may not believe this," she answered wistfully, "but I'm so numb from everything else that's been happening that I was actually *relieved* to hear the show's been dropped. When you think of all the *real* tragedy and unhappiness that's going on, who cares? It isn't that important!"

"I guess you're right," Neil agreed. "And even more so now, with what's happened to Liz."

"What's happened to Liz?"

"You haven't heard?" Neil frowned. "It seems I bring you nothing but bad news. It's in the late morning papers. Liz flipped out. Apparently the show being canceled was too much for her. They had to carry her out of the Oak Bar at the Plaza last night, raving like a lunatic."

"Oh, no," Leigh exclaimed. "Where is she?"

"They locked her up in Bellevue."

"Isn't that where they put Zev Brahms?"

"Yeah, but she won't be where they keep the criminals."

"How bad is she?"

"They don't know yet, but it isn't good."

"What happened, Neil?" she sighed. "We used to be such a happy show. What made everything change?"

"I wish I knew. Times change. We change. We grow . . . or we don't. It isn't just the show, it's everything."

"You're telling me." She woefully shook her head. "Nothing is turning out the way I imagined . . . or hoped it would."

"Including you and Jamie?" he gently probed.

"I knew he was married and had a child," she spoke in a rush. "But they were too far away to be real. They were like characters in the show. Like Slim Chisholm and Mata Hari . . . Then I went to California and all of a sudden I was hit with reality. First the experience of the movie. Next, it was seeing Erika—then Bucky. I don't know why it was such a shock to see them as real live people, but it was."

Neil nodded sympathetically.

"I thought I could cope with even that, so long as they were there and we were here, but yesterday . . ."

"What happened yesterday?" he prodded.

Leigh lowered her gaze to the glove she was twisting in her lap. "First Jamie came back from Europe. Then, my mother . . ."

"Jamie's back?"

"Night before last," she explained. "The commercial's been postponed for the time being."

"That's very interesting," Neil remarked thoughtfully, then returned his attention to Leigh. "I'm sorry. What happened yesterday?"

"It was early in the morning . . . We were in bed when she arrived . . ."

"Erika?"

"Yes."

"She caught you in bed with Jamie?"

"Not exactly. She called from the airport. I was able to leave before she got to the apartment. Then this morning my agent called to see if I would be interested in going back to Hollywood to be in 'Eternal Spring' . . . with Jamie and Liz. That's when it struck me. I would never even have considered a relationship like this if I'd taken the time to think of the consequences. I even told Jamie—on our first night—I told him I didn't care about the future. That only now was important. Well, the future is here. And it *is* important! Why was I so blind to what should have been so obvious?"

"Don't worry about it, cutie," Neil smiled. "It only proves you're human. The question is, What are you going to do about it? Is Jamie leaving Erika, or what?"

"That's what I wanted to talk to you about. I don't *know* what to do. Although he's never come right out and said so, it's clear their marriage is over. But with all his other problems, I don't feel I can push him . . ."

"Probably not," Neil agreed.

"Then, there's my family. If I stay with Jamie, it will be the absolute end with my father."

"You're going to have to do *something*. This doesn't sound like a situation that can resolve itself."

"I wish I knew what," she agonized. "I've been thinking about it all morning. The only thing I'm sure of is that I'd like to take an eraser, go back to the beginning, and just wipe it all out—acting, Jamie, 'Yesterday's Children.' Everything!"

"Well, you can't do that," Neil tried to console her. "But you *can* benefit from the experience and start out fresh from right now."

"What do you mean?"

"You're young enough. If acting doesn't thrill you anymore, quit and do something else. The same with Jamie. As cynical as this may sound, you'll meet another man. You'll fall in love again. Look at me, I've been through dozens of them. All you have to do is decide what you really want."

"How do I make a decision like that when I don't *know* what I want?"

"You'll figure it out," Neil responded with confident assurance. "Underneath that scatter-brained masquerade you use so well is a real, whole person. I know you, cutie. You have good instincts. You'll figure it out."

◈   "Erika!" Jamie called before he saw her seated in front of the television.

"Erika, guess what, they want me to be an executive. It'll be a regular job just like normal people. I'll be a goodwill ambassador. I'll have to quite acting, except for the Saddle commercials, and only concentrate on selling men's toiletries. I'll represent the company at various promotions, sales meetings, conventions. Wherever they need me."

"Quit acting?" she reacted with indulgent skepticism. "Jamie, it's different for me, but it's all you've ever known. How can you quit?"

"I don't know," he shrugged. "I've been thinking for a long time that if something else came along, it might be time to quit. Why not?"

"You always talk like this when you don't have a job. Has something happened with 'Eternal Spring'?"

"I talked to Fred from Sam's office. They were interested in me if they could get Liz to carry our story line into the new show. It depended on *her* decision to do it or not. After what's happened to her, that decision may be a long time in coming." Jamie stopped as he noticed Erika's suitcase standing near the door. "Where are you going?"

"Home," she answered. "Unless you've made a decision."

"When?"

"In a few minutes," she looked at her watch. "I was waiting to explain."

"Oh, shit, Erika," he complained.

"It's all right. I understand it takes time to make important decisions. I have said everything I have to say. With my words and . . ." Erika paused to purse her lips. "And last night. That was also from my heart. I believe you will be less burdened in your thoughts without my presence. I love you, Jamie. I want you and me and Bucky to be a family. If you're willing, I'll spend the rest of our lives working to make it happen."

"Erika . . ."

"Don't, Jamie," she put her fingers to his lips and kissed him on the cheek. "Take your time . . . but not *too* long. You can imagine how anxious I'll be to hear your decision."

"At least call me when you get home," he pleaded.

"No, Jamie. *You* call *me* when you have something to say."

CHAPTER

Jamie's absorption in his personal problems disappeared when he returned to his apartment and found a message from George Conley on his answering machine.

He wondered what Conley wanted, knitting his brow as he reached for the phone.

"What a lucky break it is that Neil found out you're back," George explained when he came on the line. "I've got a part in my new show that's like it was written for you. And since I saw that stuff you did with Liz in 'Yesterday's Children,' no other actor is good enough for me!"

"What kind of a part?" Jamie reacted with feigned calm.

"It's a great part. Look, we start shooting next week so I don't have a lot of time for the usual games actors and producers play before they can get together. It's a nighttime soap called 'Fort Worth.' We're doing it in Hollywood at your old studio. Your part is one of the leads. Do you want to talk about it?"

Jamie's throat tightened with excitement. "Sure, I'll talk about it. When?"

"There's a couple of network people you'll have to see . . . Hold on a second."

Jamie unconsciously checked his image in the mirror while he waited.

"Come to my office at Slippery Rock in exactly two hours," George's crisp voice came back on the line. "Everyone will be here."

Jamie quickly dialed Fred Wald in Hollywood.

"Well, what about it?" Fred questioned after explaining that he had also received a call from Conley. "You're going to have to make up your mind. An hour ago you said you were going to quit acting to become a Saddle salesman."

"Who do you think you're kidding, Fred?" Jamie admonished. "When did you ever hear of an actor quitting when he had a job?"

"I just wanted to hear it from *you*," Fred laughed. "Call me after the meeting."

Two hours, Jamie thought impatiently, after replacing the receiver. *Erika shouldn't have left so soon. She'd feel a lot better if she knew . . .*

She wants to be a family again, he reflected. *And spend the rest of her life working to make it happen. She's talking about tomorrow while I've been trying to get back to yesterday . . .*

He sat down for a moment, then impulsively reached again for the phone and called Leigh. "Leigh, honey, I've got to see you," he blurted.

"Where's Erika?"

"Erika's gone." Jamie paused only for an instant. "Sorry if it sounds like I'm rushing things, but I think we've gone on long enough like this. Anyway, when I read my horoscope this morning, it said today's a good day to get things settled."

"Mine said the same thing," she replied decisively. "If you're free, I can see you now."

"Now?" Jamie wavered. "Sure. How about Rumpelmayers in fifteen minutes?"

"All right, Jamie . . . and thank you. I was hoping you'd call today."

It took Jamie less than ten minutes to walk the few short

blocks to Rumpelmayer's restaurant on Central Park South, but Leigh was already waiting when he arrived.

"I've been thinking," they said almost simultaneously after overcoming the first restrained moments.

"I'm going away," Leigh continued before Jamie recovered. "I need some time. Perhaps a lot of time . . . I don't know. These past months have been terribly confusing, Jamie. Regardless of what I used to believe, I know now that show business isn't a fairy tale and love does *not* conquer all. I also know I have a lot of growing up to do, and that's why I'm going away. I think it might help to see how the rest of the world lives. There must be more to it than the view from *TV Guide.*"

"Where are you going?"

"I'm not sure . . . I thought I'd start with those places you told me about. The Roman Forum, the ruins of that little theater near the base of the Acropolis, where the Greeks put on the first plays . . . I want to see if I can get in touch with what made being an actress so important to me in the beginning. Maybe, then, the rest of me will be easier to understand."

"Well," Jamie reacted. "Looking into the past makes sense for you, but I've spent enough time there. I've decided to head full gallop into the future."

Leigh's new resolve masked her distress as she looked at Jamie. "You're going back to Erika and Bucky, aren't you?"

"I have to," he answered thoughtfully. "No, I *want* to. Whatever happened to Erika—to our marriage—is largely the result of my refusal to accept the fact that time is marching on. If I don't smarten up and fall into step, I'm going to be left behind. By Erika, by you, and by anyone else I get involved with."

"I'll always love you, Jamie," she said, reaching to touch him.

"You're right about love," he replied, struggling to control his emotions. "It won't conquer anything by itself. Except, maybe, good sense."

Leigh nodded in silent resignation.

"Have you made up your minds?" the waitress intruded, cheerfully indicating the menus. "Yeah, we've made up our minds," Jamie said, rising abruptly to his feet. "We've decided we're leaving."

The wind swirled around their ankles as they stood facing each other on the sidewalk.

Leigh pulled the collar of his coat up over his ears, then lifted her face to kiss him on the lips.

"Good-bye, Jamie."

"Good-bye," he responded more brusquely than he intended. But before he could explain, she was already moving away.

"Good-bye," she repeated, thrusting her chin into the cold wind. "Good-bye, Jamie."

CHAPTER

How did I survive living here as long as I did? Neil asked himself, as he stepped out of an air-conditioned taxi into the stiflingly hot, humid September afternoon. It had been nearly a year since he was in New York—since "Yesterday's Children" had folded.

"Yes, sir?" the doorman of Leigh's apartment building greeted as Neil hurried into the relatively cool lobby.

"I'm a friend of Leigh Fisk's," he explained. "Her answering service says they haven't heard from her in months, but I talked to her mother in Palm Springs yesterday and she told me Leigh is here."

"I see," the doorman responded noncommittally. "I can't tell you anything for sure. If you care to leave your name."

"I don't have time for all that," Neil interrupted impatiently. "Look, have you ever heard of 'Fort Worth'?"

"You bet, it's my favorite TV show."

"Did you watch the Emmy awards last week?"

"Yeah . . ."

"Good, I'm the guy who won the Emmy for *directing* 'Fort Worth,' Neil Decker. Don't you remember?"

"Well," the doorman searched his recollection. "You do

look kind of familiar. I remember some of the actors . . . and that girl who did the dance. Yeah, I guess I remember," he became more friendly. "You make a good show, Mr. Decker. Like I said, it's my favorite."

"Terrific," Neil said with a chummy air. "Well, tonight the Federated TV Network is giving a ball to honor its Emmy winners."

"I read about it in the paper."

"Great. If I can find Leigh in time, I want to take her with me, but there's no way if I can't get ahold of her!"

"Why didn't you say so in the first place?"

"I thought I did," Neil snorted in reply.

"She's been away for months, you know."

"Yes," Neil answered, helpfully urging the man along. "She's been out of the country. Her mother told me. I see her mother often in Palm Springs. It's quite near Hollywood where I live. But that's not what I'm here about. I'm here to see if you can help me locate her."

"She's here," the doorman admitted. "She arrived from Europe day before yesterday."

"Where is she *now?*"

"She left early this morning with a nice young fella to go visit some friend in a sanitarium down in Jersey."

"Must be Liz," Neil muttered.

"Yeah, Liz," the doorman nodded."That's who they were talking about. She mentioned she'd be back some time this afternoon."

"Well, I can't wait around," Neil said, taking a note he'd already written from his pocket. "When she comes in, please make sure she gets this and calls me at the Park Sheraton, right away. I don't have to tell you how important it is."

"No, sir," the doorman replied. "I've known all about the Emmys since 'Mr. Fisk' won one back in the seventies . . . or was it the sixties? She'll get the message. You can depend on that."

"Thanks," Neil pressed a five-dollar bill in his hand. "Thanks a lot," he said moving to the door.

"Let me get you a cab," the doorman insisted. "There's no

reason for you to go out in this heat if you don't have to. Just wait right here."

He walked to the street at the same moment a taxi arrived to discharge one of its passengers. Neil watched as he opened the door, then began jabbing his finger toward the lobby as Leigh stepped out onto the curb and waved good-bye to the remaining passenger.

◈ "What do you mean, you don't know if you have anything to wear?" Neil hooted as he followed Leigh into her bulging closet.

"Most of these things belong to Mother," she replied, while critically picking through the selection. "And everything I bought since I've been away, I took to the cleaners when I unpacked. I hadn't planned to be here more than a few days so I didn't think I'd be needing anything fancy."

"If you'd bothered to check with your answering service, you would have known."

"To tell you the truth," Leigh conceded, "it's been so long, I forgot I still have an answering service. And except for Chris Knight, who I ran into when I stopped for a bite at Kerry's, I didn't think anyone knew I was in New York."

"I'm sorry I didn't notice it was Chris in the taxi with you. I'd have liked to say hello."

"He's working tonight. If you like, we can stop by Kerry's on the way home from the party."

"That might be fun," Neil agreed.

"And since you're such a big deal now," she continued as she began sorting through a shelf of shoe boxes, "maybe you can help him get some work. Except for a few commercials, he hasn't done much acting recently."

"There isn't a lot going on here, but I'll see what I can do. It was nice of him to go with you to visit Liz."

"He goes every once in a while. Quite a few people do. The network redid her room at the sanitarium so it's just like her office at Webster. She decided she's in charge of the Alumni Association now. She keeps track of everybody, sends out bulletins."

"Do they think she'll ever get well?"

"Maybe. But as far as she's concerned, why should she? She's happy and content where she is. Everybody loves her."

"I was going to see her a couple of months ago, but her mother advised against it. Liz doesn't remember why, but she resents me a lot."

"I think she had a crush on Eddie."

"I know she did," Neil nodded. "Maybe I should have done something. I felt at the time it was important for Eddie to decide for himself which way he wanted to go."

"Why didn't he come to New York with you?"

"He's busy scoring a TV show and taking care of our new condo." Neil's familiar grin crept across his face. "And anyway, no one travels with their spouse anymore. Think how daring and butch I'll look with you on my arm."

"Oh, Neil. You're impossible!"

"Yeah," his grin widened.

"And you're lucky," she added, digging out a handbag to go with the dress and shoes she had put together. "What would you have done if you hadn't found me?"

"But I did find you."

"Why didn't you call Cathy Allison?" Leigh persisted. "You used to be such great friends and Chris told me she and Sam are divorced."

"Cathy fascinated me, but we were never 'great friends,'" Neil answered, wrinkling his nose in distaste.

"I don't understand you," Leigh stopped to look at him. "I wonder if anybody does!"

"Not *anybody*," Neil smiled defiantly. "Least of all, myself. It's what makes me so interesting. Anyway, I couldn't call Cathy. She's living with somebody."

"Chris mentioned that Sam had remarried—an Italian girl, I think he said—but he didn't say Cathy had gotten involved too."

"Chris doesn't know *everything*," Neil sniffed. "Remember Pam Godfrey?"

"The woman who replaced Jim Hennigan?"

"Bull's-eye!"

"Oh, Neil," Leigh grimaced disapprovingly. "You're always teasing. You don't expect me to believe Cathy and Pam Godfrey are . . ."

"You know me, cutie," Neil shrugged. "I'm the last one to spread idle gossip, but the way I heard it, they've been living and working together ever since Sam caught them *playing* together in bed."

"No! Not Cathy!"

"I told you, Cathy fascinates me. It wouldn't surprise me if she and Pam take over the whole network. They'll be at the ball tonight. Don't expect them to dance together. But that's all right, Eddie and I don't dance together either—at least not in public."

"This is too much," Leigh said, shaking her head. "I'm thirsty. Let's go see what's in the kitchen."

"I'll take a Pepsi, if you have one," Neil requested, following her down the hall. "What else did Chris tell you?"

"Not a great deal," she replied, peering into the refrigerator. "Vico comes into Kerry's now and then. He's as bad-tempered as ever. And Joyce Pagent starred in a pilot for an all-black soap that Marnie produced at her cable network."

"I heard about it," Neil nodded. "But I haven't had a chance to see it. It's a great idea. I hope it works out."

"No Pepsi," Leigh announced. "How about some diet cranberry soda?"

"Diet what?" Neil laughed. "Never mind. Those diet chemicals all taste the same anyway. If it's cold, it'll be fine."

Neil couldn't help recognizing a new aura of maturity about Leigh as she prepared two ice-filled glasses of soda. "What about you?" he said. "We've talked about everyone else. What have you been doing these past nine months?"

"Trying to understand who I am," she answered with a vague smile. "Not an especially fashionable pursuit."

She studied Neil as she drank from her glass, then decided to ease the conversation in another direction. "My friend Mindy seems to have found herself."

"And Stanley Gordon along the way," Neil laughed. "I never thought *she'd* end up in show-biz! Since she's gotten into movie financing, her picture is in the Hollywood papers more often than most stars!"

"Their wedding is the main reason I came back," Leigh explained.

"I'll be there too. So will your mother. I see her often in Palm Springs. I know all about how happy she is and how your father's been hanging around, trying to get back into her good graces since he realized what a better deal she is than that Lipton broad. What I don't know is what's been happening to my favorite ding-a-ling, Leigh Fisk."

"That's a longer story than I care to go into before my bath," she responded measuredly. "However, I'll meet you for a glass of wine at the hotel before we go to the ball and I'll tell you everything."

"Everything?" he grinned.

"Everything, you creep."

"Swear on your grandfather's Bible?"

"Only if you tell me first what *you've* been doing," she bargained. "I know you're a hot director and 'Fort Worth' is the hit of the season. It's even a sensation in England. What I'd like to know is . . . Well . ."

"You want to know about Jamie?" Neil anticipated softly.

"I've read about him in papers and magazines. Even in Egypt, I saw his picture on a cover. Is he as well as they say?"

"He's terrific. Maybe it's because he's securaf0le, but he's really mellowed out."

"And he's happy?"

"Listen, cutie," he answered earnestly. "I know you're asking because you really care, so I'll tell you the truth. It was a little rough at first, but he and Erika have been really working at their marriage. It seems to be getting better all the time."

"I'm delighted for them," she nodded solemnly, then

finished her glass of soda. "I'd better take my bath. What time
do you want me to meet you?"

"Six-thirty. I'll be waiting in the lobby bar."

◈   Neil was smartly elegant in
his newly tailored tuxedo as he jumped up to meet Leigh,
sweeping grandly across the Park Sheraton lobby.

"You look ravishing," he greeted, kissing her on the cheek.

"And you, sir, look very chic," she returned.

Neil led her to his table in the lobby cocktail lounge where
he signaled to the waitress before assisting Leigh into her seat.
"For a poor dear who didn't have a thing to wear, you'll
probably be the best-dressed girl at the ball."

"Thank you," she smiled. "You wouldn't be so flattering if
you'd seen me last month, sifting through the sludge in the
ancient harbor area of Alexandria."

"Alexandria, Egypt? What on earth for?"

"Well," she formed her answer, "I told you it would take a
while to explain. It began when I was stumbling around the
ruins of Greece and Rome trying to make sense of what I felt
about acting—and life—and people."

"What did you come up with?"

"First of all, I started to analyze what had happened: my
story with Jamie. Mom and Dad. Erika . . ."

Leigh hesitated a moment as she made the decision to skip
the more intimate details.

"The more I thought about it, the more I could see how
ordinary we were. We were a little different, but we weren't so
special. Stories like ours were probably used at one time or
another on 'Yesterday's Children,' and most of the other soaps
on TV. I began to realize I was like Alice in her looking glass.
Was I looking in or looking out? Which life was real, the one
inside the TV studio? Or the one outside?"

"That's heavy," he reacted with an affectionate grin.

"You're right. It was quite a load."

"And the acting?"

"Acting," she repeated sourly. "I *thought* I was an actress. I was totally dedicated, but not to what acting is really about. I was dedicated to a fantasy. To an idealistic dream of acting that doesn't exist in the real world. The real profession of acting is a cold, calculating business. It doesn't hurt to have talent, but knowing how to sell yourself is what's really important."

"You sound bitter."

"Maybe I am. I try not to be, but I put a big piece of my heart into it. Sometimes the truth is painful."

"You got that right," Neil responded, glancing toward an exhilarated cluster of young celebrities as they moved across the lobby. "But everyone may not agree with your version of the truth."

It's true for *me*, that's all," she answered, following his glance. "They can have their own opinion." She forced a smile. "We all have the right to our opinion, don't we?"

"Absolutely! We can't always voice our opinion, but we have the right to have them! And it is my present opinion that you're developing into someone very special."

"Wait until you see the next stage of my development."

"Do you mind if we have some bubbly first?" Neil asked with a smile, as the waitress appeared, offering a bottle of champagne for his approval.

"Dom Perignon, '69. Is that correct, sir?"

"Perfect," Neil confirmed.

"Pretty extravagant wine," Leigh commented whimsically.

"Nothing but the best for my deep-thinking little sister," he crowed as he tested the splash of champagne the waitress poured in the bottom of his glass, then nodded for her to fill both glasses. "Especially now when I've become a celebrated director and can sign for this on the network expense account. Here's to you, cutie," he toasted. "And to the next stage of your development. Has all this developing brought any interesting new men into your life?"

"One," she conceded demurely.

"Where is he? When do we meet him?"

"He's somewhere along the Iraq/Iran border, checking on the ruins that weren't destroyed in their war. Stephen's a young archaeologist I met with my mother before I left New York. We spent a month together on a dig in Sicily."

"What do you mean, together?" Neil asked suspiciously.

"I mean together the same way you mean together," she responded evenly. "He's a sweet man, but there was never any thought on either side that it would be more than it was. An interesting, enlightening experience."

"When you start developing, you move right along, don't you?" Neil reacted good-naturedly. "So now you're going to be an archaeologist. Why?"

"You remember I told you I was stumbling through the ruins of antiquity in search of reasons for my life today? Well, when I started learning *how* to search, I discovered that goals are often not nearly as important as the way you reach them. Maybe it's enough if I can learn to be a little better . . . and a little happier at whatever I'm doing."

"What about love?"

"That comes later," she looked at the bubbles rising in her glass. "I'm still working on the basic stuff. I'll get to love a little farther down the road."

"You're on your way, cutie," Neil smiled proudly, then paused to follow Leigh's gaze to the excited mob of fans and photographers who were noisily announcing Jamie and Erika's arrival at the hotel entrance.

Neil reacted with poignant concern as he caught an unwitting flash of pain and regret in Leigh's expression as she followed their progress into the lobby.

"I'm trying," she responded, bracing into the semblance of a serenely regal pose as Jamie and Erika, unaware of her presence, breezed past them.

Neil reached to comfort her, then looked up to notice Jamie hesitate, as though restrained by an unseen hand, to glance back over his shoulder.

Jamie's smile for Neil evaporated as he recognized Leigh; and in that brief instant, Neil was startled to witness an impassioned display of suppressed longing in their silent exchange.

The spell was broken as each glanced away self-consciously; and before Erika could discern what had caused Jamie's sudden change of attitude, she and Jamie were bathed in the glare of a television interviewer's lights.

Leigh slumped back, ashamed to meet Neil's gaze. "You must think I'm pretty foolish," she sighed, "after everything I've just said."

"Hey, I think you're terrific," he smiled supportively. "You never said you've *reached* your goals. You said you're still *looking*. There's nothing wrong with that!"

"No, I suppose not," she smiled through the tears welling in her eyes. "And I'll get there, Neil. I promise you, I'll get there!"

ABOUT THE AUTHOR

Brett Halsey, author of the best-selling, award-winning, *The Magnificent Strangers,* has an intimate understanding of the soaps. He has appeared in four daytime soap operas: as Spencer Garrison in "Love is a Many Splendored Thing," Clay Collins in "Search for Tomorrow," Doctor Adam Streeter in "General Hospital," and John Abbot in "The Young and the Restless."

He has also starred in his own nighttime series, "Follow the Sun," and has had guest roles in countless episodic television shows including "Fantasy Island," "The Love Boat," "The Dukes of Hazzard," "Matt Houston," "Fall Guy," "Knight Rider," and "Mike Hammer."

Throughout his long acting career, he has starred in over sixty feature motion pictures in the United States, Canada, Italy, France, Germany, and Spain.

Mr. Halsey is an active member of The Academy of Motion Picture Arts and Sciences, The Authors Guild, The Authors League of America, The Screen Actors Guild, ACTRA, AFTRA, and Actors Equity. He resides in Toronto, Canada, where he is currently working on a new screenplay and researching his next novel.